INTO YOU

A Novel

By

Alexandra Y. Caluen

INTO YOU

The Playlist:

Difícil - Juanés

Nothing's Changed – Chris Isaak

Leyenda – Andres Segovia

Don't Tell Me – Madonna

Don't You Wanna Stay – Jason Aldean & Kelly Clarkson

Tied Up, Tied Down, and Twisted – Kellie Rucker

Fever – Peggy Lee

I Want It All – k.d. lang

Solamente Tú – Pablo Alborán

A Mi Manera – Robin Williams

INTO YOU

Contents

CHAPTER 1

January 2015

"Happy New Year," Manny said as the dollar fluttered down into his guitar case. He said it every time, glancing up. If the giver was looking at him, he'd offer a quick smile. He wasn't out here to make his rent, but every dollar still counted.

This giver wasn't simply looking at him; the guy was next-best-thing to studying him. Manny blinked, caught up to what his fingers were doing, and wrapped up the song. It wasn't really the end, but he could always play it again in a little while. The guy obviously took that as an invitation to say something. "You're pretty good with that thing."

"Thanks. It's not my day job, but it's a nice way to pay for a day at the beach."

The guy laughed. "I remember having more than one job."

Manny studied him right back. "You look kind of familiar."

"Maybe." It sounded a bit sly, and came with a wicked smile. "Depends on how you spend your leisure time."

Whoa, that was kind of flirty. Manny leaned back on his folding chair, grinning, letting his left hand stroke down the neck of his guitar in a suggestive way. "You out here by yourself today?"

"No," someone said behind the guy. An older woman, who took his hand with an indulgent sideways glance. Manny thought *oops, shit* but the guy didn't seem worried, or even embarrassed. "He's just a sucker for a good-looking kid with a guitar."

1

Now Manny was blushing. Were they out to pick up a third? He wouldn't be averse – they were both sexy – but this was an awfully public approach. And he'd only been playing for an hour; he'd barely made back his parking yet. Before he could say anything, the guy said, "We're on our way to a movie, but it was nice hearing you play. Have a great day."

"You too." Manny watched as the woman dropped a business card in the guitar case, along with another dollar. Then the couple walked away. It took a real effort of will to start playing again, instead of taking a look at that card. A couple hours later, he counted and stowed the money, then paused to look at the card before packing up his gear. "Whoa," he said out loud. Now he knew where he'd seen the guy. Because that woman was Monica Wilder, a director for Stroked, which happened to be Manny's favorite porn site. He wondered why she'd dropped off her card. It couldn't be because she thought he'd be into making porn. Could it?

"Can you believe that?" He directed the question to a framed photo sitting on his nightstand at home. "Met an honest-to-God porn star today." Lobo would have gotten such a kick out of that. He'd have laughed his ass off. Manny was smiling as he got online, looking for something starring that guy. Rick Wilder, married to Monica, but a longtime star on both sides of the site. A new clip was up, Rick and another guy going at it in a garage. Manny debated the cost of the download for a minute, then decided to go for it. The scene was not so different from moments in his own life. "Think that could be me?" he said out loud after a while, when the laptop was closed and he'd wiped himself off. He and Lobo made a sex tape once. They thought they were so fine, so cool, but that tape made

2

them crack up every time they looked at it. *Not as easy as they make it seem*, he thought. Still smiling. This morning he'd been feeling kind of gross about the impulsive, beer-and-weed-fueled New Year's Eve hookup with his neighbor Angel. Now he felt better about life.

He chucked the card into his nightstand drawer, thinking he might call someday. He was no worse-looking than Rick's partner in that clip, and they gave him the opening. He'd be able to say hey, I was the guy playing guitar that time. More likely by the end of the week – after six days packed full of his three jobs – he'd forget all about it.

The next day, out in the San Fernando Valley, Monica cornered her partner Irv and showed him a picture on her phone. "Saw this guy in Santa Monica yesterday."

"Whoa."

"Yeah. Looks like a bad guy when he's serious, but when he smiles it's kind of special. I dropped off my card." She shrugged. Probably nothing would come of it. "His name's Manuel Figueroa."

"He tell you that?" Irv wouldn't be surprised if she asked. Monica wasn't shy about recruiting. A lot of guys took it as a compliment when a woman did the asking.

"No, he had his busking permit where I could see it. You might want to look him up. I'm too busy to chase him down."

"Oh, and I'm not." His tone was dry, but Irv was amused. They were all busy. Time spent developing new talent wasn't optional, though. So he asked her to send him the picture, and then he got online to see if he could find out anything about this guy. Sent out a few casual queries to contacts, did some Googling. Didn't find a website, but there was a YouTube channel: Figueroa was a bicycle racer. He rode for one of the big-name gym chains, and was a spin trainer in their Hollywood location. That happened to be Irv's workout, but he never went over the hill for it. He put the prospect's information in a follow-up file and forgot about it for a while.

Then he went in for his workout and almost said 'what the fuck' out loud, because Figueroa was there, standing in for the regular Northridge trainer. A perfect opportunity for Irv to scope him out. What Monica said about the smile was true. It was all Irv could do to resist taking a phone picture or two. The gym management wouldn't like that, so he didn't. He'd have to make contact somehow, though. This guy was exactly what Irv was looking for. Young enough to appeal to just about everybody, not so young that it'd be skeevy to some. A different kind of face. A body Irv would like to photograph, and that smile.

He caught himself later with his hand down his pants, thinking about that smile. "Stop it," he told himself out loud. If he made the approach and the guy gave him a flat No, *then* Irv could fantasize about him.

Manny finally got sick of Angel's attitude. It was two months later, and the fucker should have been the fuck over it. There wasn't even anything to *be* over. Hooking up with a co-worker was not uncommon. Things shouldn't have been awkward at the gym. It wasn't like either of them asked the other guy out and got turned down. They weren't dating, so it wasn't a breakup. All Manny could figure was, people didn't say no to Angel very often. He wouldn't have himself if he

4

hadn't been a bit too clear-headed New Year's morning. Should have been clear-headed earlier. Then he wouldn't have ended up with the nasty sore throat that turned out to be gonorrhea. He couldn't help being pissed at Angel, even though it was his own damn fault. Should have known better. He was lucky it was something they could treat.

They didn't see much of each other at work. The spinning room where Manny spent most of his time was at the other end of things from the high-intensity interval training room. They only intersected when Manny went in there for his own workout, and when their comings and goings coincided at the apartment building. The whole reason Manny wanted this particular apartment was because Angel lived in that building. He felt like an idiot. Twenty-six was too old to have that kind of stupid crush on somebody. Well, he was over it now. He wasn't so much of an idiot that he needed a slap-back to involve an actual slap.

They were both in the locker room. Angel was starting his shift, Manny was ending his. Angel said something about people who thought they were too good. Manny shoved his sweaty clothes into his gym bag, zipped it up, and said, "I was after you for six months and you know it. You told me and showed me, about a hundred times, I'm not your type. But I guess you'd feel better about yourself if I kept trying?"

"I don't want you to keep trying! I never wanted you, you little bitch."

"Who the fuck you calling a bitch, coño? I'm not the one tracking someone around, whining about how he won't get on my dick." They were not alone in the locker room. There were some mutters, ranging from 'oh snap' and 'dude what' to 'ooh child,' along with a

5

few stifled snorts and giggles. "And you might want to get your filthy ass to a clinic. You gave me the clap."

"The *fuck*?!"

Manny brushed past him and left, heart pounding, hearing Angel slam his locker door with another curse. There was an outburst of laughter and cat-calling from the other trainers. This was not going to improve things. He couldn't regret it, though.

Irv heard every word of it. He watched the spin trainer leave the locker room, walking fast, wearing an expression that said anyone who got in his way was probably going to regret it. That conversation answered two big questions. Rick read this guy as queer, and he was right as usual. And now Irv knew he was single. It wasn't unheard-of for married or partnered men to work with Stroked – Rick was a prime example – but single was less complicated.

There were countless good-looking guys in Los Angeles, a fair percentage of them were gay, and more than you would think were willing to pose for some dirty pictures. Enough of those were willing to do dirty things on video. Especially after the usual seduction. A meal, a tour of the filming house, a look at a sample contract and some samples of the product. Everything clean, health-conscious, non-obvious, and as respectful of boundaries as porn could be. And Irv had a way about him, a way that reinforced what he always said. "The quid in this quid pro quo is not you fucking me or me fucking you. It is you fucking yourself or somebody else of your choice on camera, me selling that picture or video, and us all making money. It's legal and it's legit. It's not fine art and it's not going to get you far unless you have talent, you behave like a professional, and you keep yourself clean. But you'll make some money. What do you say?" An amazing number of them said yes. It was like they almost couldn't believe they weren't being lied to, promised the moon and the stars in exchange for a blow job.

This one had a lot going for him. He obviously had boundaries, plus some pride; he was well-spoken and not afraid to stand up for himself. He was also fantastic-looking. Not too tall, well-proportioned, hair and beard trimmed close. He could have been anything from Middle Eastern to Brazilian; might be a mongrel like Irv, despite the probably-Mexican name. Whatever went into the mix worked out a lot better for him than Irv's mix, that was for sure. He jolted into action, taking an intercept course, and caught up at the exit as planned. "Mr. Figueroa?"

Manny looked around. "Yes?" He didn't get spoken to outside the spin room very often, especially not by people who didn't do spin classes. He almost never was addressed as 'Mister.' This guy didn't look like gym management. A couple of inches shorter than Manny, stocky, and kind of odd-looking. Strangely monochromatic. Had to be mixed. A mix of what, who knew. Skin nearly the same tone as Manny's, but reddish hair, greenish eyes, and freckles. "Can I help you?"

Irv couldn't help noticing he was being assessed. Couldn't help appreciating the unobtrusive speed of it, and the polite inquiry. "Do you have a moment to talk?"

"Yeah, sure, if you don't mind walking with me. I have a gig across town."

"No problem." He had to stretch to keep up, actually. Irv didn't do a lot of walking, and never walked fast. "I'm a photographer and filmmaker.

Spotted you when you subbed out in Northridge a few weeks ago. Have you done any work on-camera?"

"A few extra gigs here and there. I've been trying to work up some skills but it's hard to fit the classes into my schedule." Manny glanced at the guy. He couldn't honestly say he'd noticed him in Northridge.

Irv appreciated that Figueroa didn't say oh yeah I remember you. "Sure, I get it. Look, I don't want you to think hey, this guy is a big shot. I'm not." They'd fetched up at a big red pickup truck. "So you don't ride a bike to work, huh."

Manny laughed. "No. I do races. That bike does not belong on the street dodging SUVs."

"I'll bet it doesn't." A racing bike was expensive. Irv dug into his pocket for his card case, flipped it open, extracted a card and handed it to Figueroa. "Irv Morton, that's me."

Manny took the card. STROKED INC. His eyebrows went up. This was so weird. "Wait a minute." He couldn't help dropping his volume. Everybody he knew bought porn, but still. "Did Ms. Wilder send you? You want to put me in porn?"

The tone was not thrilled, or excited, or even flattered. Irv held up both hands, palms out, poised to retreat. "Hang on. I just wanted to introduce myself. I mean yes, I'd love to take your picture or put you onscreen. Monica spotted you out in Santa Monica and we thought we'd follow up." He looked around, couldn't repress an exasperated little sigh. "This is not a conversation to have in a parking lot on the spur of the moment."

For no apparent reason, the next thing of Manny's mouth was "What kind of accent is that?"

8

Irv was surprised by the swerve, but he answered anyway. "Queens, New York."

"How'd you get out here?"

"The usual way. Look, Mr. Figueroa, you know who I am and what I do, you know how to reach me. If you have any interest give me a call. Drop me an email. Or Monica, whatever. Nice to meet you." He held out his hand.

Manny took it, shook lightly, let go. His mind was racing. He said, "You too," which was slightly ambiguous, as he took out his wallet and slid the card into it. Then he opened up the truck, slung his gym bag into it, and climbed inside. "Might want to step back."

"Sure." Irv took several steps back. If the kid took off like an asshole he might re-think this. But he didn't. Started up with no obnoxious revving, fastened his seatbelt, pulled slowly out of his parking space, and signaled before turning onto Sunset Boulevard. *Well, mission accomplished.* Contact made, and no punch in the face. That had only happened once, but it wasn't the kind of thing you forget. Irv turned around and went to find his car. He had to get back out to the Valley, pick up groceries, and set up for his next shoot.

Manny thought about Irv Morton and his offer (or whatever it was) all the way to his gig, most of the way through it, and all the way home. Wondered why he was the one following up, and not Monica Wilder. He'd be lying if he said he was completely turned off by the idea. The truth was, he was flattered. It was nice to be sought out like that. The only reason he hadn't jumped at it was he really knew nothing about the porn business. How it worked for the actors, or models, or whatever they were called. Reading the site, doing a little Googling, and watching 'Boogie Nights' filled in some blanks. It might be fun. On the other hand, it might completely torpedo his chances of ever making it as a legit actor.

Ideally he could talk it over with someone, but he couldn't imagine who that someone should be. Definitely not his parents. His pop worked for Recology and his mother for the LAUSD. They were sober blue-collar people who went to church and prayed for their bent son. His brother and sister were on the 'we'll follow you on Facebook and stay in touch that way' side of things. If he posted something about a race, or some gig he did that was kind of buzzy, they'd always drop a thumbs-up or a comment. But he hardly ever saw them, and that was probably for the best. His sister was sure he was going to hell, and his brother wouldn't shake his hand.

He couldn't talk to anyone at the gym, either. For all he knew half the trainers there did porn, or worked as escorts, or whatever. They all had pretty high expenses. You had to look a certain way to be a successful trainer. He knew people who'd had lipo, nose jobs, boob jobs. The management wanted all their people camera-friendly, if not camera-ready. Certifications had to be up-to-date, new skill sets were acquired at the trainers' own expense, and teeth had better be straight. The hourly rate at the gym wasn't bad, but they all made their real money from side gigs. Competing with each other half the time. No, it couldn't be a co-worker.

Which didn't leave a lot of options. Manny worked too many hours to have much time for hanging out, getting to know people. His whole social life amounted to a drink here and there, a meal here and there – typically after a training session with one of the

10

company's other racers – or a resigned trip to West Hollywood to pick someone up at one of the clubs. The New Year's Eve thing with Angel skeeved him out so much he hadn't done that at all so far this year. Had to think back beyond that.

There were some people he met on Thanksgiving weekend. He helped someone move out of the apartment he was in now. That person was a yoga teacher, twice Manny's age, moving in with his lover. Angel helped, mostly because he had a hard-on for the yoga guy. The age thing didn't seem to faze him. But that was irrelevant. That guy, Kevin Park. Manny knew where he taught. He seemed really mellow, and he was old enough that he'd probably seen it all. Even if he was shocked or disgusted by the idea of porn, it wouldn't matter because Manny never had to see him again.

He made the approach in a way that would at least ensure Kevin didn't feel like his time was being wasted: he booked a private lesson. There was no way learning some yoga was going to be bad for him, after all.

And it turned out to be a great strategy, because it was actually private. The tiny windowless training room was tucked between the bigger street-facing and alley-facing rooms. The owner gave it a spa feeling with grasscloth on the walls, soft lighting, quiet music, and high-end mats. Kevin was already there when Manny stepped through the door. "Oh," he said. "I remember you."

"I hoped you would." Manny offered a hand. "How are things with you and Mr. Xiao?"

"We're getting married next month." Kevin smiled. He was really happy about that, and never tried to hide it.

11

"Congratulations!" Manny wanted to ask for details. He didn't know any queer couples who were married. It hadn't been legal for very long. But they weren't that kind of friends, so he minded his own business. "Look, Mr. Park, I have an ulterior motive."

"Call me Kevin. Let's get on the mats. We can talk and work at the same time." Something told him this young man would find it easier to talk when he was moving. "How much yoga have you done up to now?"

"Like, nothing. I know what a sun salute is. I'm a spinning trainer."

"Oh yes, I remember. Let's see your sun salute." Kevin sat in lotus by the wall, watching. A natural mover, but clearly hadn't been taught the purpose of this particular vinyasa. Tight hamstrings, to be expected. Tight chest, tight hip flexors, compromised posture. "Hmm. What's your goal here, beyond this ulterior motive of yours?"

"Can I sit?" On Kevin's nod, Manny sat cross-legged on the mat. "It might be all tied together. My body's too tight. I need something else." Something for his body, for his mind, for his soul. Maybe for his heart. "I'm twenty-six. I'm on the audition round like everybody else. Spinning won't last forever and one bad crash in a race might finish me." Kevin nodded comprehension, said nothing, simply waited. Manny didn't want to get into all the other reasons he felt limited. Confined. Going nowhere. "Somebody approached me. A photographer, filmmaker guy." He hesitated, nearly bailed out, sucked in a breath. "Guy who makes porn."

"Oh." One syllable with three notes. Kevin could tell Manuel was not horrified by the idea. He wasn't himself, though he'd declined the offer that came his way thirty years ago. "Are you familiar with the company?"

"Kind of." He didn't want to say it was his favorite site; that would sound like he watched porn all the time. "I knew the name, and I looked up some of their stuff. It's not gross." That came out sounding a little like a question, because Manny's idea of gross might not be Kevin's. "I mean, it seems like each model has his own kind of thing. Like I'd be able to do my own thing. I mean, as long as the guy likes it. My God this is weird to be talking about."

Kevin laughed under his breath. "I'm sure it is. Did you want advice, or simply to tell someone?"

"I think just to tell someone, but if you have any advice I'm all ears."

"Let me think about it while we fix your sun salute. Watch mine." Kevin stood up, waited for a second while Manuel moved back, then went into his version of the vinyasa.

"Jeez, your posture is so good."

"Mmm." Kevin breathed out and straightened up. "Your turn again." He put Manuel through it in slow motion, describing the body mechanics, helping the younger man tune in, giving adjustments. Adding a couple of poses to the sequence to address this particular body more effectively. Twice, four times, eight times. Manuel was sweating. "Once more. I'll put it on video for you so you can review."

"Great, thanks." Manny handed over his phone. He let Kevin talk him through the sequence. "I'm going to be feeling this tomorrow."

"Yes." Kevin handed back the phone after Manny dropped to the mat. Gave him a towel. "I'm free for the next hour if you'd like to walk down to the coffee shop."

"God, I'd kill for an iced coffee right now." Probably not how you were supposed to be after yoga.

Kevin laughed. "If you really want to open up your chest and shoulders, do this four to eight times a day. Come back and see me in a month and we'll fine-tune it. I would also recommend some ballet."

"Ballet?!"

"Do you remember the dancer who was at our house last fall?"

"Oh yeah, he was amazing."

"Dmitri Vasko. He has a few private students who are more in the fitness space like you."

"He won't try to teach me how to, like, do the foxtrot, will he?" Manny was half-kidding. According to the comments, that show dance they watched on YouTube was partly foxtrot. Any athlete would have been impressed.

Kevin was stifling laughter again. "Only if you ask him to. If you go in and say, fix my posture, that's exactly what he'll do."

"What about if I go in and say, teach me how to lift a lady over my head like you did." Manny was smiling for real now. The room was tidy, the exhaust fan was on, and they were walking out.

"He'll want to fix your posture first." Kevin listened to Manuel laugh. He hoped the young man would come back in a month, to tell him what was happening. At the end of their slow walk up to the coffee shop, into the park, and back, he said, "Personally, I try to be open to opportunities. Some things look strange from head on but different from the side. If the general idea doesn't bother you, why not meet with the man? Find out what he has to say. See what kind of facilities he has. Ask for a sample contract."

Those were exactly the same thoughts Manny already had. "As long as I don't sign anything till I'm pretty sure I won't regret it, huh."

"Exactly." Kevin hesitated for a moment; they were right outside Tidal Flow again, and he had to go teach. "You might consider using a stage name, if you decide to proceed."

"Oh my God yes." They both laughed. Manny held out a hand. "Thanks so much, Kevin. I'll see you in a month or so."

The first couple weeks, every single repetition was painful. He felt like the work he did at the gym was the exact opposite of the yoga and they were almost cancelling each other out. Plus, he had a race to do in there, and it didn't go well. He crashed, and while he wasn't really injured he was sore for a week.

Both those Stroked business cards were on top of his bedside table now. He didn't add the contact to his phone, and he didn't make the call. It wasn't like he was ready to roll up and say 'let's take some dirty pictures' yet. He wasn't desperate for money. There was a little bonus for the race even though he crashed. Had some serving gigs that sent him home with good tips, and picked up an extra role that was three days' work. If he got halfway good at this yoga shit, he could put that down as a skill. It didn't take much Googling to find out how much yoga showed up in commercials.

The thought made him remember Kevin's suggestion about ballet. Manny liked to dance; it was the second skill on his resume, right after bicycling. He did all the club stuff. Salsa, merengue, bachata, plus what passed for dancing at the gay bars. Once in a while people would be in there doing stuff that you thought, wow, that's like Dancing With the Stars. Most of the time it was just grinding on each other. There was a place and time for that. Manny still wasn't feeling it. And he couldn't afford ballroom lessons. That shit took forever. He'd heard all about it from a couple of girls who were in one of his spin classes.

But ballet, fixing his posture, that was maybe three lessons. If the guy was as good a teacher as Kevin. It was worth finding out, anyway.

Midweek was a good time to make a hole in his schedule and cruise over to WeHo. The dance studio had its own parking lot. Manny put the truck in the spot furthest from the door, where he could pull straight out when he left, and went inside. Music was playing, something Latin. A young couple was over by the mirrors. The woman was a ringer for Salma Hayek; the guy was probably Filipino. He was cute as fuck. There was a white lady, working with a black guy not much older than Manny. It looked like she was a teacher, but there was something else going on too. A few other people, working in couples or by themselves, in front of the completely-mirrored side wall or at the barre on the end wall.

One of those was Mr. Vasko. Manny recognized him from that dinner after helping Kevin move. He was wearing yoga pants with a close-fitting black tee shirt that had BALLROOM DANCERS DO IT in rhinestones on the front, and WITH RHYTHM on the back. Manny could see both sides because of the mirrors. It made him smile. Fifty-something, maybe an inch taller than Manny, not quite as wiry as he was five months ago. Well, he retired from competition, they said. That probably meant he could lighten up on how he ate. He appeared to be ignoring everyone else in the

16

room, but within a few seconds of Manny stepping inside he took his foot off the barre and came over. He didn't say anything, but his expression was welcoming. And inquiring. Manny stuck out his hand. "Hi, Mr. Vasko. Manny Figueroa. We met for a minute last fall."

"Mr. Figueroa. I am Dmitri. How may I help you?"

He jumped right in. "I had a yoga lesson with Kevin Park last month and we were talking about my lousy posture. I'm a spin trainer and I do this all day." He mimed being hunched over his bike; Dmitri grimaced. "Yeah. Anyway he suggested maybe a ballet lesson or two would give me some more tools to keep working on it at home." He wanted to make it clear he wasn't there to become a ballet dancer. Judging from the amused expression on the studio head's face, he'd made his point perfectly.

"Let us discuss," he said, indicating the office. Manny followed him in. "Your schedule?"

Manny blew out a breath, shaking his head. "It stinks. I mean, for any kind of regular class. That's why I was thinking of a few private lessons." Dmitri nodded. "I have a lot of flexibility, I mean in my schedule, not in my hips like you." That almost got a smile. Manny reminded himself what Kevin had said: he does not often laugh or smile, but he is a warm person; watch his eyes. He did that while he said, "If I make an appointment I will keep it. And I'll do the work at home."

Another nod. "Is only way." Dmitri opened a drawer, lifted out a sheet of paper, and handed it across the desk. It was a schedule of the regular classes at the studio, with the hours the instructors were generally available. And their rates, which was good to know. They weren't as high as Manny half-expected. "Sunday

17

mornings," Dmitri said. Manny looked at those; there were three classes listed under a line of bold type reading COMMUNITY CLASSES – PAY WHAT YOU CAN. One of them was a yoga class. "All are walk-in."

Manny glanced up. "So there's no progression? I could drop in any time?" Dmitri nodded again. "That's great. Sometimes I have a gig on Sundays but a lot of times I don't. Okay, so." He pulled out his phone, checked his calendar to confirm the recurring gaps, and suggested a date for a lesson at the barre. Dmitri countered after a glance at his own schedule. A few minutes later they reached an agreement. After shaking hands again, Manny headed out. He would have liked to hang around and watch the dancers, but he had work to do.

CHAPTER 2

The private ballet and yoga lessons were definitely a good investment, even if Manny was mostly fighting the effects of spin training. Going to the Sunday drop-in yoga class turned out to be great for his social life. He met a lot of the Shall We Dance regulars. Even hooked up with one of them. They negotiated for about five minutes over coffee down the street from the dance studio. Went back to Manny's place and had a good time. The guy was just a bit shorter, which he liked; a bit thinner, which was okay; and really good-looking. The hours they spent mostly in bed, with a couple orgasms apiece, would have made a damn fine sex tape. He didn't have the thought till it was too late, and might not have made the suggestion anyway. Maybe it was only in mind because of those Stroked business cards in the nightstand with the rubbers and lube.

Almost three months after meeting the porn guy, having spoken about it with nobody but Kevin Park, Manny still hadn't quite made up his mind. He'd had a string of extra calls in the past six weeks. Most were single-day, which were the easiest for him to manage. One of them was a totally-fun night shoot at a legendary salsa club downtown. Manny had never been there before. There was a gay guy on the crew, and for a minute Manny was tempted to make some kind of suggestion. Then he heard the guy say something about a boyfriend, so he walked away, thinking he didn't especially want to reach thirty without a boyfriend himself.

On the other hand, if he was actually interested in this whole porn thing, he ought to look into that first. Because he could see how some people would be turned on by that, but other people might be turned off. Even if it was nothing more than pictures of him by himself. If he started doing that after getting into a relationship, the other guy might have a problem with it. And the fact he hadn't thrown out those cards meant he was interested. *Why am I interested.*

That was something he needed to clear up. Was it simply curiosity? Was it the ego boost, that someone would make that approach? Or was it something more? Was it about, maybe, the idea of being desired. Being the object of desire, knowing people were using you for sexual gratification, but without having to actually interact with them. Was this a different way to have a sex life? Was he that messed up about what he'd lost? Because it had been a long time since he really seriously thought about finding a person who could be more than stress relief. Then there was the practical question: would doing porn be remotely useful for the acting dream?

So many questions. Well, he could ask the guy. Ask him, will I learn anything about performing, about acting. Would he learn more about how to present himself to a camera. Would he be *directed*. Would he learn about staging and blocking and camera angles and all that shit in a way that he'd only read about on the internet.

He'd never been in a position to play an actual character. He was Guy at Table Five, or Pedestrian Six, or Retail Customer Three. Background, always background. To the extent he was directed, it was 'don't look at the camera and don't focus on the people giving lines.' He was always supposed to be going about his own business, unconscious of the people doing the meat of the scene. Living his own life as Guy at Table Five, not involved with the TV cops at table three or the romantic couple at table one.

But doing porn – doing *good* porn – meant engaging with the camera. Engaging with the people on the other side of it. Trying to turn them on, even if it was him by himself, doing himself as if nobody else was there.

Doing himself as if Lobo was there. The thought set him back. He was sitting on his bed, with that card in his hand. Was this all about having the sex he wished he was still having with Lobo? They hadn't had nearly enough. "I miss you," he said out loud, looking at the one actual picture he had, the one Lobo's parents gave him seven years ago. He had to burn this out somehow. Maybe porn was the way. At the very least, he'd learn something. He reached over for his phone.

Irv had not precisely forgotten about Manny Figueroa, but when two weeks went by without a phone call he shrugged it off. There was always another hot guy looking to make a buck. His spring and summer were fully booked with shorts and photo shoots. Plus there was always the actual business to manage with his partners. Festivals and awards to submit for, promotion to do, ideas for long-form videos to fool around with. Competition was fierce in this field; some of their competitors pulled no punches and had no standards. Stroked released plenty of hard-core and kink, but even the kinkiest stuff had some story.

Irv hadn't always done porn; he'd worked in legit film for years. Unfortunately, the fact that he now did porn meant that most legit writers didn't want to work with him. The average short didn't have much of a script. But if you looked at the history of the genre, you saw things like 'The Devil in Miss Jones,' which had an actual story. Irv hadn't completely given up on the

21

idea of making a film that would stand up to that one. A film people might consider a classic someday.

It wasn't something he spent much time thinking about, though. 'Be practical' was kind of his motto. About everything, because being an idealist got him exactly nowhere. He was making a good living, with an acceptable degree of risk. Doing something he was good at, namely filmed entertainment. And he *was* practical. He would rather be making a living as a filmmaker whose subject was sex and whose object was getting people off, than holding out for Art and working in an office somewhere. Fuck that.

He was getting ready for bed when his phone rang. The day's shoot over at the house was finished hours ago, and he'd already spoken to his partners that day, so he frowned at the phone. Picked it up anyway, because you never know. "Hello?"

"Hi Mr. Morton. This is Manny Figueroa. We met in March?"

I'll be damned. "Yes we did. I'm surprised to hear from you after all this time."

Manny huffed out a laugh. "Yeah, I'll bet. I've been kind of busy. And I had some thinking to do."

Well, it was always best if people did their thinking before they showed up for a shoot. "And then you called me."

"Right." Manny stalled for a second. "Are you still interested in talking to me?"

"I'm talking to you right now. But sure. Any time. Always looking for a fresh face." Or fresh meat, but whatever. No need to be too crass about it. "When did you have in mind." Figueroa offered a day and time. Irv counteroffered. They negotiated down to a dinner hour the following week. Irv said, "I'll be picking up the

22

check but that does not mean you're obligated. For anything. Right?"

Manny took a moment to let that settle. It hadn't occurred to him, because he'd never been in a casting-couch kind of situation, but he knew that happened. And it probably happened a lot in porn. It was nice of this guy to get that out in the open. "Thanks. Good to know. I'll see you next week."

"Looking forward to it." Irv disconnected without another word, added the contact, entered the appointment in his calendar, and told himself quite firmly to forget all about it until the actual day. He didn't entirely succeed.

Having ideas was an occupational hazard. Any person in a creative industry, even if the industry was porn, always needed ideas. You *wanted* to be having ideas, because turning out the same tired crap over and over again was no way to stay in business. A high-budget TV show could get away with recycling the same storyline every season, swapping in occasional new characters or a different mysterious cabal behind the latest conspiracy. Movies got re-made all the time. But you always needed something a little different, and maybe especially in porn. Because what you were doing was giving someone a way to get off in private, and the only reason they came looking for porn in the first place was because they needed something different from what they already had. Or maybe it was just something *more*.

Irv had no problem at all with people calling romance novels 'lady porn,' except he thought they were missing the point. He believed people read romance novels because they needed something they were not getting in real life. If you read enough romance novels, it was really fucking easy to pick up

23

what that something might be. One of three things, usually, or a combination of those things. A lifetime love, meaning commitment and fidelity; words of love, meaning main characters who told each other they were loved; and great sex.

The combination meant a guaranteed happy ending, which not enough people got in real life. It was really fucking sad, if you thought about it. But if you were a person who produced those things for people to get in their fantasy life, it was a road map.

Irv would not have copped to being a romantic. He did think 'happy ending' should mean more than 'come shot.' So did his partners, which meant even the hardest hard-core porn they produced tried to provide a hint of romance along with enjoyable images of people having sex. Give the viewer a reason to believe the people having sex really cared about each other, and you got repeat business. It might have been counter-intuitive, and there were people in their industry who swore anonymous hookups were the number-one scenario. That hadn't been the case for Stroked.

So they had a tendency to look at new talent with the 'what kind of story' lens. All Irv knew about Manny Figueroa was, basically, that he knew his shit as a spin trainer; he wasn't afraid to call out a one-time partner who acted like a dick; and he was a romantic. If anyone asked Irv why he thought that last thing, he would have said, because he tried to get with somebody for six months, and when he finally did and that person was a dick about it, he was hurt.

He was a guy who wanted more. Which meant he knew all about the people on the other side of the camera. Now if Irv could just get him on *his* side of the damn thing.

24

Irv half-expected Figueroa to cancel on the day of their meet-up, but he didn't. They convened at Jerry's Famous Deli as arranged, talked about bullshit until they had their entrées, and then got down to business. Irv gave him the rundown on how things worked. Showed him a sample contract, answered questions, gave him an idea about the earning potential. Pulled out his netbook and played a couple of non-explicit clips from his own backlist. Then put it away again. "So what do you think?" Irv honestly couldn't tell which way this might go. The kid had a hell of a poker face.

Manny gave himself another minute to think about it. He felt like he ought to say no. But the thing was, he couldn't think of a single reason to. Not a reason based on his own life, who he was, or what he had to lose, which was basically nothing. He knew if his parents ever found out they would be horrified. Mortified. Hurt. Well, it hurt being told (not in so many words) that you weren't welcome in your parents' home anymore. He'd always tried to be respectful, without giving up entirely on who he really was. He'd never stopped loving them, and that was not what this was about.

He sat back and studied Irv for a few seconds. *Dude looks smart*. Patient, too. Letting Manny take his time, not pushing. "Do you think I could make enough from doing this that I could give up one of my jobs?" Because he sure didn't want to find himself spending days filming and then still have to do everything else. That was the whole problem with being an extra. Without special skills, he could put in a twelve-hour day and only get a hundred and fifty bucks. He was better off taking a catering job; it was only the dream that kept him logging in to Central Casting.

Irv could guess what the kid's other jobs paid. "Oh, yeah, definitely. I mean, okay. I don't want to make promises. But if you enjoy it, that will show. People like to watch people enjoy themselves. Did you ever see 'Fame,' the original one?" A nod. "You remember where Coco gets into that mess, crying on camera? Nobody wants to see that. So if you hate it, call it a day and try something else." He studied the younger man for a long minute. He didn't even know how old Figueroa was. The hairline was in retreat, which might account for how short he wore his hair – embracing it instead of fighting it – but the skin around his eyes said 'under thirty.' The eyes themselves were ancient. This kid needed something, and he wasn't getting it in the rest of his life. "I haven't seen you with your clothes off but I'm guessing you're worth looking at. We could come up with a character for you, a stage name with a persona. Design your shoots around that. Maybe there's some skill you have that people find sexy. Bicycles, well," he made a face that he knew said 'that ain't it.'

Manny huffed out something like a laugh. There really was not much sexy about a man riding a bike. "I play the guitar. And I used to work with horses. One of my first jobs was at a riding school."

Irv perked up. "That's fantastic. I know a guy with a stable and a couple of horses. So," he did a 'how about it' thing with his hands, "what do you think? Want to give it a try?"

"Yeah. What have I got to lose, right? Nobody knows who I am, nobody will care."

Oh shit, Irv thought, because he didn't want this to be a revenge-against-the-world scenario. "For the record, payback is a nice idea, but it has an awful tendency to boomerang on you." A sideways smile,

26

which did amazing things to those eyes. *Oh Lord.* "If you smile on camera we'll make a fucking fortune. No pun intended."

Manny laughed out loud, waving that off. "Sure, I'll bet. Look, this isn't about payback. This is about maybe stepping sideways in order to find a better path up. Going off-road, maybe. I could learn more about acting doing this, couldn't I?"

"You definitely could."

"And if I'm no good at it, I can always go back to the other bullshit. I just hate," his voice went wrong for a second, taking him by surprise. He inhaled slowly, controlled the exhale, inhaled again to say, "I don't want to be just another tired old faggot bringing out eggs Benedict till I die."

The mental image made him wince inside, but Irv nodded. "How old are you?"

"I'll be twenty-seven in a minute."

"I was about your age when I decided to quit trying to be a serious filmmaker and make some money instead. It's tough how God or whoever gives idealism to young people. So many of us get it beaten out of us and then we're bitter the rest of our lives. Idealism should come when you're older, I think. When you're secure enough to take disappointment."

"I don't want to be bitter." Manny was studying Irv Morton's face now. Trying to imagine what kind of films the man might have made when he was young and idealistic. It must have been tough. He'd noticed that even people behind the camera tended to be more successful when they looked a certain way. And this man wasn't ugly, far from it, but he wasn't conventionally good-looking. Of course, neither was Manny. He had a good body and good eyes. And, according to at least one person, a nice dick. "I'd like to be secure someday. I don't think I was ever really idealistic. Is that something you learn in college?"

That made Irv laugh. "Yeah, maybe. You didn't go?"

College was a dream, one that went along with a different dream. Both gone now. "Where was I going to find the money or time to go to college? Maybe I'll go when I'm old." The beer bottle was empty. Manny was tempted to order another. He couldn't remember ever having a conversation like this.

Irv had never had a conversation like this with a potential subject. There was something awfully engaging about this one. Part of it was his looks, which were not your conventional good guy looks. If anything, he looked like your conventional bad guy: aquiline nose, heavy eyebrows and beard. But those sad old eyes, and the way they lit up when he smiled: the camera was going to love him. Even if he didn't work out on video, Irv was positive he could do some great pictorials. Figueroa was nothing like any of his other models. And Irv was much too interested. He told himself to concentrate on finding the most marketable niche. "Well, Mr. Figueroa. Want to get another, and tell me about you and horses?"

Manny glanced up. He couldn't read the guy's expression. It might have been personal interest, probably wasn't, didn't matter. He told himself they needed to figure out a way Manny could distinguish himself. He'd seen plenty of boring porn. "Sure. Call me Manny. Do you mind if I call you Irv?"

Did he mind. "That's fine."

May 2015

Manny hadn't told Irv everything about him and horses. Or at least, not about why he gave that up. It wasn't a case of a better job coming along. It was the need to get away from reminders of something else.

Irv was pretty sure there was more to the story. He arranged for them to meet at the filming house in the Valley, which happened to be where Irv was living. He stayed in the apartment over the garage after forming the company. It was convenient, the partners didn't have to pay for security, and if a shoot was going too late or getting too loud, he could stroll over and tell them to wrap it up or keep it down. The neighbors might suspect what kind of filming happened here, but it was best for everybody if they didn't know for sure. The company had all the proper permits. That wouldn't keep them out of hot water if somebody decided they didn't want a porn house next door.

The new model rolled in right on time, politely declined the offer of refreshment, and offered to drive to the stable. Irv was okay with that, though he didn't generally like being a passenger. He also wasn't a fan of big trucks that you had to climb up into. At least the pickup was clean; no fast-food wrappers littered the footwell.

They didn't talk much on the way. It was sufficiently far that the silence could have been awkward, but it wasn't. The radio was on, Latin stuff, not too loud. Figueroa might have been genuinely calm or he might have been a better actor than Irv expected. He was also a good driver. Irv gradually relaxed.

Today was not meant to be X-rated. Today was set up as a pictorial, sexy pictures, not explicit, meaning no erection. As naked as the kid wanted to get without being explicit. The kind of naked pictures that people weren't embarrassed to be caught looking at, the kind they could say 'check out the composition' or shit like that. Though if he decided to get explicit Irv was certainly willing to roll with it. If the kid was actually good with the horses, and the pictures came across, they were talking about using El Vaquero as his stage name. Irv had other Latino guys but all of them were very urban. He knew there was a potentially-huge, so-far-untapped (by him, anyway) market for a country angle.

When they were about five minutes out – off the 101 and onto the road heading into the Santa Monica Mountains – Irv said, "This place is owned by a friend of mine, Red Warner. He just bought it. We met on a film set a long time ago. You might have seen him in a thing or two. Huge guy with red hair down to his ass."

"Oh yeah." Manny smiled. Unforgettable guy. "What's he up to these days?"

"He's got a big part in a movie that's filming this summer. Still doing props, stunts, weapons training. Got married a minute ago."

"Good for him. So he's big on horses?"

"He plays a knight at those Renaissance festivals. Been doing that for years." Irv had done plenty of taping for Red in the fifteen years they'd known each other.

"What kind of weapons? I always wanted to take that training. There are so many calls for people to play cops or soldiers, whatever."

"Everything from knife fighting to broadswords, nunchaku to machine guns. You don't have any weapons skills?"

"It's not a great idea for a Mexican kid to be dicking around with weapons. Everybody thinks you're

30

in a gang anyway." A pause. "My folks kept us busy after school." Manny glanced over at Irv with half a smile. "I do know how to cook. So I can use a kitchen knife." And boy was he glad to move out of *that* job.

Irv snorted. "Well, that's a start. Turn right up there."

The dirt road to the stable was well-graded. Manny drove along slowly for about half a mile, then pulled through the open gate and parked under an oak tree. "Nice place." A big paddock with freshly-painted white rail fences; a small red barn; a tiny wood-frame cabin. A hammock was strung up between metal poles under another oak tree, not far from a picnic table. The owner was sitting there with a Klean Kanteen in his hand and a contented expression on his face. "I think he likes being married."

Irv gave a startled bark of laughter. "Yeah, I guess. Come on, let's introduce you." They got out of the truck and walked over. Red stood up to greet them. "Hey Red."

"Hey Irv." Manny offered a hand; Warner shook it. "You must be Manuel Figueroa."

"Call me Manny. It's a real pleasure to meet you."

"Well, thanks. Call me Red. Irv told me you guys are doing some pictures for Stroked."

"Uh, yeah." Manny knew he was blushing. "It's my first, well." He didn't even know how to talk about this. It was so much more abstract when he was talking to Kevin.

"Don't feel weird about it. I've done some beefcake in my time. Irv says you've worked with horses before." With that, Red started moving them toward the barn. Once they were in there, and Manny had three bright-eyed animals to greet, he forgot about feeling weird. Red exchanged a glance with Irv when he saw how at ease the kid was. "This is Merlin, my horse." A huge gray, well up to carrying Red's six-foot-three, two-thirty. He gave Manny an arrogant snort and turned his back. "That's kind of typical. Don't take it personally." Across from the gray were the others. "This is Freyja, and this is Jarvis. They're new but they're settling in pretty good. I'm teaching my wife to ride."

"Oh yeah? What does she do?"

"She's a dancer. Actor, model. You know. We all do everything we can to get a gig."

"For real. Freyja." Manny leaned on the stall door, letting Freyja come to him. She snuffled him thoroughly. "Preciosa." He was smiling. He put a hand on her neck and scratched under her mane. Jarvis, in the next stall, made a sound that might have been irritated. "You jealous? I'll be right there."

"Have you done any riding?" Red got Manny to talk about the sum of his experience with horses, well aware that Irv was taking mental notes from his position away from any of the stalls. He was also well aware that Irv was not all that comfortable with horses, or with big things in general. If it weren't for their history, he probably wouldn't have considered bringing the new kid here. They moved down to Jarvis, letting him get acquainted with Manny. Both the new horses were plenty big enough for him; Red's wife was six feet tall. "If you want to take either of them out in the paddock, feel free."

"Wow, Red. You sure? They're awfully nice horses."

"I'll be right there if they give you any trouble." Unspoken was, of course, the reverse.

Manny gave the big guy an amused sideways glance. "I got you."

Red was sure he did. "There's a bathroom and snacks and stuff in the cabin. I have a guy who stays out here overnight, he's not around today. Make yourselves at home. I've got some work to do out back but yell if you need me."

"Thanks Red." It was the first thing Irv had said since they went into the barn. He directed the next words at his model. "I'll get the camera stuff out of the truck." A reminder of what they were here for. Not that he would have minded simply watching the kid bond with the horses, but they had a job to do.

Over the next two hours, while Red installed a small satellite dish so he could get internet and cell reception, Manny took full advantage of the situation. He started with Freyja, putting her into the show halter with her name on it and leading her out to the paddock. There, he turned her loose to wander around, watching as she examined the fence and gazed down the dirt road. "You want to get out there, don't you lady. Sorry, not with me, not today. You gonna give me a little ride? How about it?" He kept talking softly, letting the horse come to him again.

Irv was taking pictures continuously. Figueroa was dressed for this in well-worn cowboy boots, jeans, and a long-sleeved plaid shirt that had to have come from a western-wear shop. Perfectly in character, in fact, except for not having a hat. *Or chaps. God would I love to see him in chaps. And nothing else.* Irv was laughing to himself, or at himself, when the kid went to the mounting block and simply stood on it. Freyja came over. He said something to her, stroked a hand down her back, and swung a leg over. The next thing Irv knew, Figueroa was riding bareback around the paddock with one hand wound into Freyja's mane and the other resting on his thigh. *Jesus Christ.* Irv was not a country-western kind of guy. He'd never been to a rodeo, never even watched any kind of rodeo thing. The sum total of his experience with horses was dodging the occasional mounted policeman back home in New York, and watching the fancy riders in the Rose Parade. He could have watched this all day. The photos were going to be great. He was taking way too many, considering his model had all his clothes on. It was clear the kid would happily have stayed on the horse forever. But after a few minutes he dismounted, said another thing to the horse, and led her back to the stable. Irv followed, wondering what came next.

It turned out to be a brief grooming session. Manny used the currycomb and a chamois cloth to brush and polish the glossy brown coat. Then he made sure Freyja had fresh water and some hay before giving her another pat and turning to Jarvis. The whole program repeated itself. Jarvis was bigger, and clearly had a different personality. His behavior with Manny in the paddock was a lot like a dog's. Slightly challenging, but as if he wanted to play.

After a few minutes, Irv said "What the fuck" out loud because damned if the kid and the horse weren't playing some kind of keep-away game. It was almost like a dance. He looked over to see if Red was watching, but the big guy was nowhere in sight. Irv switched his camera to video mode and let it run until the horse went over to the mounting block, looking over his shoulder as if to say 'let's go.' Manny had to jump a little to get on his back, but Jarvis stayed put and let him do it. Then it was a few minutes of riding around before Manny dismounted and took the horse back to the barn.

34

This time, after finishing up with the horse, Manny took off his shirt. "Got hot out there," he said, not quite making eye contact with Irv.

"Feel free to dump some water on yourself." Irv's tone was slightly dry. He saw the laugh in Manny's body, rather than hearing it.

"I could do that." And damned if he didn't. He went to the end of the passageway, where there was a hose curled up on a slab of concrete. Shook out the shirt and hung it on a convenient nail. Took off his boots, stripped off his jeans and boxer briefs, and sprayed himself down. "Fuck that's cold!" He took his time with it though, the whole thing. Irv shot pictures like a maniac. He'd given Figueroa only the vaguest suggestions about what to do today. It wasn't quite a test, or at least he hadn't consciously intended it to be. Now, watching this happen with next to no direction, he thought *I should have given him a script*. It wasn't really fair to bring someone out like this and make him improvise, his first time. But he was rocking it. The pictorial was going to be great. The background looked like genuine country, not like they were only a few minutes from a major freeway in the middle of a metropolis. The angle of the sun ensured that the subject, while in the shade, wasn't in the dark. Every line of that body, every muscle, was showing up perfectly. The way his nipples tightened under the cold water, too. He hadn't touched his dick but plenty of people who saw these pictures were going to touch theirs. Zero ink on that tawny skin; it was the first time Irv had shot a Latino model with no tattoos. There was zero fat on those thighs, and the ass was perfect. Literally perfect. Well, it should be, the bicycle-racing motherfucker. Figueroa was drying off now, using the inside of his shirt. Drying *everything*. He wasn't

35

looking at Irv or the camera. Was acting as if he was all alone, and as if he had something on his mind. Something that from the look of things might have reminded him of lovemaking, but also something sad. God, those eyes. Irv didn't say anything. He kept on taking pictures while the kid got dressed again, or mostly dressed. He didn't button up the damp shirt.

Then he went back to Jarvis, collected a big soft nose to the neck, patted that giant head. Took a couple steps to Freyja and did the same thing. Except he leaned in to rest his forehead against hers. Irv said, "You okay?" Then, like the asshole he was, he switched to video mode.

"Mmm. When I worked in a stable before, I had a friend. The guy who owned the place, it was his son. We went to school together. He was my first." He wasn't moving. "We were together all through high school. Then he joined up, the Marines. We talked about when he got through. He was going to do six or eight years, then get out and go to college. We talked about the future. I came out to my family for him, after we graduated." He inhaled audibly. Irv got the idea that didn't go so well. "He came home after basic training. Had himself a Marine Corps ring, he was so proud of that. We went down to Venice, and there was this metalsmith on the boardwalk with silver bands. He could do a message on it, right there while you waited." He held up his right hand. "Lobo got me this. The guy stamped in a word, it says Semper. Always." Another deep breath. He rubbed Freyja's face with both hands for a long moment. Irv felt a little sick; he was pretty sure he knew what came next. "He was killed in a training accident. Never even got deployed." Manny wiped his face on his shirt sleeve and turned around. Freyja draped her head over his shoulder. He reached up absently to fondle her soft muzzle. "I mean, who knows if we would have made it. If we would have lasted. The odds were never good. But it would have been nice to have the chance to find out."

Irv gave it a second, then said carefully, "Was Lobo his real name?"

"No, it was Lowell. He was white. He was like, of all the fucking names." A trace of a smile.

"Is that why you're single?"

Manny shrugged. "Probably. After having that, someone to look at the future with, it's hard to settle for less." He huffed out half a laugh. "The next person I was really interested in was that fucker Angel. I don't even know why, now."

You were lonely, Irv thought. "Does it help to talk about it?"

"Yeah, actually. It helps to think someone else knows. Thanks for listening."

"You're welcome. Ready to call it a day?"

"God, yes. Did you get what you need?"

"Oh, you were terrific. I'll let you know when I've got it ready to launch. Think you might want to come back here sometime?"

"I'd love to. Would he let me?"

"I'm going to find him, talk to him for a second. Take a load off. Maybe go in the cabin, see about a snack."

"Yeah, okay." Manny turned his head, regarded Freyja for a second, and said, "You're a nice lady." She made a whuffling noise. Irv didn't say anything. He turned off the camera and lugged the tripod over to the truck. Tried to decide if he needed to come up with some kind of cover story for his partners about all the extra footage, all the extra shots. Well, the only person who was likely to see any of it was Lauro, and he wouldn't give Irv any hassle. But another person might be interested.

CHAPTER 3

Red was in sight now; he was lying on his back on top of the picnic table. "Hey," he said without moving. "All done for today?"

"Yeah."

"Get some good stuff?"

"Jesus, yes. I want to show you what that big horse was doing with the kid." Irv took the camera over there. Red sat up, leaned over, watched the playback of that file. Made an interested sound. "That's what I thought."

"How old is he?"

"Twenty-seven."

"He's probably going to look exactly the way he looks now for about twenty years. You're going to get rich." Irv laughed. Red was grinning at him. "I don't suppose he lives anywhere near here."

"Red, nobody lives anywhere near here except hippies and religious fanatics. If there's a difference. He lives near the Beverly Center. I think he'd come out here again, though. If maybe you could use a hand with the horses from time to time."

Red gazed at him thoughtfully. Irv was not in the habit of suggesting ways for his subjects to connect with his friends. "I could, actually. When I go out on that shoot especially. My guy can't be twenty-four-seven, and Mary might not want to come out every day." They talked about things for a few minutes, half-watching Manny leave the barn and go into the cabin. "So what's the quid in this quid pro quo."

Irv laughed under his breath. "He wants weapons training. He's doing the extra calls and stuff, but you know."

"Yeah, I know. Working as a trainer is rough." It sounded like a change of subject, but it wasn't.

"Says the guy who nearly broke his neck on a set."

"Accidents happen. I'll talk to Mary and get in touch. We'll see what he wants to do."

"Fine. Thanks. Thanks for this," Irv added. "It was a great shoot. I'm glad you finally got your piece of the country."

"Jesus, me too. Mary loves it."

"Which horse does she like better?"

"She likes Jarvis. He's such an asshole sometimes, though. I'm glad we got Freyja too. She calms both the guys down, and when Jarvis is in a mood it's good to have a spare."

"Little ménage à trois. Am I ever going to get you in front of the camera again? I know you're hanging with that other guy from time to time, the guy who shoots the Underground Cabaret."

"Who, Andy Martin? I hardly know him. I don't think he's doing much photography these days. There's some talk about him shooting this new dance thing we're doing at the end of summer. But I should get you out to our place. Take some pictures of Mary." There was a soft look on Red's face now.

"Yeah, sure. I'm gonna go drain the lizard." He felt kind of awkward going in the cabin when Figueroa was still in there. Couldn't for the life of him have said why. He was in close contact with subjects all the time. Alone with them pretty often. This hesitancy was both new and annoying. Only years of practice hiding his reactions kept him from shaking his head impatiently as he walked back over to the cabin. *Keep it professional.* He shouldn't have to tell himself that.

Manny was grateful for a few minutes alone. He'd managed to forget he was being photographed when he was working with the horses. That was such a joy, after so many years away. He guessed it was true what they said, you never forgot something you learned as a kid. He worked at the riding school right up until they got the news about Lobo. Had actually been there when they got the news. His boss knew, in a kind of 'don't tell me' way, that Manny and Lobo were together. He thought the military would cure his son. His tall, strong, football-playing all-American son, who took a girl to homecoming and prom but spent most of his free time with that Mexican kid. He was kind, even in that moment of what must have been terrible grief. Manny was done in the stable, heading out to the truck that preceded the red one. Lobo's dad stopped him. Said come inside, we have to tell you something. Sat him down at the kitchen table. Didn't let him leave until he thought Manny would be safe driving home. He didn't cry, not then, not in front of them. Sat in the truck for ten minutes after parking outside his shitty little apartment, trying to get his head around the fact that he would never see Lobo again. Finally went inside, got in the shower, and stayed there until the hot water ran out.

The riding school was closed for a week. Manny never went back. Lobo's dad called him the next day and said, we'll understand if you don't want to work here anymore. Manny heard, we'd rather you didn't work here anymore. That might not have been what the guy meant, but by the time Manny was over the worst of the grief and able to think things through, he had a different job. So many jobs since then, working up to the one he had now. If only it were a full-time job, one with benefits, one he could actually live on. Well, it wasn't, and that was that. If taking his clothes off for Irv meant he could call the catering company and say I'm out, he was okay with it. He didn't feel bad about what they did today. Irv wasn't skeevy or gross about it. He was all business. Manny was really curious how the pictures would turn out. He'd never had a portrait taken except for school, or a work ID. Even his head shot was just from someone's phone.

The cabin was set up for occupancy by the kind of guard who knew he wasn't going to be disturbed much. There was a closed-circuit monitor to the stable; Manny noticed the cameras when he was in there. A flatscreen, now surely connected to the dish Red was installing that day. A decent little kitchen, full-sized bathroom, and a pull-out couch. A place like this would be perfect.

He was leaning against the counter, absent-mindedly working his way through a snack-sized bag of gorp and scrolling through some shit on his phone, when Irv came in. "Hey kid. I'll be ready to go in a minute."

"Sure." Manny checked the time, blinked at how late it was, shrugged. It was weird to have only the one thing to do; he usually filled up the days he wasn't scheduled at the gym. This time, not wanting to feel rushed, he didn't book anything else. After he dropped Irv off, he'd have the whole evening free. Too bad he didn't have something better to do with it than watch videos online, or fool around with the guitar. He didn't do that much at home in the evening. Was always afraid to bother the neighbors. But there were a few hours yet before the time most people seemed to shut down for the night. Playing for a while would settle him down. And then he'd probably jerk off, because for a minute there he was getting turned on. Being watched like that kind of worked for him.

It was another quiet drive back to the filming house. Irv could tell that the kid was tired. It didn't seem like so much work, but when emotions got involved they could wear a person out fast. And while the experience had obviously been a good one, it had brought up those memories. Irv couldn't stop hearing him say 'someone to look at the future with.' It was almost twenty years since Irv had someone like that. They must have been about the same age when their dreams died. He hoped the kid wouldn't go the same way Irv did, getting cynical and closed-off. Was it better or worse that the kid was still in love when his dream ended? Irv's ended the way most adolescent love affairs did, with someone saying they were through. He would have sworn he was over it.

I should think about this stuff, he realized after he was up in the apartment, putting together some dinner. It wasn't a question of needing to process his heartbreak, or anything squishy like that. There were plenty of conversations on that topic over the years. With his parents, with classmates in college, with other boyfriends or partners. Irv was never at a loss for someone to go to bed with when he really wanted another body. There were plenty of not-so-good-looking guys who couldn't make it with the really hot ones. He could remember more than one evening with a guy, spending hours bitching and laughing about their various traumas before (or after) going to bed.

That might make a hell of a film, actually. He wondered if he could get a few of their regular models interested in doing it. It would need an actual script. One couple playing the through-story, a night of reminiscence in between sex acts. Each of those guys playing two or three scenes with other partners. They

43

could get a lot of guys involved. It wouldn't count toward 'best group scene' (though they could certainly include a group scene, so who knew) but it might catch people's attention when they were looking at 'best actor.' GayVN awards wouldn't boost a career the way an Oscar did, but everybody liked to be recognized. Even if it was only by the other people in their particular industry.

He should have been working through the hundreds of photos from that day's shoot. Instead he spent the evening writing up his idea. Most of the films he made were short. Five or six setups in a single scene, with a single objective. The long-form films were time-consuming and expensive to produce, which meant they cost more on the consumer side. Most people went for a thing they could watch in ten or fifteen minutes. Get turned on, take care of business, and go on with their day. The same way people watched short comedy pieces, or music videos, or whatever. This would be the kind of thing the company only made once or twice a year. Once he was satisfied with the write-up, he'd send it out to his partners and see if either of them wanted to jump in with him.

The next day he had a shoot scheduled, so he didn't get to Figueroa's photos till evening. He caught himself pulling some into a blank folder. *What are you doing.* It seemed he was making a marketing set. All the kid had was that lousy head shot. No wonder he couldn't get any traction. *Not my problem.* He didn't stop separating them out. The naked pictures, those were obviously for Stroked. And choosing the usual number of them was going to be tough. Then he had those two video clips, and fuck knew what he thought he was going to do with those. All those damned pictures with the horses. *Screw it.* By the end of the session he had a

44

dozen images in the folder now labeled 'marketing.' When the kid came back out to review the proposed pictorial, he'd mention that. Say, I could put together a web page for you in about an hour. Give casting people a way to find you. Maybe even load the clip of him playing with that big horse. You didn't see shit like that every day. And he was smiling in that clip. Laughing. Calling the horse terrible names in both his languages.

It wouldn't cost anything but time. Buying another domain was trivial. Constructing the actual page could be done on the same template he used for everything else. Link it to the email address and the YouTube channel the kid already had. Nothing to it. It could be his good deed for the year.

What with one thing and another (gigs with the catering company, a race, covering another trainer's absence), Manny couldn't manage a meet-up with Irv until the back half of June. "I'm really sorry it's taken so long," he said, after they settled on a day.

"Not a problem," Irv lied. He would have been happier if the stable pictorial had gone up within a week. But then, offering to review it with the kid first was his own idea, so this was his fault. "I'm going to ask for some of your time. Couple things to show you."

"Once I get out to the Valley I'm all yours." Manny heard himself say that and winced. He didn't want to give the impression he was making a pass. Or up for a pass. He liked Irv fine, but he wasn't looking to hook up. With the whole naked-pictures thing, that would be too weird.

After a few weeks to convince himself Figueroa was only a model, Irv didn't even hear any innuendo. "Great. I was talking to Red the other day and he had an offer for you, told me to pass it on. See you at the house later."

"Okay, see you." Manny was curious about the offer. Maybe the big guy needed an extra hand with the horses from time to time. He put the question aside and went to lead his last class of the day. In the locker room later, there was another skirmish with Angel. Or attempted skirmish. This time Manny didn't react to the snotty comment, except to make eye contact with another of the HIIT trainers, who rolled his eyes in an 'ignore that dick' way that made Manny smile. Then it was out to the Valley, with a stop at a taco truck before finishing the drive to the porn house. It didn't occur to him to wonder why they were meeting there until he arrived and saw half a dozen vehicles crowding the driveway and parked on the street in front.

Irv had a street-view window and was watching for the red pickup truck. As soon as the kid parked, Irv jogged downstairs to meet him. "Hey. There's a shoot happening in the house. If you want to see how it works, we can go in."

Manny blinked. That would be smart, if he was serious about doing this. "Yeah, okay." Seeing Irv come down the stairs alongside the garage, Manny figured there must be an office up there, which answered the question about why Irv was here. He followed the older man into the house.

There was generic-sounding music playing. A man's voice, giving directions. Then the music was replaced by some obvious porn sounds, a man and a woman getting it on. Manny could feel himself blushing as they approached the working room.

God, it was so crowded. The couple on the bed. A person who had to be the director, with a video camera on a tripod. A person holding a boom mic. Cables trailing everywhere, and two lights with diffusers, set on tripods. A box fan stood against the wall. Two people loitered in the hallway. One of them was obviously a production assistant – he looked ready for anything – and the other one had his eyes glued to a tablet. Manny could see the scene being shot, on-screen. Everybody except the models was completely silent.

Even with those other people acting like this was just another day at the office (which he guessed it was), Manny was embarrassed. Watching porn at home on a screen was so, so different from watching real live people fuck. It was nothing like the few times he'd been in a room where people were doing it. He'd been involved then, not simply standing around watching. There was a word for that, but he couldn't remember it.

Irv could tell the kid was mortified. He hid his own amusement, keeping his face neutral, breath steady. There were times watching a scene (even a straight scene) got him hot, but most of his attention was on the technical stuff. The composition, the lighting, was the boom guy letting the mic droop, was there too much clutter in the background. The director, Irv's partner Payton, must have dressed the room this way for a reason, but to Irv it seemed messy. Oh well. Different strokes for different folks.

The room was easily twenty degrees hotter than the hallway. By the time Payton cut the scene, both models were glistening with sweat. "You want us to stay sweaty?" the guy said. He was still fully erect. Manny wondered how long he could keep it up. Maybe he took Viagra.

"We're just changing angle here. Wipe down a little." The lights had to move – the production assistant did that, while the dude with the monitor tablet viewed the last shot again – then the camera, then the boom guy found a new place to squeeze in. "Is that thing out of the shot? Good. Re-set to the start of this scene." The P.A. set the box fan in the doorway and switched it on. Then he brought in bottled water for the models, patted away the worst of the sweat, touched up the woman's makeup, consulted another tablet and adjusted the set dressing.

Manny was fascinated now. One person handling all the jobs that he'd seen a whole team do on a real movie set. Meanwhile the monitor guy and the boom guy left the room with the director. When they came back, the assistant cleared out and the director called for action. The models gave some dialogue that sounded like they were making it up on the spot. Manny hoped so. Nobody should get paid for writing that. There was some really slurpy kissing, with lots of groping. The woman had these huge fake-looking tits. She was pretty enough aside from that. The guy was a bodybuilder. Not Manny's type. By the time they were fully fucking again, he was used to it. Not blushing, not embarrassed, watching the same way Irv was. Before the director cut the scene, Manny glanced over. Caught Irv's eye and tipped his head to indicate he'd seen enough.

Irv was aware of the moment Figueroa got over it. There were some guys who simply couldn't take it, so he was glad this one settled down. Having seen how businesslike everyone was, the kid should now have a better idea what it was like in front of the camera. When they got outside he said, "Sometime you might want to see how we do a solo video. Basically the same when we shoot here. On a location, it might be only the camera, plus a P.A. to make sure the model is comfortable and camera-ready."

"I've seen some amateur porn," Manny said, following Irv up the stairs outside. "The kind where it looks like they took the video with their phone."

"Smartphones can take some damn good video. It still helps a lot to have someone managing sound and lighting. Your average guy jerking off on camera at home, there's always shadows and bad angles and background noise. Zits, bad hair, whatever. Plus they never have rights to whatever music they use, so if a company like ours picks it up, we have to dub in something different, which means if the person said anything or made any useful sounds, those get lost. We try to have a consistently high-quality product."

They were inside the apartment now. Manny forgot the thought he'd just had about music, and went on alert. "Do you live here?"

"Sure do. We need someone in residence, for security. You can't leave a house vacant and expect people not to fuck with it. The alarm service is for emergencies." Irv watched the kid study the place. It was divided into three spaces. Sleeping area and bathroom were at the back. Then there was an eat-in kitchen. The biggest space was Irv's office. He hadn't had anyone but his partners or Lauro in here for a long time. What was Figueroa thinking about the editing suite with its three big monitors, and all the other computer gear? The wall of DVDs, interspersed with books on filmmaking and cinema? The front half of the apartment had windows on three walls. Irv hardly ever turned on the ceiling lights during the day. "I figure the lack of privacy is countered by my view of the pool."

Manny registered that aside from the barstools at the kitchen peninsula, the only seating was a high-end task chair. This was not a bachelor pad; it was a workplace that someone happened to sleep in. He

49

relaxed, turning his head, shooting Irv an amused glance. He indicated the wall of shelves. "Is that every movie ever made?"

"Jesus, no. I have some standards." That got a laugh. "Hang on." Irv went to the closet on the far side of the bathroom and pulled out an upholstered folding chair. He didn't want to put Figueroa in the task chair and have Irv hanging over him, or vice versa. A reminder of what the kid looked like laughing was also a reminder that a little professional distance was advisable. "Want something to drink?"

"Water would be great, thanks."

Irv poured filtered water into a pair of insulated travel cups and took them over to the desk. He indicated the folding chair for Manny, then sat in the task chair. "Red's out on a shoot. Mary's also got a thing out of town. Their watchman person is still out there overnight, and he's going to handle the daily maintenance."

Manny said, "Okay." It sounded like a question.

"Red mentioned he'd be glad to have someone who knew the horses going out there from time to time, to give them some exercise. He already told me I can use the place for filming again if I want. If you want to go separately to do horse stuff, all you'd need to do is text the overnight guy to let him know you're coming." Figueroa looked so excited, Irv thought he probably didn't even need to say the next thing. But it was going to be good for the kid long-term, and for whatever reason Irv was still riding the do-good-for-the-kid wave. "He also said he'd be glad to give you some weapons training once he's back in town. He and Mary are going right into another dance concert, but it's not all day every day. You might want to go see that, too," he suggested. "He said it's tango and cowboys, whatever the fuck that means."

Manny almost laughed. He barely knew what tango was, but a dance concert with cowboys? This he had to see. Especially if Red and his wife were dancing in it. "I'd love that," he said. "All of that. I wanted to ask if I could visit the horses again sometime."

"Well, this was a specific invitation, and he's serious about swapping you some training in return. He wants those horses in good shape when they get done with the dance thing in September. Says the, what's it called. The big brown one."

"Jarvis."

"Says he's a real asshole if he doesn't get out on the trail regularly." The kid laughed. Irv grinned back at him for a second. "Anyway I'll give you those numbers before you go. Now let's have a look at that pictorial. I'm not gonna lie, I want to get you back out there to do a solo video. If you want to, let me know if you have any ideas for the scenario."

Manny nodded, but he didn't say anything right then. He was cringing a little at the idea of looking at naked pictures of himself. Irv turned to the keyboard, moved his mouse, and the biggest screen woke up. It was a search view, but a second later he opened an index view with what looked like a thousand thumbnails. "Damn!"

"This is all of them. You want to see, or you want to go straight to the ones I want to post?"

"Could we look at that first? How many is that?"

Irv sighed. He'd tried to cut it down to the usual number. "It's kind of a lot. What you did turned into a perfect slideshow. Like an old flip-book animation, almost. I know people are going to view it that way."

Manny didn't know the term, filed it away for the future. "Can I see it that way?"

"Sure." Irv set the viewer, selected the file, and sat back as it began to run.

There were a lot more pictures than Manny expected. He wasn't counting how many images there were, but Irv was right; it was basically a whole continuous scene. Undressing, one shot for each garment. Close-ups of his face, chest, and bare feet. Then rinsing himself down. Another close-up of his chest, when he'd had chicken skin and his nipples were tight from the cold water. Shots of his bare back and front, including his ass and his half-hard dick, with water running down it. *Damn*, he thought, surprised. *This is sexy*. It didn't even seem like himself. The way the light hit him, he almost looked like a sculpture. There were a few shots of him drying himself off, including a close-up of his hand rubbing his shirt between his legs. A back view of him shrugging into the shirt. He'd been walking past Irv, toward the horses. That one was really artistic. Had Irv used a flash? There was light on Manny, showing off the hollow of his back, but the horses were almost silhouetted against the bright daylight at the far end of the barn. The last shot was Manny leaning his forehead against Freyja's. Not a single one had him looking directly at the camera. "Was that bad?" he said uncertainly. "That I never looked at you? I thought I did."

"Oh, you did. I didn't use any of those for this. I like the way it reads, as if you're all alone. A private moment. What do you think?" He put a slight emphasis on 'you.'

"Is it sick to say I think it's sexy?"

Irv stifled a laugh. "No. You good with posting this?"

52

"Yeah, I'm good. I like it. I wish I had some of those pictures to put with my head shot." Manny sat back, thinking of the contract he'd signed. It had only now occurred to him that Irv really didn't have to show him these pictures. He could post whatever he wanted. *Why is he doing this.*

"Well," Irv said, drawing it out. "I kind of did that. Your head shot is crap. And we had these pictures anyway." The kid was looking at him as if he were speaking some unknown language. "I made you a new marketing set. You want to look at the rest of these?"

Manny started to say something, recalibrated, started again. "Um. Could I see the marketing stuff first?" He was excited again, but also worried. A full marketing set could be hundreds of dollars. Maybe that was why. Maybe people saw what good pictures looked like and decided to pony up.

Irv didn't say anything, only navigated to a different folder. All the photos opened at once, a full screen of Manny. A great head shot framed by the doorway of the barn: eyes slightly narrowed against the sun, half-smiling. Several action shots from out in the paddock. A picture of him bare from the hips up, hands at his waistband as if fastening (or maybe unfastening) his jeans. And another portrait, with Freyja. Irv pointed to that one. "Re-do your resumé to play up the horse angle, if you haven't already. People will notice this picture, how at ease the horse is with you. There are more shoots using horses than people realize, and nowhere near enough good handlers. Let alone good handlers who are good on camera."

"Irv, these are fantastic, but I can't afford –"

"No charge. Like I said, the pictures were already done. Personally I'd like to get you out from under the caterer because I have about a million ideas for shoots I want to do with you." A million filthy ideas, which he'd spent a little more time visualizing than he should have.

Manny was smiling. "You don't even know if people will like this one." Irv gave him a look. "Okay, I guess you do. Are you sure? That's a lot. I mean, I really appreciate it."

"Well, there's more, and don't feel weird about it. I know that gym job isn't full-time. You need to be earning other ways, and it suits me if you get more work in the pictures. Anyhow I threw together a website. It cost basically nothing," he said, cutting off another protest. "Took me no time. I have a template. All it is, is a landing page with a few of your credits from the resumé you showed me, some different pictures, a contact link, and a link to your YouTube channel. Here." He handed over a flash drive. The kid took it mechanically, mouth open as if he was about to say something. Irv kept going. "Couple of videos from when you were doing stuff with the horses. Now, you want to go back to the full set from the barn, or you want to talk about doing a video out there?"

Manny could see he wasn't going to get anywhere saying Irv shouldn't put so much time into him. The guy had his reasons, and he wasn't being creepy about it at all. Nothing like, I did this for you, maybe you could do something for me. In fact, Irv clearly wanted to get off that subject immediately. Manny sighed, put the flash drive in his shirt pocket, and organized his thoughts. "I guess I don't need to see the full set. I did have an idea for a video. It's more clear now that I saw what you did with the still pictures."

"Okay, tell me." Irv took a swig of water, relaxed now that all his overly-enthusiastic helpfulness was out

54

of the way. "Bear in mind it'll be like I said. Me on camera, a P.A., maybe a sound guy."

Manny nodded. There were plenty of times he'd wondered if it might be easier to get a job as a production assistant than as an actor, but he guessed it probably wasn't. "That guy in the house today seemed like he was really on it."

"Lauro? He's very good. He's full time with us. Anyway, go."

Manny drank some water. "Okay. I was thinking, what if I'm out there because I was supposed to be meeting someone, and he stood me up. I'm on the phone with him going what the fuck, where are you."

"I like it, leaves a lot open to interpretation." They wouldn't even have to specify that the person Figueroa was talking to was another man.

"Right. I mean, if we might make a few of these, the guy who's not in them is my story, right? He's not with me, that's why I'm doing it for myself. All kinds of reasons he might not be there." Manny shrugged. He'd put a lot of thought into this, because if he had some kind of reason to be doing what he was doing, it would be easier to do it. Even if that reason was fictitious. "Anyway, so I'm out there alone and I'm like, damn. I was looking forward to that. Might as well, you know." It was so weird to be talking about this. *I am going to get myself off in front of people I barely know, on camera, so that other people I don't know at all can get off. La vida loca.*

Irv tried not to react, even while he wondered if Figueroa suspected what a thrill it was to have a model approach this as an acting exercise. Not simply posing for the camera, making fuck-me faces and getting himself off, but creating a character. Jesus, he couldn't wait to shoot it. "That's all good. That'll definitely work. Are you going to play it angry, disappointed, or what?"

"I thought maybe disappointed. Like I understand why he can't be there even though I'm not happy about it. Then a little bit of man, you're gonna wish you were here when I tell you what I did. Maybe Red wouldn't mind if I use those hay bales."

"You could be on the phone –"

"Telling him I was going to bend him over right there." Manny laughed at Irv's expression. "Or let him bend me over." He probably shouldn't have said that; Irv might be blushing a little. Did he think Manny was coming on to him? *Cállate hombre, keep it professional.* "Maybe we take that both ways, then you can decide which way is better for the viewer."

Take it both ways. Jesus Christ. Irv told himself very sternly not to speculate about whether that was a hint. Manny – no, Figueroa – was not acting flirty. He was not going to flirt with Irv, for fuck's sake. Steer this some other way. "You know if you only do solos, these could run on both parts of the site. Crossover."

"Oh!" Manny hadn't thought of that. "I guess so, huh? Do women watch porn?"

Irv laughed. "So I've been told."

"Damn, I guess. I never thought about it." Manny was laughing now. "But sure, there must be lonely ladies out there too. Should I do anything different? Oh, that whole hay bale thing, that should be different." They both cracked up. "Unless a lady's into pegging."

Shut UP. Irv tried not to picture that. "Use of toys is always an option." He almost laughed again at Manny's expression. Jesus, give up already, he was not going to keep thinking of the guy as 'Figueroa.' That ship had sailed. "Sure, why not?"

Manny shook his head. Somehow this ridiculousness was making him feel much more comfortable about the whole thing. Comfortable with Irv. *Irving*, he thought for some reason. He didn't know anybody else with that name. *Concentrate.* "I'll be thinking about how to play it," he said. "When you want to do that?"

Irv pulled up his calendar and they talked about a schedule. Manny wouldn't have another race for a while. Catering jobs could be worked in around things he was doing in the Valley. A video shoot would take at least as many hours as they'd spent at the stable the first time. "Personal question," Irv said after they had a date blocked out.

"What's that."

"How long can you edge yourself?"

Manny felt his face heat. Oh, shit, he had to be bright red. A sip of water, a breath, clearing his throat. "I, uh, I never timed it. Usually, you know. Eyes on the prize."

"Uh-huh. I get it. Might be worth doing a little bit of practice. It can be more efficient if you can, you know." Jesus, why not simply say it: if you can manage not to come till we're at the end of the scene. Of all the things to be shy about saying. This was about porn. They were going to make porn, which Irv did all the damn time. At some point, Manny was going to come, because nearly all people who watched porn wanted to see that. *Oh fuck what is that going to look like*. Irv was way too interested. He changed the subject to something he forgot ten seconds after Manny excused himself to the bathroom. This hadn't happened for a very long time. Irv was going to have to be careful with

57

this one. Ten years in the business without a harassment complaint, and he wanted to keep it that way.

He was still thinking about things he shouldn't be thinking about when they shook hands and Manny left. The kid was too damned likable, was the problem. On the other hand, if that came across on video, he was going to be a hit. For now, Irv needed to post the pictorial, make sure the shoot next door was wrapping up, and find something to watch. Something he had to pay attention to, so he wouldn't keep thinking about his sweet, hot, new model.

CHAPTER 4

The funny thing was that right when Manny was getting comfortable with the porn stuff he got too busy to do much of it. Thinking about the scene Irv wanted to do, thinking about how he wanted to do it. Practicing for it, which was going to make a funny story someday. But there was a race, there were lessons, there were weddings and graduation parties and whatever to be catered, and while a solo scene was worth more than a day as an extra it was still not 'I can quit this job' money. Manny didn't want to do a million random scenes that were just like everybody else's, not when he could make steady money other ways. He'd do porn as and when he could, right up to the point where he stopped learning stuff that helped in the real world.

He learned a hell of a lot from doing the first video. One thing he learned was that he enjoyed it. Which might make him a little bit of a perv. On the other hand, it was like Irv said at that first meeting: most people don't want to watch somebody be miserable.

They arranged to meet at Red's stable, because Irv was bringing Lauro and a carload of gear. Manny arrived early to give both the horses a little exercise in the paddock. He finished up their grooming, gave them both some fresh hay and water, and still had time to stretch out on top of the picnic table and enjoy the almost-country silence. When Irv's car rolled in Manny looked over, but otherwise didn't move.

"Nice hat," Irv said as he got out of the car. "You look comfortable."

"It's a nice day. I don't have any outdoor space where I live." He sat up. "Hey Lauro."

"Hey Manny. You ready for this?"

"I don't even know."

Lauro laughed. "Any scene-setting we need to do?"

"No, I already did it." Manny picked up his new black cowboy hat, set it on his head, stepped down from the table and struck a pose. Plaid shirt hanging open over a white tank top, thumbs hooked in his pockets so his fingers framed his groin, weight on one leg. Chin up and eyes narrowed, the way he practiced at home. "Cowboy enough?"

"Looking good, El Vaquero." Irv had not suggested the hat; he was very happy to see it. No chaps, but you couldn't have everything. He made a mental note to take a few shots in this exact pose. "Any other props?"

"Come and see." Manny had set the stage a little in the tack room, which was really nothing more than a double-wide stall. The bridles, saddles, and other leather all belonged to Red, as did the coil of rope hung on the wall under a rack of grooming tools. Sacks of feed were piled up along another wall. Hay bales were arranged like a daybed, with a serape draped casually over the top. "I wanted it to look like I was expecting to mess around with someone else in here, like we were talking about." There was even a cooler, with some bottled beer on ice. "We can use this if we don't show the label, right?"

"Right." Irv looked around, nodded his approval, and went back to the car for the gear. The tack room got some natural light, but he'd want the tripod lamps. A tripod mount for the boom mic too; Lauro was getting that set up. Then was time to try a few positions, figure out where the tripod for the camera should go. He'd film handheld until Manny settled into place. "Still going with the phone thing, right?"

"If you think that's good."

"Yeah, it's a good lead-in." They didn't waste any time. Started with a few silent takes of Manny doing stable things. Then went to half a dozen takes of the one-sided phone conversation. Irv noticed slight differences in what Manny said and how he said it. "Come and watch this back," he suggested, after he thought they had enough to work with. "This was your third take." He played it, aware of how close they were standing and trying not to like it too much. "I think the disappointment really comes across here. But it's still kind of flirty."

"Yeah." Manny glanced over to make eye contact. *Damn he's right there. I can feel his heat.* "I wanted it to feel like this is someone I really care about. I'll forgive a lot."

That was interesting. They'd have to talk some more about through-story. "Uh-huh. Well, have this one in mind and we'll go to the next setup."

Then it was a few takes of Manny off the phone, talking to himself and to the horses, deciding to make the most of his afternoon. Opening a bottle of beer, taking a drink, setting it down. They cut there to let Manny pour out the beer, refilling the bottle with water so he could actually drink. Then there was a take of Manny standing in the aisle with his shirt unbuttoned, bottle in one hand and the other down his jeans. Jarvis made a snorting sound. Manny looked at him, said, "Get a room? Yeah, you're right," and went into the tack room. They cut again so Irv could set the camera on the tripod and frame the next setup. Manny lounging on the bales with his back to the wall, unbuttoning his jeans. Stroking himself to full arousal, but only half-exposed. So tantalizing. Irv wouldn't have thought of suggesting that, but it really worked.

It was definitely weird doing this, but after a while Manny was in it. He was remembering his first time with Lobo. Such a good memory. They'd been friends for years, working together at the riding school, dating girls. Of course, 'dating' before they could drive was mostly meeting up at school events and making out between classes. Then one day they were in the stable, and Lobo asked how a date went. Asked if Manny kissed the girl. Manny said yeah, it was okay. Lobo said why just okay? He was standing real close. Eye contact turned into Manny looking at Lobo's mouth. He said, truth is there's somebody else I'd rather kiss.

That was all it took. Lobo kissed him. A few minutes later they were rubbing off against each other, Manny's back to the wall, Lobo's tongue in his mouth. In the here and now, Manny made a frustrated sound. Leaned forward to pull his boots off, shucked off his jeans, and got back to business.

He thought he did pretty well. Held out for two more setups, never lost his hard-on, and when Irv said "You can go whenever you want" he went for it. Lying on the bales, breathing through his mouth, chest slick with sweat and belly wet with come. Irv made some kind of move and Manny flicked a glance his way. *Not done yet.* Somehow Irv read his mind. Kept still, kept the camera running.

Manny groped around for his phone and took a selfie. Pretended he was sending it as a text. "Bet you're sorry now," he said. Dropped the phone, closed his eyes, and relaxed. "I'll clean up in a minute."

Irv understood that to mean he could stop taping. "Okay. Cut. That was great. How you feeling?"

"Feeling fan-fucking-tastic, to be honest." He looked over at his crew. *My crew. I just made a porn video*. Lauro was switching off equipment. Then he pulled a hand towel out of the gear bag and tossed it to Manny. "Thanks." A minute later, he was tidy and dressed. "Anybody else want a beer?" They all took one, went to sit at the picnic table to drink them, didn't talk. Manny had no idea if this was what people usually did at the end of taping a scene. It was nice though. He was going to sleep well tonight.

Irv and Lauro talked about the nostalgia feature on the way back to the filming house. That was their usual topic of conversation these days, when there wasn't another project in front of them. Discussing Manny's scene would have meant opening a giant can of worms. Irv wasn't even going to review the footage that day, much less start editing. He was basically waiting for Lauro to get the hell out so he could jerk off.

Around nine o'clock his phone rang. He was watching a movie, trying to distract himself so he wouldn't jerk off again. Glanced over to check the caller ID and connected. "Hey Monica, what's up?"

"How'd El Vaquero do today?"

"He's a natural."

"Hey, that's great! Tell me about it."

Irv gave her the run-down on the storyline and staging. Mentioned Manny's advance planning about the costume and beer. "I'm going to look for some stock country-western music to score it. The way Red's place is situated, you can't see the city at all, and inside the stable you can't hear traffic. Perfect place to shoot."

"Think he'll let us use the place for other shoots?"

"Oh, bound to. He told me having people roll in there regularly is good for security. Maybe Payton's preppy guy wants to do something with that blonde and some polo gear." Monica laughed. Irv got off the phone thinking he'd done a pretty good job pretending it was an ordinary day. Then he stared at the screen, sighed, and un-paused the movie. *You better watch yourself.*

"Fresh meat," Irv muttered, and only realized he'd said it aloud when Lauro snickered. Irv turned his head, got an eyebrows-up half-shrug, and rolled his eyes. "It's always this way."

"I know." Lauro was up in the office to help Irv organize his nostalgia film. They'd barely even begun before they got distracted looking at views and downloads of the El Vaquero scene, which resulted in reading comments. Comments were important sometimes. Amongst all the pointless drooling, one could occasionally find a useful note about the actual filmmaking. The comments on Figueroa's first video were mostly drooling. He wasn't conventionally handsome, wasn't a pretty little twink, wasn't a big beefcake kind of guy, wasn't the typical tough tattooed Latino. Nevertheless, a lot of people were joining Team El Vaquero. Lauro glanced at Irv. "You like him."

"Yeah, so?"

"He likes you." Irv made a growly, dismissive sound. Lauro countered with a *tsk* sound. "You're allowed to like each other. Monica and Rick are doing fine." Irv's partner and her top model were twenty years into his career and sixteen years into their marriage. "They're not the only ones."

"I barely know this kid," Irv said, hoping uneasily that it didn't sound like protesting too much. Thank God nobody else knew about the website and the marketing kit and the other stuff. They'd never let him hear the end of it. He changed the subject back to what they were supposed to be working on. "Is it worth trying to get a writer on this, or do I have to write it?"

"You don't like writing," Lauro observed. "But it's not a lot of script." After a team meeting and a deep dive into the archive, Irv and Monica decided to work on the nostalgia thing together. Rick was going to play one of the leads, and Irv's longtime top model Zane Ryder would be the other. They were both versatile, with crossover appeal. Instead of shooting a ton of new scenes with each guy, Monica suggested recycling previous material that hadn't been promoted for a while. "You have all those memory scenes." Lauro tapped a pen on the graph notebook he was using to chart the film. "Those other models, they'll be thrilled to get paid again, and we can put them in this order." He scanned the list and quickly numbered each of the archive scenes. "That's chronological. So Rick and Zane will be aging up through the backstory."

"Good," Irv said, staring at the list, thinking. "That's good. That's way better than shooting a ton of new shit." If they opened with one hot new scene between Rick and Zane, and closed with another, that was, "Holy shit, that's a lot of fucking." Lauro laughed. Irv counted it up again. "That's sixteen scenes. How long do you think it'll take you to go through the old ones and mark up the parts to use?"

"You want to start there? Pick the material first, then write the script?"

"Might be easiest." If they already knew what the guys were going to be talking about, writing the voice-over and the filmed dialogue would be a piece of cake. Irv still didn't want to do it, but somebody had to. "We're doing a ninety-minute DVD. The new material goes on the site later, but the thing is a movie." Monica was firm on that. It was time to give their top guys another shelf title, she said.

Lauro did some quick math. A solo might be anywhere from six to twelve minutes long, but couple scenes averaged twenty. The one group scene they'd found with both Rick and Zane was thirty-two minutes. "If we go with eighteen minutes for the opening scene and a little longer for the ending scene, like twenty-two, you need fifty minutes of new dialogue and old scenes."

"Hmm. That's not going to leave much breathing room. We can't use all fourteen of the old ones." They went through the list again and cut it down to seven. With two new scenes at the suggested length, they'd be able to take plenty of material from each old scene. The very best parts, no filler. This was going to be high-value porn.

"Okay." Lauro reached past Irv for a red pen and muttered to himself while he did more math. "That's three with Rick, three with Zane, the group scene. Five hours, minimum, for me to view them, take notes, tag the clips I think we should use. You really want me to do that?" He put some emphasis on 'me.'

"I think you've got a sense of how to shape this. Opener, the old stuff, the closer. If you want to take a crack at the script, feel free. The only thing is, we want to shoot the new scenes pretty soon. Get the thing in position to submit for awards." The deadline for that was the end of September; the very thought of it was exhausting. Irv had three or four days of shooting on the schedule every week through October. Of course, Lauro was working six days a week too, but delegating it was worth a try. The kid had proven himself so far.

Lauro blinked. "I haven't written a screenplay since college."

"It's not a whole screenplay," Irv pointed out.

Lauro made an incredulous face. "It kind of is."

Irv gave him a look. "Whatever, you know what sells here. You know what these guys are like on camera. The idea is Rick and Zane have hooked up. The whole first scene is them having better sex than they expected. Then the middle section is them shooting the shit about other people they've been with. Having a drink. Maybe having a snack. It's bringing them together. So when they get rolling again it's different."

"It's better," Lauro said softly. "I wish I knew what that was like."

"They don't have sex in that group scene, so maybe the voiceover on that is them going, I wanted you then. Maybe we run a little more of that one, have more conversation over it." Irv caught up to what Lauro just said. "What do you mean?"

"Um. About?"

"About you wish you knew."

Lauro fiddled with the red pen, not making eye contact. "I wish I liked sex."

Irv opened his mouth to say something, thought better of it, and redirected. "You don't like sex at all?" Lauro shook his head. "What have you tried?"

"Jesus, what *haven't* I tried. Not liking sex puts a guy on Freak Street." Lauro turned his head a few degrees, trying to read Irv's expression. "I thought there had to be something out there I would like, but." He shrugged. He wasn't exactly comfortable talking about this, but on the other hand, the boss didn't go directly to mockery. Not to mention he'd just handed Lauro a writing assignment, plus a job that was basically assistant director. And this company gave

67

credits where they were due. The least Lauro could do was tell the truth.

"Huh." Irv sat back in his chair. "I don't think I've ever met someone who identified as asexual."

"I'll bet you have, and they just didn't say so."

"I will be damned." He thought for a few more seconds. "What's your favorite kind of romance to watch, then? Bollywood?"

Lauro laughed under his breath. "Yeah."

"What about kissing?"

"Kissing's okay but if someone gets turned on and you don't then you end up getting called a tease, or someone starts asking what's wrong with them. Girls, they automatically assume something's wrong with *them*."

Irv noted the emphasis, wondered if he should say 'there's nothing wrong with you,' decided maybe later. "You've tried with guys."

Lauro nodded. "I thought maybe I was gay and didn't know it, but no. The guy I went out with was not happy."

I'll bet, Irv thought, observing his assistant in more detail than usual. Back when they did the first round of interviews, he thought the kid was cute. Not quite Manny's height, a year younger, soft-bodied in a cuddly, appealing way. Full head of wavy brown hair, big hazel eyes and a pretty mouth. But as usual, once they were working together Irv stopped noticing. And after an initial round of ribbing about getting in front of the camera, everybody else accepted him as part of the team. Lauro was good at what he did. Someday he'd make a fine director. "Jeez, you were born to make porn."

Lauro laughed out loud. "Why, because I'm not going to get inappropriate with anybody?"

"Right. We've all had our struggles. Well, you should hear Monica on the subject." Irv was not above getting his partner and her spouse talking about those first few years of Look But Don't Touch.

"I have." He was still smiling. This was a conversation he never wanted to have, but it was painless. Such a relief. "So how you want to work it with the media."

"Copy those seven pieces to this." Irv opened the middle drawer of his desk and lifted out a laptop. Reached back in for cables, and passed it all over to Lauro. "Work on it whenever but ASAP."

"Okay. I can work on it at home." Lauro rented a room from an agent who had a big house out in Woodland Hills.

"How's that going, anyway?"

"Oh, it's great. Raquel's cats act like my room is their room, but I like cats."

"Well, I'm allergic, so wipe that fucker down before you bring it back." Irv pushed his chair back. "Gonna get a drink. Want anything?"

"No, I'm good, thanks." Lauro got busy, on the assumption that Irv was ready to have the office to himself now. He never said so. Never said, get the fuck out. A non-shitty job working for a non-asshole was a sufficiently rare combination that Lauro didn't mind taking work home. It didn't happen often. And this was a big project. He was still quietly excited when he left.

Irv could tell. He sent Monica an email summarizing the plan, then couldn't resist looking at the El Vaquero material again. *We're allowed to like each other*. Yeah, but him liking Manny was a slippery goddamned slope.

August 2015

Irv did not verbalize his wish for Manny's second explicit video. He didn't even admit it to himself. Maybe because it felt borderline abusive to use the story he heard that first day at the stable as the basis for a scene. It wasn't overt, Manny sitting on a bed with a uniform across his lap crying like in some cornball chick flick. But if they had props to clue the audience in, they could set up a few shots subtly emphasizing those. He could ask Manny to focus on the props, connecting what he was doing with the person who was far away, maybe in danger. Maybe gone. Fill in the subtext with music. He hesitated to admit that he wanted to do more than make a simple porn clip here.

But then Manny called him up, a week in advance. "Would it be okay if I showed up an hour or so early? To talk?"

Irv was a little surprised, and a lot worried. Hoping this didn't mean the kid wanted to bow out. "Sure, if you want. Or you want to talk now? Is there something specific about the staging?"

"Maybe. Well yeah. It was," Manny paused, huffed out an irritated breath, and said, "You know, maybe the shit with the phone? Maybe we don't need that this time. This should be about the person left at home when somebody goes to war."

Irv took a second to answer, because of course it should, but was it even fair to do that? After debating with himself about whether he should try to blow this off, he sighed. He couldn't lie. "I thought about that

70

story you told me. About you and Lobo. Are you sure you want to set it up that way?"

"No." Manny smiled. He might have known Irv would make the connection. "I'm not sure. But I can't be the only one. Think how many people are in the service." Both of them were silent for a moment. They'd talked about shooting this one at the house, with sufficient set dressing to suggest a connection to the stable video. His boots in a corner, western shirt hanging on the doorknob, framed snapshot of him with Freyja on the dresser. "What about if you added in some different props. Enough to make it clear it's a military person I'm missing. But not to the point that anyone has to visualize my person. Only enough that they could visualize *their* person."

"It would be really easy to do that," Irv admitted, without mentioning that he'd already been thinking about how to do it. Storing away a moment of being impressed by the way Manny articulated that. "Dress the room a little bit more and cut from you looking somewhere to what you're looking at. Get some music in there that'll lead people to the conclusion."

"I could play it. It's cheaper if it's a cover, right?"

Irv blinked. The things this kid knew always surprised him. "You pay attention, don't you? Yeah, you're right. We don't have much of a budget for music licensing, that's why it's almost always stock music."

"You know that song, 'Tie a Yellow Ribbon?' For the longest time I thought that was about a soldier, because there was that whole thing, support our troops, with the Iraq war. I was in middle school. Our whole neighborhood was yellow ribbons. In the song, though, it's a guy who's coming home from doing time."

"That could work for people too. Double meaning." Irv was trying to hide his excitement, and probably failing. He didn't get a chance to bring art into these videos very often. To give them meaning. "I'll get the props. You care what branch of the service?"

He's so nice. People were going to see this; somebody might recognize Manny and make the connection. Lobo probably wouldn't have cared, but he wasn't around to say so. Not the Marines, then. "Can we go with Army? And can you get rights to that song?"

"Pretty sure I can. I'll get my lawyer on it and let you know. If you want to score things yourself, I mean it really works with the vaquero thing, I'll look into finding you public domain music to play."

Manny took another second. "You sure take a lot of trouble for me." The 'why' was implied.

Irv, deeply uncomfortable, said, "I told you I used to make real films."

"Have you missed it?"

Irv was silent so long Manny thought he wasn't going to answer. But finally he said, "Yeah, I have. There's no money in going the extra mile with porn. Get in, get off, get out, that's where the money is. But sometimes I miss having an actual story to tell. You're not going to make more this way," he added, because he had to be honest. "I can pay you a little extra for doing the music."

"Mmm." Manny didn't need to think that over. "You don't have to. It's going to cost you something to get the license. I'm going to play the guitar anyway. If we can use that to make the product better, why not? Why wouldn't I want my shit to be as good as possible?"

Because most people only want to do the bare minimum, Irv thought. "Okay. I'm in if you're in. Let's make it good."

So he talked to his lawyer, they ponied up for the song license, Manny recorded it. They shot the video, which felt like it took longer than the one at the stable; maybe because it was a new environment and another new experience. But fuck, it was good. There was no hesitation when he saw the finished scene a week later. He took a second to make sure his voice was steady – this really did spark some memories – and said, "Roll it out." Then he got too busy to check the response on the site. Too busy to call Irv for a follow-up conversation, especially since he'd found himself making those conversations last a while. So busy he didn't hesitate to decline a catering gig on the same night he had a ticket to go see that tango-and-cowboys dance show at Chrome.

By the last Sunday in August, he'd had time to do a little internet research on tango. The website for the show had a ton of links; digging into all of that occupied his spare time for a whole week. It was a little bit funny: never in his life had he thought about whether other countries had cowboys. But the U.S. sure wasn't the only country where people ate beef. Finding out that Argentine cowboys were called gauchos was cool. Seeing pictures of the country, a place he'd only vaguely heard about before. Maybe someday he'd have enough money to travel. There were so many places where people spoke Spanish. He'd only even been to Mexico twice, to race, since the last time he went with Lobo.

There were a few too many things he'd only ever done with his first love. After he found a seat at the nightclub and got his order in, while he was waiting for the show to start, he remembered those thoughts he had before he called Irv. At the time, he wasn't thinking of basing any of his scenes on real life. It was possible the porn thing was doing exactly what he'd hoped it would. Giving him a different way to think about his sex life, a way that let him remember the best things about being with Lobo, without having to compare the person he was with to the person he'd lost. Distancing himself a little, in an intentional way. Working through some of the leftover pain. Did he still miss the guy? Of course he did. He probably always would. They'd been friends for seven years, lovers for five. That was a non-trivial relationship.

The thought made him smile. He was getting some new vocabulary out of working with Irv, for sure. And Lauro. That guy was smart as a whip. He had a film degree too, wanted to direct someday. Manny almost asked if he wanted to come to this thing, but everyone he'd met at the porn house was so careful about staying on the right side of the line. He wasn't sure if going out together, even if not on a 'date,' would cross the line, so he didn't mention it. Maybe after the next video, when they knew each other better.

The lights went down for a few seconds, then back up. The house music faded out, but there was a burst of noise as people scrambled to get last-minute drink orders in. A couple minutes later the lights went off and a voice came over the P.A. "Good evening, and welcome to Chrome. You're here for the final performance of Gaucho, directed by Alison Jarvet. Silence your spurs and hang up your hats. It's time for a vision of tango, cowboy style." A projected title card hit the stage curtains, and music began. It sounded strangely familiar, but Manny didn't try to pin it down. He just sat and finished his meal, swallowed some of the strong red wine that came with it, and prepared to enjoy as the curtain opened.

He wasn't prepared to think *Wow*. It was the first time he'd ever been to a live dance performance. This had an actual story. A grown-up, real-world, sexy story.

Three main couples were all broken up at the end of the first act by one guy, whose original partner happened to be another guy. That blew Manny's mind right there. Then it was amazing how the homewrecker guy messed everything up over the course of a single song. He'd never seen dancers change partners like that, weaving in and out of different combinations, actions and reactions spelling out exactly what was happening.

Another mind-blowing thing was how many of the performers he recognized. He'd seen almost all of them at Shall We Dance, either when he went in for Sunday morning yoga or when he met up with Dmitri for a ballet lesson. Because of his crazy schedule, he hadn't been in for one of those since late July. It was a kick to see his teacher right there in the cast, part of the six-person troupe playing the background roles. He must have been the oldest one there by a lot of years, but he sure didn't dance like it.

Red and his wife Mary were one of the main couples. She'd been out at the stable a couple times when Manny went to exercise the horses. He loved seeing her like this, on a stage, dancing to this wicked music. It was a shame the person sharing his two-top was a complete stranger. He'd have liked to spend the intermission talking about the show, but that person was away and cruising the room before Manny had a chance to say anything.

The same thing happened at the second intermission. By then Manny was fully invested. There were only three dances in the second act, but the last one really got to him. It was a solo from the guy whose partner left him to mess around with all the others. He couldn't help hoping they could get back together somehow.

How did people think this shit up? The director had to think like a person who wrote plays *and* like a DJ. And who did all the choreography? Well, maybe he could ask Red sometime. They knew each other now.

Act three started with a solo for the homewrecker. He was played by a Filipino guy Manny knew from the dance studio. The troupe was looking dangerous in the background. They followed up with a number that flat-out said 'he's so fucked.' And oh, here it came. Red and the other two main guys danced together, like a gang. Then one of the others beat the hell out of the homewrecker. It wasn't an actual fight, but it was the meanest dance Manny could ever imagine. Then there was another number with all six of the main dancers, back in their original partnerships. The five people who'd been messed with all took bites out of the homewrecker guy. He was so grateful when his original partner, this tall black guy, finally held him with forgiveness. You could see it in their bodies. Manny wished he could see this about twenty more times. He never thought of dancing as acting before.

He wasn't the only one to stand up and applaud at the end. The place was going nuts. Manny looked around after the stranger at his table disappeared again, wondering if the performers would be coming out. He'd have liked to shake a few hands, tell people how great he thought the show was. Was knowing somebody by sight because you had lessons at the same studio enough of an introduction? Well, it had better be. No reason to think it wouldn't be. None of those people seemed like the 'don't speak to me' kind of people. Dmitri definitely wasn't.

Decision made, Manny drained his glass and relaxed, leaning one elbow on the bar-height table and people-watching. A lot of folks down here had gold wristbands on. That must mean something. When the performers started coming out from backstage he overheard the words 'after-party' and figured it out. Then Dmitri came out with the tall black-haired woman from the troupe, listening to whatever she was saying. They headed for a loveseat up front, where a good-looking guy with silver hair was sitting with a pretty blonde woman. Judging from the body language and the rings, those were Dmitri's husband and the tall woman's wife. Manny edged closer and waited for a few seconds.

Dmitri noticed him almost immediately, raised his chin with the slightest smile, then offered a hand. "Manuel."

"Dmitri. Loved the show. Found out about it because I take care of Red's horses sometimes."

The other three all heard that; somebody said "Oh, you know Red?" and before he knew it Manny was in the thick of a conversation that lasted until it became clear the after-party was about to start. He hadn't even spoken to anyone else from the cast, but that was okay. After another round of hand-shaking and congratulations, he started for the stairs before one of the club staff could push him that way.

The mezzanine lounge was full; all of the tables overlooking the downstairs lounge were occupied. Manny would have liked to hang out a while longer and do some more people-watching. This kind of night out was a rare treat, and he didn't have anything he had to get to early the next day. A glance toward the bar told him he wouldn't be getting a seat there anytime soon.

Maybe he looked disappointed; a woman sitting by the railing said, "Want to hang out for a while? My fiancé's downstairs." She indicated the empty chair across from her, then pointed over the railing. Manny tried to guess which guy it was. "The one in the white suit like a Chinese John Travolta."

It made him smile. "You wouldn't mind? It's my first time coming to a show here and I didn't know about the after-party."

"No worries. Have a seat. My name's Kate Pok."

"Manny Figueroa." He offered a hand; she shook it. Her left hand was on the table, loosely resting on her phone. "Wow, that ring is amazing." Two black pearls with an infinity curve of diamonds around them.

Kate smiled. "Thanks. Danny gave me this when he proposed. He designed it."

"Is that what he does?"

"No, he's a DJ and producer, but his father's in the jewelry business. I manage a dojo in Santa Monica."

"I'm a spin trainer. Trying to be an actor."

"Ooh." She winced; Manny laughed; she grinned back at him. "So what brings you to Chrome tonight."

He told her about taking lessons with Dmitri, and about the Red Warner connection. "Went riding with Mary a few times since she got back from Chicago. They're both super nice. Red promised to give me some weapons training so I can beef up my skills."

"What kind?"

"Couple kinds of illegal knives." Kate laughed; Manny smiled and went on, "But otherwise it's all going to be guns. I've never even held one before."

"You have any martial-arts background?"

"Not a thing." He shrugged. "There's only so much time and money." The fees from Stroked went right back out the door for lessons; the whole porn adventure was an investment in being a better, more bookable actor. One thing was for sure: after jerking off on camera, he was never again going to be shy about whatever a regular film set might call for.

"You should get some hand-to-hand training if you can. Come by my place sometime. I'll give you the friends and family rate." She flipped her phone over, extracted a business card from a slot on the back of the case, and passed it across the table.

Manny took it with a smile that he hoped covered his confusion. "That's awfully nice of you."

"Any friend of Dmitri is a friend of ours. Danny's been doing mixes for people in the Underground Cabaret for a couple of years now. And a lot of people who do the Cabaret are in the Shall We Dance orbit. But," she gave half a shrug, "it's good for me to train people in the business. It's a credit for me."

"Oh. I didn't think of it that way. I should put that on my website, huh? Dance training with Dmitri Vasko. Weapons training with Red Warner."

"Kung fu training with Kate Pok." She grinned at him again. "You'll dig it the most."

He laughed again. "You don't wear that ring when you're sparring, do you?"

"Nooooo."

A server swung by and asked if they wanted anything. Kate looked over the railing, noted that her fiancé was dancing with somebody, and said she did. Manny ordered something too. They were still talking when Danny finally came upstairs, ready to go but happy to meet this guy talking to his lady. Manny thought he could be forgiven for mentioning he played the guitar. Anybody you met could be a person you worked with someday, and since he and Kate were getting along, he might see this guy again. And you never knew, the guy might need a guitar sometime.

October 2015

Irv was going through his calendar, looking at what was in the pipeline and getting in contact with his models about what they wanted to do next. Some of them did new scenes every week. They all had to be conscious of not doing the same exact thing too often, and not doing something exactly like what other people were releasing that month or quarter. Most of the guys in his stable did fully explicit videos and pictorials, mostly with the usual kind of scenario. Pizza guy. Parcel delivery guy. Gardener, pool boy, electrician, whatever. The company had a fat binder full of short scripts. Lauro (thanks to briefly dating a musician) started calling it the Fake Book, and everyone else now called it the Fucking Fake Book.

There was always the wish to get out in the world and film a pick-up scene in an actual bar or gym or something, the way people were more likely to meet in real life. But the second you thought about doing something like that, you were talking thousands more dollars a day. Permits up the wazoo, extras, license fees, and union rates paid to any actors who were giving lines. All the partners lived for the day the houses on either side of the filming house might be vacant. They were going to throw together the fastest, dirtiest pool party you ever heard of. Get a ton of footage they could use as stock, get all their regular people in there to film a million daylight set-up scenes, and have something a little fresh to work with. And probably end up filming the biggest orgy of any of their careers. Group scenes were not easy to do in the normal-sized rooms of a normal-sized house.

They made the most of the interior; every room that was big enough to hold a model or two and a crew was in regular use. A surprising amount of set-up could be shot outdoors. The patio adjacent to the house was under a pergola covered with bougainvillea. When they turned the place into a filming house, they installed a row of breezeblock along the top of the existing cinder-block garden wall, then added sheltering panels of redwood lattice close to the patio. Whatever happened on that patio couldn't be overlooked from the houses on either side, and not from the house behind them either, thanks to a stand of palm and banana trees. Those damn things drank water like marathoners, but they made a terrific tropical-looking backdrop.

The patio was dressed, at the moment, as a tiki bar. Inside the house, a straight couple was filming a prologue scene in the living room with half a dozen other men. All pretending to drink, pretending to eat, pretending it was somebody's bachelor party. The girl in this scenario was the groom-to-be's sister and the boy was the best man. As usual, they were all improvising their lines while a professional striptease artist put on a show and the groom got 'drunk.' The main sex scene was scheduled for the afternoon. Tomorrow they'd shoot the morning after. That was going to involve the central couple having an embarrassed wake-up moment, then a shy coffee moment, and then a funny OMG moment when they stepped out onto the patio and saw the groom passed out with a big kahuna tankard by his head. Bonding over getting him up and dressed. A little bit of kissing and hands, and a suggestive "So what are you doing

81

after the reception?" It wasn't a bad little script; it set up a sequel (already on the schedule) perfectly.

Irv knew the product would be a hit. Bachelor-party scenarios often did well. He personally would have done a twist on it, having the groom crash out with another of the guys and then wake up to a 'wait what the hell oh okay' fuckfest. But this was straight porn, so even though the guy playing the groom was gay, he'd be getting some lap-dance action from the stripper. Only that, though. Monica never did adultery storylines. She'd broken out because of a really popular early film, a ninety-minute explicit rom-com. In this one, the groom was faithful to his bride. The best man and the groom's sister might fall in love.

If Manny wasn't so definite about no interactives, Irv would have been trying to come up with some way to do a romantic piece with him. The kid was sweet, there was no other word for it. Even a scaly old cynic like Irv wanted to give him a hug. They only had the five pieces up so far, three solo videos and two pictorials. The El Vaquero persona wasn't fully formed, but the yellow-ribbon video got a huge response. So many comments from people who had people away in the armed services, or people who'd lost people. If they made an interactive that was a reunion, he was going to break out.

Quit thinking about it, Irv told himself. He had something else to throw the kid's way. It might not go anywhere, but on the other hand it might. And if it did, Manny probably wasn't going to be in front of Irv's camera for much longer. He looked at the casting notice again, picked up his phone and sent a text: *Hey Cyrus I'm looking at your notice for something called Countdown and I see they need a bicycle guy. I've been working with someone recently, could I send you his kit?* He wanted to write more, which was another of those surprises that kept sneaking up on him since he met Manny. More would be too much. At least this wasn't completely out of the blue. He'd thrown a model at Cyrus Garrett a couple times before.

The phone rang. Irv picked it up. "Hey buddy. How's things. Yeah? That's good. Tell that wrangler of yours if she ever wants to get down and dirty, one of my partners still has the hots for her." He laughed. "Yeah, I know. Okay. This is a new kid. We've only done five things and none of them are interactive. Yeah, uses a stage name. His day job is as a spinning trainer and he does bicycle races for the gym chain he works for. Five foot nine, one fifty-five or so. Latino, no ink. Yeah, he's been doing extra gigs for years. Mm-hmm. You want to see it? I can send it right over. Oh, you know me. Yeah, I'd be a rich man if I would just exploit people like I ought to. Give my regards to the wife. Yep, as soon as I'm off the phone. See ya." Irv blew out a breath as he disconnected. *Here goes nothing.* He swiveled around to his computer and sent the email from his drafts folder. The email with Manny's new resumé and the photos that Irv had selected from their shoots to date. Then he sent a text to Manny to let him know what he'd done.

Manny saw the text at the end of his shift at the gym, thought *what the hell*, and didn't have time to deal with it; he was heading to a serving gig at a wedding. He looked at it again after he got home, but he was tired and it was late. When he got a break in the middle of the next day, he finally texted back: *Hey Irv, sorry delayed reply, been working. Are you my agent now?* He put a smiley face on that to show he didn't mind.

A reply came fast: *I probably shouldn't have done that but I know the guy who's casting background and*

U5 for this movie. It shoots here in LA next summer, action comedy, they need a bicycle person so I thought what the hell. I sent the kit we worked up

I really appreciate it Irv. Manny had a feeling he knew why Irv was doing him all these favors. Or maybe he only hoped he knew. Just because he hadn't had someone like this in his life for a long time – someone who would not only think about what might help, but actually do something – didn't mean it was all that rare. Maybe everybody had that one person. He wanted to ask about a million questions, starting with 'is this not a regular extra gig,' but all those questions were premature. Or at least they were until six hours later, when he got a call from the casting guy.

CHAPTER 5

He almost didn't pick up the unknown number, because he'd worked two sixteen-hour days in a row and he was beat. But he remembered Irv's text, so he connected. "Hello, this is Manny Figueroa."

"Hi Manny, this is Cyrus Garrett. I'm casting a movie called Countdown and a friend of yours sent me your head shot. Got a minute?"

He managed to say "Sure" instead of 'holy shit yes.'

"You're not a member of SAG."

"No sir."

"Done any dialogue before?"

"No sir."

"What kind of races do you do?"

That was a swerve. "Road races. Not the Tour de France," Manny said cautiously, smiling because Irv told him that would make his voice sound warm. "All local. Some of them are sponsored. Our team does fundraisers."

"Promotion for the gym, huh. They get you out there pretty often?"

It sounded so cynical, but he was right. Manny said, "I've seen a lot of SoCal from a bike, let's put it that way. I could send you some links." It almost sounded like a question.

"Yeah, do that. I want to have you come in and read something, too. Are you available tomorrow?"

Read something?! Was this a speaking part? Manny's heart thumped. The timing was perfect; he didn't have classes to lead tomorrow, and the evening's

85

serving gig was only a maybe. "I can be available all day."

"Then how about," a pause, "eleven-thirty."

"That's fine."

"I'll send you the address, you send me those links."

"You got it. Thanks, Mr. Garrett." Tired as he was, Manny set his alarm early so he could read up on how to audition. He'd done it before, of course, but he felt like the stakes were higher this time. Someone else was going to know if he screwed it up. As soon as he got the address from the casting guy he sent the website link, and links to a couple specific videos on his channel. Bicycle races were not the most exciting things to watch if you weren't a true fan, but he had a supercut from start and finish lines, plus one epic multi-rider wipeout. It was worth saving because it looked like he and the other guys should have been dead, but they all walked away with nothing worse than road rash. There was also the thing Irv gave him, a three-minute edit of Manny playing around with Jarvis that first time at the stable. He was tempted to send the other clip, the one where he was playing guitar. But this was an action thing. They wouldn't care about guitar. Done with that, he emailed the staffing coordinator with the catering company to let them know he wasn't going to be available. When he got done out in the Valley, he'd want to chill for a while, not go rushing around trying to get to a gig. He could afford a day off.

The casting office was in Sherman Oaks, in a strip mall a couple blocks up from Ventura Boulevard. It didn't look like anything from the outside. Not really on the inside, either; only a shallow room full of file cabinets with a closed door in the back. There was a reception desk, but nobody was sitting there. It didn't even have a computer on it. Manny looked around for a way to signal his arrival, maybe one of those bells that were on every restaurant expeditor's shelf in the world. Then he noticed a closed-circuit camera. *Okay*, he thought. He consciously relaxed, taking advantage of the moment to study the big whiteboard calendar on the wall. Finding out how other people did their jobs was always interesting. Somebody here had to start her day really early sometimes.

A minute or two later, a sixty-something white guy came through the door and said, "You must be Manuel Figueroa."

"That's me. You must be Mr. Garrett." Manny offered a hand, the other guy shook it.

"Call me Cyrus. That was quite a crash video. That happen often?"

"No. If that happened my first year racing I would have been like, I'm out." Manny was smiling. You had to be really lucky not to take a spill sometime. He'd been lucky not to be seriously injured so far.

"Yeah, I'll bet. Come on through." Cyrus led the way to the bigger office in back. "Take a seat. You have a number of skills on your resume. Any credits with those yet?"

He was happy to be able to say yes. "I did a gig last week, a healthcare commercial, doing yoga. Mr. Park, my yoga guy, he sent me to Mr. Vasko. Then I've been working with Mr. Morton." Manny could feel his face heat. But this guy had to know all about that, and he called anyway, so whatever. "Irv connected me with Mr. Warner, who was in a dance thing in August, and I went to see it, and I met Ms. Pok there."

87

Cyrus made a note. "Interesting." He tapped his pen against his notepad, studied Manny for a few seconds, dropped the pen and reached for a couple of script pages. "So, I'm not the person making the ultimate decisions here. This is a prelim because you're non-union. All right?"

"All right."

Cyrus handed the pages across the desk. "The bicycle part is a messenger. The scenario is, we have an NSA guy and an ATF guy who are on a case together for some reason, don't ask me how realistic that is. Anyway, the case is really time-sensitive, which you might guess from how the movie is called Countdown." Manny stifled a laugh. "So these two guys are connected by phone, but in this scene there's a physical thing that has to go from point A to point B."

"A MacGuffin," Manny hazarded.

Cyrus looked pleased. "Yeah, exactly. Take a minute."

That clearly meant 'to read this.' Manny scanned the pages. The NSA guy grabs the bicycle guy off the street and says get this to my pal at this place, it's a matter of national security, and then there was an action sequence with the bicycle guy doing his thing. It sounded really cool. Manny had dodged traffic plenty of times. "I jumped a car once but I couldn't swear I could do that again."

"If they decide they want actual stunts, they'll get an actual stunt rider. Ready to read it?"

"Sure." Cyrus read the NSA agent, Manny read the bicycle guy. "Next page." That one was at the other end of things. Cyrus gave him half a minute and then they read that one too. "Okay." He thought for a few seconds, then held up his phone. Manny understood he was about to be recorded. "What would you say if this was you and you were cutting through a traffic jam in downtown Long Beach."

"You mean in real life?" The guy nodded. Manny let fly with fifteen seconds of high-speed, full-throated Spanish profanity. Cyrus laughed out loud, clamping his free hand over his mouth to stifle it. Clearly he knew what mierda, culo, pendejo, cabrón, puta, and coño meant, if not every verb and modifier used in between.

Cyrus put the phone down again. "All right. I'm going to pass this on to the production team, and someone will be in touch. Thanks for coming in today."

"Thanks for asking me." Manny stood up, offering his hand again. Cyrus shook hands but didn't get up, so Manny let himself out. The whole thing took half an hour. *What do I do now.* He had the entire afternoon and evening to do whatever he wanted. It seemed like even if he didn't get the job he'd have a good story to tell. He walked to the donut shop at the end of the strip mall, got himself a coffee and a cruller, and sat down to write it up in Evernote. Then he surfed the web for a little while. He found a story from when the star Jonathan Morris was cast. This was his first above-the-title part. Manny didn't know that guy, so he had to dig a little to get an idea. Used to be a WWE wrestler, got drafted into a villain part, and stole every scene according to some reviews.

A lot of athletes got a start in movies that way. They brought some fans with them, and if they weren't completely talentless as actors – which most of them weren't; a high-profile athlete usually had a dose of charisma and a reasonably quick wit – they had a decent run before they either got tired of it or the filmmaking fashion changed. Manny didn't have any fans, obviously. Except possibly a few people who'd seen the stuff he did with Stroked. He finished his cruller and did a new search. "Oh verdad?" The co-star was Latino. On top of that, he was gay. It was Victor Garcia, who'd been playing a cop on a series called 'L.A. Vice' for a long time. He came out about two years ago, and now here he was with a second lead in a feature. That was major. That was the kind of stuff Hollywood dreams were built on. Gay Latinos didn't get to see those dreams come true very often.

Manny didn't have cable or a DVD player. He decided to treat himself to some good takeout for dinner, and spend the evening watching Morris and Garcia clips on YouTube. Till then, Red wouldn't mind if he spent some time with the horses. Being around Freyja and the others would feel like a reward for taking another step out of his comfort zone. He sent a text to the watchman and another to Red, letting them know he was heading over there.

December 2015

Irv was not the kind of guy who tried to keep up with everything. He didn't have a Fear Of Missing Out problem. But he tended to treat entertainment consumption as work research, and once in a while a person needed to get away from work. Outside of his own business, his primary interest was photography. The last time he'd been to a show, it was not in a gallery but in a live/work space at the Brewery, north of Downtown. The artist was a bit of a celebrity; he'd joined the cast of 'L.A. Vice' in the spring for a ground-breaking (and controversial) arc as the love interest of one of the regular male characters. Irv had no idea where the guy got the energy to do an exhibit. It was pretty obvious why he decided to, though. It was a way to remind people what he did and who he was. A real person, not this bartender character who'd launched a million flame wars on the internet.

When Irv got to the space he was surprised to learn that the guy was imminently moving out of it. A bigger surprise was that Irv looked around and thought *I want this*. It was such a blank slate. All of his personal stuff and his work gear would fit just fine, leaving room to do shoots. The apartment at the filming house was convenient, but if he wanted to shoot something he had to use the house. Not too surprisingly, he rarely did shoot anything that wasn't for the site. And lately he'd realized that the job had become his whole world.

He contacted the Brewery management the next day to find out about the rent, and immediately put in an application. It might have been overkill to include a short letter about why he wanted the unit, the kind of work he planned to do there, and his business references. On the other hand, they approved his application fast. Then he had to talk to his partners about how they would handle security at the filming house. "I wondered how long you would stick," Monica said, after Payton was off the call.

"What do you mean?"

"The rest of us have outside lives. We keep sprawling out. Partners, travel, kids. I was afraid you were going to let your life get smaller and smaller until you disappeared."

Irv blinked at the phone. "Wow."

"I mean, you're still young." She ignored his dismissive snort. "Shut up, you're not even forty. And it's been good for the business that you were so single-minded, but I'm really relieved that you're looking at getting a little separation."

"Even though it's going to be a pain in the ass dealing with security now?"

"Let's ask Lauro if he can camp at the apartment for a while. We'll keep an eye out for the right person to take over the space. Ideally it's somebody else who works with us. There's a lot of new blood since last year."

Irv thought about that for a second. "Yeah. Okay. That could work. He's here all the time anyway."

"And it's not too far from Woodland Hills, when he wants to run home for something. I'll talk to him tomorrow after my shoot." She wound up the call and disconnected.

Irv put down his phone, swiveled around in his chair, and stared at the space. It felt perfectly adequate six years ago, when they bought the property. Why did it not feel adequate now? He shook himself, dismissing the question.

The email from gym management sat in his in-box for nearly a week before Manny answered it. He usually got back to them right away, but he wanted to make sure his initial reaction (specifically, Hell No and Nunca Más) wasn't simply the product of a long day. There was another of those moments: being in the locker room at the same time as Angel, seeing on the man's face that he was primed to say something bitchy. This time Manny gave him some kind of look, or moved some kind of way, and Angel turned aside. It felt like a victory. Manny was never much of one for trying to control a situation. He was just tired of dealing with the same old shit all the time.

And that's what the email promised: same old shit. Another race, meaning hours of extra training that would eat into all the other stuff he wanted to be doing. Training that he had to do on his own time, unpaid.

Another chance of a fall or a crash. All the benefit going to the gym. The fee he got for the actual ride wasn't enough to make it worth doing anymore. It took a while to compose a reply that sounded right. He was so used to saying yes to everything that he almost panicked after he sent it off.

But nothing bad happened. The acknowledgement didn't say anything about how he was letting them down. In fact, they said some other guy had expressed interest and now there was room on the team. Manny made a point of talking to the people he used to ride with, and then he really was done. It felt like a giant weight off his neck.

Maybe he shouldn't have been surprised that he enjoyed his classes more after that. He'd chosen spinning back in the day because he liked to ride indoors, where it was safe to listen to music. Where he had filtered air to breathe, and didn't need a helmet, and didn't have to worry about people in cars who didn't want to share the road.

He was getting plenty of outdoor riding now anyway, thanks to Red. There was no comparison between a bike and a horse. Every time he was there with Red or Mary, he felt like they were closer to being friends. It was nice to be doing something for no reason other than you wanted to.

Ironically, the next extra gig he landed called for him to ride a bike. But it was a classic cruiser, out at the beach, and he spent most of his time in the saddle sitting straight up. Riding hands-free, looking at the ocean and the sky.

"Nice day for it, huh?" said the extras wrangler when she signed him out.

"Can't complain," Manny said, glancing at his time card. "Thanks."

"You were good today, so thank *you*." She checked the line behind him. "Hang out for a second?"

"Uh, sure." It sounded like a question, but he stepped aside, zipped up his jacket, and waited, eyes narrowed against the ocean breeze.

Not too much later the rest of the gang was processed out. The wrangler turned around and stuck out her hand. "Rita Johnson."

"Hi." He shook her hand, smiling.

"I work with Cyrus Garrett. You read for a thing recently."

"Yeah, I did." And was he excited?

"There's another thing coming up. Where are you on firearms?"

Holy shit, now he was *really* excited. "Did a live fire course a minute ago."

"Oh! Great! Send over the certificate, will you? And I'll be in touch."

"Sure thing." All the way home, Manny wondered what was going to happen next.

February 2016

It was cold as fuck up in the hills, but Manny didn't care. The scene they called Esperando was a hit for Stroked. That one was at night, with a camp stove (plus some ingenious lighting) and the guitar. It was like an X-rated music video; he totally loved it. Now they were back to do another one.

Manny told Irv he wanted this one to be called Soledad. It was another overt call-out to the absent-

94

military-partner theme, opening in late afternoon with Manny reading a censored letter. Red gave them permission to load some hay bales in the truck and use those as a bed for the scene. Manny promised to cover them with a serape again so the hay wouldn't get too gross for the horses. When Red heard about the scenario, he referred them to an ex-military pal who actually had a censored letter they could copy for the prop. It seemed important to get the details right.

By this time Manny was an expert at edging himself. They shot half a dozen setups before he finally came and Irv wrapped the scene. Lauro was there a few seconds later with a towel, the rest of Manny's clothes, and a thermos full of hot coffee. God he was glad to see that. "Thanks. You think of everything."

"That's my job." Lauro was smiling. "You did great today."

"Yes he did," Irv said. "I'll have that ready for review after the weekend, Manny."

"That's fine." He drank some more coffee. "Guess I better get these bales back in the stable where they belong." He rolled down the sleeves of his flannel shirt, pulled on his boots and gloves, and got to it. *He's taking pictures again.* Manny never called it out. Never said, Irv, what the fuck. There was always some great new shot to put on his website, or a new non-explicit clip to put on his channel.

And there was all the other help. That one audition with Cyrus Garrett led to other calls. When Red heard that Manny got the bicycle-messenger part, he passed the latest version of the marketing kit to Reina Salazar, who worked in the casting department for one of the big companies that owned Hollywood. She called Manny in for an interview, and it turned out she was the mother of Red's college girlfriend. When she heard how Manny met Red, she just shrugged. "Everybody does it. My girl Tanith, she's done some very sketchy stuff. I mean, I'm her mother. A scene where she has to be in her bra seems sketchy to me."

Manny tried not to laugh. "What's she do?"

"She's a voice artist now, but she writes and directs. Mostly for the stage. There's no money in it. Anyway, tell me about this Countdown thing."

It was bizarre, but he was loving it. He was getting into skilled background with Central Casting. The biggest thing so far was a week as a soldier. The movie wasn't set to come out for a year, but that was a great credit. Irv told him to sign up with IMDb; one more thing to maintain, one more way to get seen. And people were seeing him now. He was still signed up with the catering company, though he hadn't taken a gig since New Year's Eve. When he got home from that, it was just like last year: Angel's door wide open, music, laughter, a haze of pot smoke. Manny wasn't even tempted this time. He was holding out for the real thing now.

When the stable was locked up and they were all ready to go, he almost regretted it. Going home alone was so unappealing, and it wasn't that late. "Anybody else hungry?"

"I am," Lauro said. "Want to meet up at Denny's?" There was one not far away, in Sherman Oaks.

"Sure." Manny glanced at Irv and the tech guy; they both shook their heads. Manny was aware of being disappointed, was slightly surprised by that, and told himself to think about it later. He actually thought about it all the way down the hill and onto Ventura Boulevard. The tech guy and Irv both had another shoot earlier in the day, but so did Lauro. *Okay, you'd have liked Irv to join.* Why be disappointed because Irv wasn't coming along? He had to get all the way back over the hills, now that he was living at the Brewery. Manny hadn't seen the place. Irv moved there in December, and kept saying he was going to start setting up photo shoots because it was a blank slate (unlike the house) but he hadn't scheduled anything there with Manny yet. *Why.* He was still chewing on the question when he parked at the diner. Fortunately, Lauro was already seated, so Manny could slide into the booth, ask him how he liked living at the porn house, and stop thinking about Irving.

That lasted until Lauro asked him a personal question. "It's none of my business, but I wondered if anyone in real life knows about these shoots you do. I mean, aside from Mr. Warner and his watchman."

"Oh sure." Manny smiled. "Lots of people know. That's one of the reasons I'm doing solos."

"Especially now that you're getting so much legit work."

"You ever miss that?" He knew Lauro had some gigs for mainstream films before hiring on with Stroked.

Lauro ate a piece of bacon while he thought about it. "There's part of me that would like to be working on shoots for Sony, or Disney, or whatever. But I feel like this is actually better. This is a full-time job. I've got health insurance. And I'm getting a lot of different credits."

Manny fiddled with his water glass for a second. "You ever tell people you're dating? About your work."

"I don't date."

"At all?"

97

Lauro shook his head. "I'm ace. I tried dating all through high school and college, saw some people here and there after that, but the past few years it's like, you know what? I'm not looking for a sexual relationship. Took me a while to figure out, but this is who I am. I know some people online and maybe someday I'll see about meeting up in person. There are other heteroromantics out there who don't care about sex."

"Does that mean, wait." A minute to think. "So you'd like a straight romantic relationship that doesn't include sex."

"Bingo." Lauro polished off his hash browns. "Anyway, the answer to the question you actually asked is no, but I do tell people about my work. A few people from college know, and my online friends."

"Hmm. I'm not dating either," Manny confessed. "This time last year I thought, I don't want to get to thirty without a boyfriend. Since I started working with Irv I'm seeing things differently."

"Like how?"

"Like I'd rather hold out for the real thing. I had the real thing once. My first. He was in the Marines and he got killed in a training accident." It was so much easier to say now. Finally. "Since then there hasn't been anything serious, and I thought I ought to keep trying. The truth is, I wasn't trying. I was just going out to get laid." He laughed at Lauro's mystified expression. "Yeah. I've had better orgasms on my own." They both cracked up. "Man, I have *laughed* at myself. Got this big old mirror, set it up in my apartment. Had to practice, right? Make sure I'm doing the right things with my face. Figure out the best angle, what's going to look good. There's learning on the job but then there's wasting people's time, you know?"

98

"God, I never thought of that. The whole thing is just so, eh. Like why bother. I see people in our scenes and I'm thinking about composition and lighting. It doesn't occur to me to wonder if that's how they do it in real life."

"I promise, it isn't. Irv told me to practice edging myself and I was all, oookay." They were snickering. "In real life it's like, how fast can I do this. Used to be. Now everything is rehearsal. Debe practicar. Nice and sloooow. Make it laaaast." Lauro dropped his head into his hands, shoulders shaking. Manny ate the rest of his pancakes. Maybe it was good Irv wasn't here. This was a great conversation, one they probably wouldn't have had with the boss around. Next time they were on a shoot, he and Lauro would have a private joke.

And now he knew why the guy was so completely, blankly professional at all times. The rest of the team was professional too; Irv never so much as implied interest in one of his models. But he was interested sometimes. There were moments when they were in close proximity when Manny caught the dilated pupils, or a slight flush. Was that why he was disappointed tonight? Did he want Irv to be interested in him? Was he interested in Irv?

Because the guy was interesting. He was smart, talented, and a good businessman. Plus he was *nice*. Behind that gruff exterior he was kind, helpful, generous. The looks that seemed odd to Manny when they met appealed to him now. Now that he knew the guy, and liked him. He thought about that all the way home.

He was still thinking about it half an hour later, cock in hand in front of his mirror. How would it be with Irv? Manny was with someone shorter than him plenty of times. He liked it, liked being the tall one.

Liked a man who wasn't too thin, someone who felt strong and sturdy, without necessarily being some pumped-up jock. And he liked men with that kind of mouth. Liked a full, soft mouth to kiss, or on his body. On his dick. *Ay papi*, he thought, half-laughing to himself as he watched his hand move. This was working for him. He was pretty sure he'd be thinking of this the next time they shot something. Wondered if Irv would be able to tell.

Going home, now that 'home' was no longer the porn house, felt strange. Well, six years was a long time. In those six years, anytime Irv did a shoot on location, he went back to the filming house. Often as not, he went straight to the computer to start work on the day's footage or images. Since moving to the Brewery, he was making a conscious effort not to do that.

He still took the media home, and he still worked on it at home. But not the same day. Now heading home from a shoot meant the end of the workday. Assembling the pictorial or editing the video started the next day.

Except here he was, at the big-ass desk surface built across the end of the loft, all three monitors live, footage of Manny on screen. He sure hoped no one could tell he was reacting to the guy. Professional distance was still a thing; he wasn't saying anything, and he certainly wasn't doing anything overt. But in the privacy of his own mind he'd completely given up the pretense.

He liked Manny. Everything about him. He *wanted* Manny. He wasn't working on this footage. Instead he was standing here looking at the screens with his hand down his pants, and it wasn't the first time. In a minute he'd go over to the bathroom and finish himself off, and he'd be thinking of Manny while he did it, and he was so fucked.

They were doing another shoot in a couple weeks, a pictorial this time, and it was going to be here at the loft. Irv was absolutely determined not to make a pass. Not to make the kid uncomfortable, not to do or say anything that would imply there was any kind of quid pro quo. So far he'd managed it, he could tell, because the kid was so at ease with him. *Calling him a kid is not working.*

Half an hour later, the screens were black, Irv was more relaxed, and he was thinking about something different. Not that different, he was still thinking about Manny, but now he was thinking about that conversation with Lauro. *We are allowed to like each other*. There were ways to talk about that. He could introduce the subject at a place and time when it wouldn't set off flares. And he could make it clear that it was totally okay if Manny wasn't interested. Nothing had to change.

Except they'd always know, and Irv wasn't sure he could take it. "Fuck it," he grumbled, and picked up his phone. It wasn't too late to call Monica.

Her answer made him re-think that. "What?"

"Bad time?"

"No, not really. Problem on your shoots today?"

"No. Mental problem."

"What is it?"

"Figueroa."

"Oh." Three long notes in that single syllable. "A Rick kind of problem?"

"Uh-huh. Except you knew Rick wanted you."

"Oh, shit, Irv." There was a pause. Irv could hear Rick's voice in the background, then Monica's answer. She came back with "Have you talked to him?"

"No, and I'm not going to. It's bad enough he's a model, but I'm almost ten years older than he is."

"What the fuck does that matter? I'm older than Rick."

"Yeah, and if Sports Illustrated did a seniors version of the swimsuit edition you could be the cover model."

She snorted with laughter. "Seniors?! Fuck you!"

It made Irv smile. "Masters?"

"Fuck you some more. You're seriously not going to say anything?"

"Not unless he says something first, which is about as likely to happen as Brad Pitt rolling up to the house saying he wants to remake 'The Opening of Misty Beethoven.'"

Monica laughed again. "Right, fine. So do you want me to take him? I like what you've been doing. I get it, the whole El Vaquero thing."

Irv sighed. "No. I want to keep working with him. I have this idea that maybe someday once he's getting more steady work on the legit side, he'll stop doing our shit, and then maybe." It was hopeless, and stupid, but it was the best he could come up with.

"So are you the man behind the curtain there? The new kit, the website, all that shit?" Irv made an embarrassed sound. Monica made a *tsk* sound. "You're a mess."

"I know. I don't want him to be with me because he's grateful."

"Right. It's completely impossible that he might actually like you and think you're fuckable. It's only a little obvious that he is completely not interested in any of the studs in our stable." In the background, Rick made a whinnying sound.

Irv laughed. "Tell the big guy hi for me. And thanks for listening."

"You're an idiot."

"Yeah, I know. Good night."

"Night." She disconnected. Irv put the phone on its charger and went to get ready for bed.

Getting through the next pictorial was a trial. To give it a little of the El Vaquero flavor, Manny's cowboy hat (now showing some wear) hung on the wall of the big black plywood shooting box. His old boots were in the corner. There were other props: a black leather pouf, a black-and-white serape. Plus the pile of black leather straps, and the glint of chains, under a coil of rope. Manny was wearing only his black zoot suit pants for the first few shots, with new black cowboy boots and a loop of chain on his hip. He took his time getting naked before buckling on the ankle cuffs, wrist cuffs, and collar.

Irv never questioned why porn viewers wanted to see bondage. He liked bondage pictures himself, in moderation. Manny agreeing to do it was kind of a surprise. Him suggesting ways to use that rope was a big surprise. Of course, Irv had to help. Had to participate. The whole point of bondage was that the person getting tied up (or whatever) couldn't get out of it by himself, which generally meant he couldn't get *into* it by himself. So it was Irv experimenting with the rope. This wasn't his thing personally, but he knew the drill: even though this was work for hire, he checked in with Manny every step of the way. Safe, sane, and consensual was pretty much the Stroked motto as well as BDSM best practice.

The shoot took what felt like forever. Most of the time the restraints didn't let Manny put a hand on himself. He got hard several times, most notably when Irv did the thing where the black leather collar around his neck was chained to the cuffs around his ankles. When he was sitting on the pouf, wide-apart knees on the serape-covered floor of the box, hands cuffed behind his back. It took forever to get all the angles. Irv thought he could be forgiven for thinking *I want that for wallpaper*.

Manny could tell this shoot was different. Not only because Irv had to be hands-on this time. He kept averting his eyes, as if he didn't want to see this. Manny kept staring at him. It wasn't intentional; he wasn't trying to be obvious. He just kept catching those moments when Irv would glance at him as if to check the composition and the lighting and then go still. He'd blink, or shake his head as if he'd forgotten something. Manny thought he could be forgiven for thinking *I am turning you on*.

Of course, that turned *him* on. If he hadn't been thinking about how much he liked Irv, and if he hadn't been getting kind of obsessively curious about that mouth, it might have felt off. Irv was working so hard at being professional. For the same reason, Manny wouldn't say anything. Not now, not today. Not when being exposed and helpless like this made him so hard he was aching. Flushed and dripping. Especially after Irv asked him if it was okay to put on the blindfold. Hearing him move around, not being able to see him, Manny couldn't help wondering if there might be a touch. Wishing for it. He'd never understood the appeal of a blindfold before.

He was right back there during the last setup. Maybe it wasn't supposed to be the last, but after that one he was done. He was glad it was only him and Irv, though they could have used another person to help. First they had to wedge in a new vertical prop, a heavy bolster covered in black leather. Then the cuffs around Manny's ankles were chained to eye-bolts in the floor of the box. Feet apart, about six inches back from the bolster. His wrist cuffs were chained to eye-bolts in the ceiling, about the same distance in front of the bolster. It forced him to lean against the black leather, which felt so much like flesh that he was hard in about two seconds. Adding the blindfold cranked him up to eleven. There was enough play in the chains for him to hump the bolster, so he did. He could get some grip on it with his elbows, so he did that too. He could be as loud as he wanted. He came so hard he thought he was going to pass out.

When he felt Irv's hands at his wrist, Manny was still standing there (hanging there?), forehead resting against the leather, panting. Irv said softly, "You okay?"

"Mm-hmm." Feeling the support of Irv's hand as each of his own came down. Still leaning on the prop, blind and shaking. Hoping none of the noise he made included Irv's name, or anything else that would make this weird. He cleared his throat when his ankles came free. "Did you take that on video?"

A stifled laugh. "Uh, yeah."

"Good. I want to see it." He pushed himself upright and lifted the blindfold to see Irv, six feet away doing something with the camera. He was a bit flushed and was very obviously not looking at Manny. *That got to you.* It was deeply satisfying. He might have made himself last long enough for a solo scene if not for all the other stuff. Maybe some other time. For now, he turned to face the camera. "Ready to shoot me taking this shit off?" Irv made an affirmative sound. Manny straightened out the serape on the floor of the box, sat on it with his back against the bolster, and put the blindfold back in place. Rested a moment, then slowly took the blindfold off. Started unbuckling the collar and cuffs. Taking his time with it. Plenty of time to let Irv focus in on the red marks where the leather had been, the sweat on his face and chest, the come smeared across his belly. He was pretty sure he'd never looked quite so fucked-out in his life. Couldn't wait to see the images.

He rested for a minute, still feeling shaky. Kind of not good, actually. He dropped his head to his knees and swallowed.

CHAPTER 6

Irv registered the moment when reaction set in and turned off the camera. A second later he was over at the box, arm around Manny's ribs, easing him up to his feet. "Come on. Over here."

"What's, I'm, ugh."

"You're coming down. It's okay. Totally normal." He settled Manny in the recliner in the back corner, already draped with a Vellux blanket. Folded the blanket over him and watched him curl up. Stood there with his hand on Manny's shoulder until he felt the tremor ease. "Take it easy. I'll be right back."

Manny heard Irv walk away, still too involved with what was happening physically to wonder where he was going. After a minute or two he started feeling warmer, and the nausea passed off. *What the fuck was that*. He didn't move. Stayed curled in a ball, eyes closed, until something nudged his hand. "This blanket's gonna be all funky."

"That's what the washing machine is for. Here." Irv held onto the coffee mug until he was sure Manny had a good grip.

"Mmm." Hot, creamy, and sweet. It tasted so good. "So what was that?"

"Well, probably, your brain knows that was your idea, but your body was like wait a minute, I'm tied up and blind in a box and every fucking thing is wrong."

Manny laughed softly into the mug. "Yeah, okay. My mom used to have a blanket like this. I always thought it felt like marshmallow Peeps." He heard a laugh. "Thanks for taking care of me."

Irv thought about saying it was part of the job, but he didn't want to be all impersonal in that moment.

107

"You are always going to be safe here." He wondered if Manny could tell he wanted to add 'with me.'

Manny swallowed some coffee, tipped his head back, and made eye contact. He could have sworn he heard two more words. "I know." *I wouldn't be here otherwise.*

"Take as long as you need. I'll be right over there if you want me." *For anything.* He tore his gaze away from those gorgeous eyes and headed over to the tripod to disconnect the camera, then set it on the desk. No way was he going to go through those images until he was alone. Instead he put on some soothing music, then got busy cleaning up the props, putting everything away. Taking care of business. Nothing to see here. Pretty soon the kid would get up and put his clothes on and head home. Then Irv could download the images. He knew which one he was going to put in his very inappropriate private collection. A still from the video, when Manny was peaking, blindfolded face against the leather, mouth open. Every muscle in that beautiful body flexed, gleaming with sweat, as if an invisible man was fucking him.

When Manny was finally gone, Irv collapsed on the recliner and pulled the blanket over himself. It smelled like Manny, of course. A whiff of sweat and come. There was a good chance he'd take it upstairs to the sleeping loft later.

Not long after the bondage pictorial went live, Lauro was over on the westside, and it happened to be a good day to meet up for lunch. Manny got to Swingers ten minutes before their agreed time and put his name on the list.

Lauro walked up when there were still a couple of people ahead of them. "Hey."

108

"Hey yourself." They shook hands. "What's new in the Valley?"

"The partners are going nuts getting ready for the con. You're going, right?"

Manny huffed out a laugh. "Yeah, I told them I would. Have you been to one before?"

"Mm-hmm. You can imagine what it's like for me." He made that mystified face. "I had to ask what some of the toys were for. Or, like, what *all* of them were for."

Manny laughed out loud. "I've never been much of one for toys." Then the host was calling them up, sending them back to a booth.

Lauro waited till they were alone before saying, "So the collar, et cetera, that was new?" He had to wait a minute for a reply; Manny cracked up, head pillowed on his forearms on the table. "I mean, no personal experience but if you don't mind my saying so the pictures have been mentioned a few times."

"Oh God." Manny wiped his eyes and sat back. "That was a trip."

"New?"

"New. The subject came up when we were talking about what's next. I was like okay, why not try this. All that rope in the stable. Whatever, right? I trust Irv. Did not expect to dig it." He sipped some water, pretending to look at the menu, conscious that he was blushing. He glanced up; Lauro looked interested, but not like he was going to make a big deal out of this. Well, he wouldn't. "I had a feeling Irv kind of got off on it too."

"Mmm. The grapevine supports that conclusion."

"Shit, really?" Manny was a little too pleased about that. "I've been having some thoughts. Feelings," he confessed.

109

"He likes you an awful lot." The server came to get their order. When they were alone again, Lauro fiddled with his glass for a second. "He's liked you for a long time. I told him once, you were allowed to like each other. Monica and Rick aren't the only ones who make it work."

"Jesus, dude. You think he likes me *that* much?"

Lauro made a big 'who knows' gesture. "All I know is I've worked with the guy for going on four years and the way he talks about you is different. But you have to know he'll never make a pass."

Coffee magically appeared. Manny tasted it, added cream and sugar, tasted again. Made a face. "Diner coffee." Lauro snickered. "Yeah. So if I want to see if we could progress it, I'm gonna have to make the move. What's the downside?"

"Is that rhetorical?"

"Do what?"

"Sorry. Was that a statement or a question?"

"Uh, a question." Manny stored away the word, wondering how it was spelled. He'd heard it before but not in actual conversation. "I've hooked up with co-workers before. Sometimes it's a bad idea."

Lauro did some chemistry with his coffee. "Bearing in mind my complete uselessness on the sex part of things, you're not actually his employee. You're an independent contractor, and it isn't your biggest income stream. If the situation got awkward, you could always work with Monica. Or you could just bail out, without doing yourself any real damage. Right?"

"Yeah, I guess." Manny thought about it. "Maybe if I get a big legit job. I'd be away from you guys for a while."

110

"So if it got weird, you wouldn't have to work together again right away."

"Right."

"Not a bad strategy." Food was delivered. They both dug into their burgers, eating in silence. When he was down to the pile of French fries Lauro said, "I think it's worth a try. I've seen you guys work together a bunch of times now." Plus there was all that other stuff Irv did for Manny, and for nobody else. "But only if you really care about him. Because he'll never admit it but he's a romantic. If you ask me, that's why he's never pushed you about doing a couples scene. You could make a lot more money that way."

So true. "Mmm. I'll think about it." Manny changed the subject then, back to the convention and what it was like to work a booth there. That was going to be a trip, too.

May 2016

Irv checked about four times before printing up the poster from the bondage pictorial. He knew Manny was going to be tripping anyway. But the kid told him it was okay, eventually saying "Irving, really, it's fine." Hearing his full name like that made Irv's brain switch off for a minute, and by the time he recovered it was too late to go back to the subject. Monica laughed at him later, pointing out that they didn't need to get permission again once the contracts were signed. Which of course Irv knew, but half the stuff he did with (for) Manny was stuff he didn't do with (for) anybody else, and he kept tying himself in knots over it. It was a relief to get everything set up at the con and then just go through the motions.

Manny would have been out-of-his-mind embarrassed to be at a porn convention if he hadn't been thinking about the audition. He'd agreed way back in February to go to AdultCon with Irv and Monica (plus Rick, Zane, and a few other Stroked stars). Now here they all were at the L.A. Convention Center. It was a madhouse; there were mostly-naked people everywhere you looked. Piles of porn and sex toys – literally piles, bins and towers and racks – at booth after booth, everywhere you looked. And fans. It was bizarre.

People bought pictures, posters, and DVDs just so they could have them autographed by the stars. Stroked had put out a compilation DVD with Manny's three stable scenes. Every time he took the cap off his Sharpie to sign one he had a moment of thinking *this is so weird*. Signing 'Stay Hot, XXX El Vaquero,' as if that were a real person.

Most of the action at their booth wasn't about him. He had plenty of time to hang back, look approachable while staying out of the way, and obsess about the next day. He was heading out to Canyon Country to read for a part on a new streaming series called 'Alhambra.' Historical, with a little bit of fantasy, according to Cyrus Garrett. Manny got script pages for two scenes. The first was in a village. The character he was reading for was a traveling salesman kind of guy. The second scene had his character visiting a camp where the two main characters – a nobleman and his second in command – were hanging out. Attached at the back was a page describing the setting: medieval Spain. Being bilingual was a plus. Especially since the thing was going to shoot in Mexico.

He'd told Irv, of course. It was a big deal, possibly a life-changing deal, even though the odds were against him getting the part. If he at least got a call-back, though, Cyrus would get some credit for sending in a person who wasn't a waste of time. And Manny would get some credit for not being a waste of time. He felt ready for it. He'd been doing as much research as possible since he got the sides, trying to give himself some context. He was a negotiator, a deal-maker, a problem-solver. The guy you tracked down when you needed something and couldn't get it in your own town. It was wild to think about how that got done so long ago. Not only before the internet and phones, but before most people could write a letter. When he thought about a character to use as a model, he came up with Quark, the Ferengi wheeler-dealer from Star Trek: Deep Space Nine.

He'd picked up some internet gossip suggesting the nobleman would be played by a Mexican movie star. Maybe that guy would be at the audition. Maybe they'd have a horse or two, since so many of the parts were mounted.

Irv nudged Manny. "Your public wants you."

"Oh! Sorry. Was zoning out thinking about, you know."

"Yeah, I know." Irv watched the guy do his thing. He'd been pretty nervous at first. Now he was used to it. Just like that first time at the filming house. Adaptable, easy-going, smart, awesome. Looking sinister and alluring in those black zoot suit pants with chains looped across his hip, a black and blue Western-style shirt on top, a choke chain, and his cowboy hat. One of the most-dressed people there, not that his fans seemed to mind. Only a true asshole would hope he tanked the audition. Irv wasn't quite that bad. He was enough of an asshole to think it would be a lot better for him personally if Manny didn't get the job. What he

113

said, of course, was "You're going to be great. Go out there tomorrow and get it."

The audition call was so early, it was almost like a background gig. Manny gave himself plenty of time, using his nav once he got past the Highway 14 interchange, even though this was his old stomping ground; his parents still lived in San Fernando. He took the Golden Valley exit and followed the prompts to a ranch house set well away from any other homes. Behind the house was a barn, behind the barn was a paddock, and in the paddock were half a dozen mounts. One was a burro, one was a mule, and one was the biggest paint horse Manny had ever seen. It was as tall as Red's Merlin, with a long full mane and tail like a parade horse.

In front of the house was a gravel parking area crowded with cars. Manny backed his truck in alongside an unhitched horse trailer. Then he took a few minutes to prepare, drinking some water and looking over the script pages one more time. Thinking about his character, and everything he'd learned about medieval Spain. Wondering if he might get to ride the glossy pale horse that had kept itself apart from the others. After a couple of deep breaths, settling himself down, he got out of the truck and walked toward the voices.

He wasn't the only person there to audition, that was for sure. It was a good thing he'd set aside the whole day. One group of people were obviously from the production company. Another, smaller group were the ones in charge of the property and the mounts. Then there were a dozen people holding sides, like Manny. He recognized a few of them, including the really tall guy who had a high-profile arc on that science-fiction show last season. "Hey Marco," he said, taking a chance the guy would remember him from other auditions. "Manny Figueroa."

"Sure, I remember you." They shook hands. "Nice to see so many of mi gente."

"For real." Everyone there was some kind of color, which was a first in Manny's experience. "Are you reading for something specific?"

"Yeah. You?"

"Uh-huh. The trader." The reaction told him Marco wasn't up for the same thing, which was good. They were nothing alike physically; Marco was seven inches taller and probably eighty pounds heavier. Not to mention he had a voice like James Earl Jones. Manny made a bet with himself that the guy was here to read for the second-in-command. "What have you heard about the lead role?"

"They cast it for sure. Tiburon is playing it."

"Verdad?" Manny whistled softly. The internet gossip got it right. That meant two things. The show was going to get seen by a lot of people in Mexico; and they were going to need a name the American audience would recognize. Which meant Marco was positioned right. There was some Emmy buzz for his arc on 'Flagship.' Now Manny was curious. "Is this your first read?"

Marco edged a little bit away from the crowd, moving subtly, answering in a low voice to match Manny's. "No, I was in last week. They want to see how I'll do on a horse."

"You ride before?"

"Not a lot, but I've had some practice recently with a friend. Guy I worked with on a play back in twenty twelve. Red Warner?"

Manny laughed under his breath. "Oh, that was you! I've been riding exercise for him since last summer. When he said he had someone coming in to work with Merlin I was like, good. I had my hands full with that asshole Jarvis." Marco snickered. They talked about Red's horses for a few minutes, keeping half an eye on people going in and out. Manny didn't have a full cast list, so he could only guess, but there was at least one other guy there who he thought might be up for the trader. Two women, who might be reading for the trader's wife. Another big guy (not as big as Marco) with a military kind of look, who might be reading for that second lead. There was enough traffic that Marco and Manny let their conversation die pretty soon, wanting to get in the right head space for when their turn came.

The read part of it went well, Manny thought. He went into character with the attitude that this was a guy people needed. A neutral party, not on anyone's side exactly, but also not out to screw anybody up. He was there to do business. Ripe for some haggling, playing to the crowd a little, even though the crowd was imaginary at the moment. After he read his scenes he was sent back to the holding area. That seemed like a really good sign, not getting the 'thanks for coming out' yet. He stretched for a few minutes, had another mouthful of water, found a bathroom. It was in kind of a state; he tidied it up for the next person. Marco wasn't around when he got back.

There was a long enough stretch of time with nothing happening that Manny got on his phone to check messages. One from Lauro made him smile: *Get that job amigo*. It was too much to hope there'd be one from Irv. He sent Lauro a note, put the phone away, and

116

stretched some more. He was straightening up when he heard his name. "Sí?"

"Come on back, we want you to meet someone."

Manny followed, excited. He didn't get any less wound up when he saw one of the two women. Were they going to have him read with her? They were. It was a new scene, with only a few minutes to read it over, mutter to each other about it, and then set themselves up. It was a scene where they just rode into the village and were getting set up for a market day. Affectionate bickering, scolding an invisible cat that was refusing to get out of a basket, announcing themselves to an invisible local. So much fun. Then the production people walked away, talking amongst themselves. Manny turned to the woman. "Hi. I'm Manuel Figueroa."

"Patrice Diaz." They shook hands. She raised her eyebrows. "You ever hear of Moorish Spain before?"

"Claro que no." She snickered. He was smiling. "You ever work with horses before?"

"Never in my life. I'm scared to death. I've been telling myself, girl, pretend it's a big dog."

"That works. How about the cat?"

"Cats are easy. Me and cats go way back. Lord, I'm nervous. This is the biggest thing I ever read for."

"Me too. You ever see Tiburon in anything?"

"Child, I *worked* with him before, not that he'll remember. I was an extra. He is," she fanned herself. Manny stifled a laugh. She leaned in closer and spoke low. "I heard he's got some explainin' to do about that divorce. May be why he's signing on for an American project."

"Or maybe he knows someone with this company. I looked them up, this is their biggest project so far too."

117

"Cantarás," she said. "Everybody says it wrong. They do all those music videos. The main guy, Leon Silva? I have all his records. I'm on his Facebook all the time going, when's the next one coming out," she whined. Manny was cracking up as quietly as possible. Then she looked past him and said, "Ay papi," so devoutly that he had to turn around and see.

"Oh. That's Marco Hidalgo." The big guy looked kind of amazing on that tall paint horse. She was tossing her head, shaking her mane, making a scene. Marco sat still and quiet, talking to her, holding onto … what. "Mierda."

Patrice nudged him. "What?"

"No saddle." All she had on was a bridle. Manny was hoping they wouldn't actually be riding bareback all the time; saddles were definitely a thing in the Middle Ages.

"So? Oh! How the f-, I mean how the hell you stay on?" They leaned on each other, having quiet hysterics. Maybe not quiet enough; one of the production-company people seemed to remember they were still there.

"Manny, Patrice, we're going to turn you over to the handlers for a few minutes. Come with me."

Patrice gave him a big-eyed look as they followed. He was excited all over again. If they were going to work with one of the mounts, that was one more way to show they were the right couple for these roles. And he liked her. If he was going to get the part, he wanted to do it with her. "Don't worry," he said softly. "You hang a little bit behind me and I'll show you what to do."

"Just so you know, that wouldn't always go so good with me," she murmured. "But today, you the boss." She let him do it, too. The production person watched while a handler brought out the first animal, a burro. Manny thought that was smart: bring out the smallest one. He introduced himself to the animal, then led it around in a circle. Like every donkey in the world, it wanted to go somewhere else, but they got the job done. Then Patrice had a word with it, acting like she dealt with a donkey every day. Next came the gray mule, which was a lot bigger. It was either bored or half-asleep. Patrice dealt with that one like a champ, too, petting its long furry ears and crooning to it, right up to the moment it propped its nose on her shoulder and drooled on her. Then she scolded it in low-volume but high-velocity Spanish that made the handler laugh.

He dug in his back pocket for a bandanna. "Lo siento querida."

"No importa," she said, making a face as she swabbed the wet spot on her shirt. "Mule drool. That's a first." Manny gave her an apologetic face as he led the mule back to the handler. Drool was the least of what they'd be dealing with if they were handling animals all the time. She didn't seem put off by it, though.

He stood by the paddock fence as the handler swatted the mule on its rump and sent it through. "Algo más?"

"Sí." The handler walked across the paddock to that pale gold horse. Manny thought *no, no way,* but sure enough the guy caught the bridle and brought the animal through the gate. "This is Saluki, he's Akhal-Teke. Very rare."

"He's beautiful," Manny said, running a hand down the animal's narrow neck, observing the bony head and white muzzle. "How old is he?"

119

"Older than dirt," the handler said. "Retired from stud. He belongs to Tiburon."

Manny blinked. "And he's in the pool?"

"Tiburon's too heavy for him now."

Ay Dios he's a fucking pet. The thought may have shown on his face. Manny blew out a breath. "So what now?"

"Now we see if you can ride him. Just you."

Manny glanced at Patrice; she raised her eyebrows, like 'thank God;' he rolled his eyes. She bit her lip, obviously trying not to laugh. "Yeah, laugh it up, amiga. Okay." The handler held Saluki still. "Patrice, give me a leg up?" Manny talked her through it, swinging his other foot over the horse's back, and straightened up. The handler clipped a pair of reins to the bridle and tossed the ends to Manny. "Thanks." He patted Saluki's neck, clicked to him, and tapped those shiny flanks with his heels. The horse shook his head and took off. Not too fast, just enough to remind this new human who was really in charge. Manny was laughing a few minutes later, when he rode back around to the front of the paddock and dismounted.

I don't want to jinx it, he texted Lauro when he got home. *But it felt good.*

"He said it was good," Lauro told Irv the next day. "The Spanish audition." Neither of them expected to see Manny for a while. Cyrus Garrett had let Irv know that the contracts were going out for the supporting cast on that action movie with the wrestler. The scene with the bicycle messenger was a huge complicated one, filming in June. None of them could guess how many days Manny would be on location. Lauro was a tiny bit envious; he remembered what it was like to work on a

120

big movie set. The Spanish thing sounded cool, too, but he wouldn't envy being stuck in the Mexican desert for five months.

Irv shouldn't have cared and definitely shouldn't have asked. "What'd he tell you?"

"Read the two scenes they sent him, then they put him with another person for a different scene, and then they did some work with animals. I guess everyone has to be okay with all kinds of livestock."

Irv snorted out a laugh. "They're not going to do CGI animals, huh."

"Yeah, no. Look at this horse." He showed Irv a picture Manny texted, of a thin elegant animal the color of white gold. "A bunch of them have to ride. Manny said this person who was reading for his wife, if she gets the part? She has to learn to drive a mule cart." Lauro saw Irv's expression and laughed. "Uh-huh. Well, they didn't have Jeeps in the thirteenth century."

"I never worked on a period piece," Irv said. "Their location camps are going to be literally full of shit." Lauro laughed. "That's pretty hard-core. He sound excited about it?"

"Mm-hmm. Maybe we should do some costume scenes. I was online last night looking into the history, and some of those clothes are pretty. It's robes and stuff, really covered up, but you can imagine they don't have anything on underneath."

Thanks a lot, Irv thought, managing not to glare at his assistant as he instantly imagined Manny bare under some exotic Jafar business. "So what are you thinking, like the Arabian Nights?"

"Why not? We could do a bunch of scenes with different people and put out a compilation DVD for Christmas."

"Call it Magic Carpet Rides." They both snickered. "It's gotta be straight-up fantasy though, or else the culture police will come out."

"For real." They brainstormed for a few minutes, then Irv took off, leaving Lauro to write it up for the partners.

Manny was out-of-control excited as soon as he got the email from Cyrus Garrett. It had been so many months since the second contact, the one that said 'you're hired,' that it almost seemed like nothing was happening. But this made it official. The producers had approved the U5s – actors with fewer than five lines of dialogue, which included Manny – and the contracts were going out. The shooting schedule, script pages, synopsis, and location ID would follow. He had no idea how many hours he would actually end up working, hoped he'd be able to keep the gym job, was fully prepared to ditch it if he had to.

The past few months had definitely been different. He'd been contacted directly, by Garrett's assistant Rita and by Reina Salazar's assistant, for a dozen multi-day extra gigs. This was not what he was used to. He'd been registered with Central Casting for eight years and they *never* called you; you always had to be proactive. But maybe this was the next step, once people knew you had some skills. With all the new stuff he had to show, and being able to look like five different flavors of bad guy, he was getting some serious action.

One of those gigs even turned into a U5, when somebody no-showed. By the end of the year, he might get his SAG card. If he got the part in 'Alhambra,' it was as close to a sure thing as you could get in Hollywood. Getting into the union was no guarantee of steady employment, but it would open up another whole class of auditions.

None of this would be happening without Irv. Manny had been tempted to say 'hook me up with somebody' because he knew how much the guy wanted to get him in an interactive. He still didn't want to do it. Going to bed with someone else just for money was a step he wasn't comfortable taking.

He didn't mind seeing himself on camera, now that he was used to it; he could look at it objectively, compare it to other guys' work, and think of it as simply another acting job. And those two winter shoots, he couldn't help thinking of them as serious. Just like the yellow-ribbon shoot. On one level those were a guy jerking off alone. On another, they were about something. Maybe someday those could get stitched together, to tell the story. He had a feeling Irv wanted to do that too. Maybe even had that in mind all along. After all, the guy knew what the story was, the story Manny kept reaching back to. Missing his soldier, living for the day his soldier came home. He knew by now that a porn audience liked a happy ending every bit as much as a mainstream audience did. If only there could have been a happy ending in real life.

Well, there wasn't, and life went on. Life, in fact, had opened up like a piñata. The juggling he had to do last summer was nothing compared to this. He still managed to get over to Shall We Dance most Sunday mornings, and he still went out to ride exercise for Red a couple times a week. He was honestly having the best year ever, aside from sleeping alone every night.

When the 'Countdown' shoot was over, he was going to suggest a fourth video that could tie in to the yellow-ribbon story. A training montage kind of thing, like they always put in a movie about soldiers, to frame the scene. Because maybe El Vaquero and his soldier met in basic, but only one of them stayed in. The other one did his hitch and then got out, because he'd rather be a cowboy, and they couldn't be together anyway. Or if they worked it so the soldier was a woman, maybe it was a fight over getting married. Maybe she had a college degree and a shot at officer training, where El Vaquero was like Manny. But he didn't want to be a plus-one, tagging along wherever she got posted, always having to get some crappy job.

Before he could talk himself out of it, Manny wrote up an email and sent it to Irv, with MAYBE SOMEDAY in the subject line. All that stuff was only back-story, but it could frame a scene where Manny was pissed off and frustrated about being left behind. Lonely and horny and ready to give in. I miss you, I'll follow you, let's try. They'd need another prop. Fortunately Stroked – thanks to Monica and all her happy endings – had half a dozen good fake engagement rings in the wardrobe. If Irv went for it, that would tell Manny something important: Lauro was right; Irv was a romantic. Didn't necessarily mean that Irv had any romantic feelings about Manny, but then Manny wasn't a hundred percent sure his own feelings were romantic. Lonely, horny, and ready to make some kind of move wasn't 'I love you.' It might help him get there, though.

Irv got the email, thought *holy shitbuckets this kid wants to make an actual movie*, and wrote back that it was a great idea and he'd be thinking how and where to tape the training stuff. Then he forwarded it to Lauro, who was a genius at charting a scene. By the time Manny was free to shoot the thing, they'd be all set.

And in the meantime, Irv should open up his calendar, get back in the catalog, and see where he had holes to fill. Keep busy making acceptable porn with people other than Manuel Figueroa. Get caught up with the latest mainstream movies (always a good source of scenes to parody or riff on). What he should not do was watch a shelf full of movies about soldiers.

So of course, that's what he ended up doing.

CHAPTER 7

Manny ended up putting in a full week on 'Countdown.' Day one was the start of his ride, and dialogue with that ex-wrestler who was playing the NSA agent. The next day was finishing his ride, and dialogue with the hot-as-fuck dude from the cop show, playing the ATF agent. The next three days were all setup after setup and take after take of the big traffic jam scene. The bike they gave him was rigged with a trio of GoPros, hidden in a cargo box behind the seat. Unsurprisingly, those were dubbed the Ass Cams. Manny called Lauro at the end of day one to tell him what happened. "It's wild, man. They have all these cars in the traffic jam and everything's fucking choreographed. All this kind of stuff has to happen on my right side because of that camera angle. Other stuff on my left because of that angle. I never even thought about how they'd get those, what do you call them."

"Inserts." Lauro was still wheezing about the Ass Cams. "I feel like I shouldn't mention that to Irv or Monica."

"They'd probably be cool. Payton, though. He'd be all over having a GoPro taped to his model somewhere. Fuck, I'm surprised he hasn't already thought of it." Lauro was cracking up all over again. Manny grinned up at the ceiling. "Everything good with you?"

"Everything's good. Having fun?"

"You know it." Manny wound up the call, because he had to be back in Long Beach at seven the next morning. And if he was this tired now, he was going to be roadkill by the end of the week.

It wasn't all Manny all the time by any means. Part of the suspense (and humor) came from Jonathan, as the NSA guy, trying to get anywhere in downtown Long Beach. After their scene, a different unit was shooting all the ways he got blocked before grabbing the bicycle messenger to say here, take this thing to this guy at this place. Meanwhile, a third unit was shooting with Victor at the other end.

Both of the stars kept doing their lines different ways. At first Manny was afraid to roll with it, so he tried to stay on script, keeping his delivery more or less the same. But Jonathan kept nudging him off the straight and narrow, and the director kept letting them go, even though they were going way over his line limit. It was such a short scene, maybe taking it a dozen times was no big deal. They were shooting on video, too; that had to make a difference.

Jonathan and his co-star Victor were on set all week. They were both totally cool, easy to talk to, never rude to the crew or the extras. Even when they were talking together about what was going on and how to play it. Manny tried to pay attention, get some education out of this. It was never boring.

Especially toward the end of day five, when everybody was a little punchy. The city was completely fed up with the situation, you could tell. There were catcalls and walk-ons, people deliberately messing up shots. Production security had to get involved at one point. Manny was over at the craft services, because they told him they wouldn't need him for an hour, shooting the shit with some of the cast and crew. They were all watching Jonathan and Victor play around with a scene that was already shot. Victor's boyfriend was there, taking illicit video in a kind of shameless way. Nobody shut him down.

Finally the director decided to wrap Victor's scene with what they had, and sent him home. Manny had one more setup before he was done. This time they hung a camera on a cable and flew it down the street over Manny's head. They took it three times, throwing different obstacles at him along the staged stretch of road. He was wiped out by the time they were done, but the director looked happy. Jonathan was still there, and he looked happy too. "That's going to kill," he said, smacking Manny on the back. "Good work this week."

"Thanks." Manny took his helmet off for the last time, deeply glad he was done, wondering if he should hit craft again before he headed out. But he'd been eating that shit all week. He wanted some real food.

"You look hungry."

Manny turned his head, startled. Jonathan was still there. "I'm starved. I don't know Long Beach though. Figured I'd head home."

Jonathan made a 'why the fuck would you do that' face. "Got a pair of jeans?"

"Yeah, I have a change of clothes. After a full day, sitting in traffic in these? No me gusta." He adjusted himself through the bike shorts, which got a laugh.

"Go get changed then. Meet me over there." Jonathan pointed toward the background coordinator, busy processing all the extras. "I'll take you out."

Manny couldn't have been more surprised if the guy said 'let's go to Vegas.' He didn't think it was a pass, though he wouldn't have minded if it were. He'd had fun with the guy doing their scene. Even if it was a pass, it didn't have to be weird, because he was off the job now.

He must have been looking some kind of way, though. Jonathan was doing a thing with his hands up, palms out. "Not a pass. I swear."

It reminded Manny of Irv, that first time they met. He nodded, said, "I'll meet you in a few," and headed for the cast parking area. When he returned to the staff exit, Jonathan was waiting in a blue windbreaker, baseball cap, and glasses. The way he was standing, kind of slumped with his hands in the jacket pockets, he seemed shorter. Forgettable. "Had to look twice," Manny said, walking up.

"Camouflage," Jonathan said. "You ever been to Lola's?" Manny shook his head. "Oh man. You have to try the street corn. And the queso fundido, I could eat that all day. Short rib enchiladas. They do this mole negro with duck breast, it is *bomb*."

"I never had duck breast." Manny was smiling while they walked, halfway noticing the very ordinary SUV in front of them and the not-so-ordinary guy holding the second-row passenger door open. "A driver?"

"Yeah, it's been a while now since I can just roll up at a valet stand." They got in the car. "Adrian, this is Manuel Figueroa, he's on the show with me."

The driver slash security guy nodded to Manny, who returned the gesture, trying to act like he knew how to behave in the world of people who had drivers. Fastened the seat belt and glanced sideways at the movie star. "This is the biggest thing I've ever done."

"I was going to ask. I could see you hanging back soaking it in. That was me on my first movie."

"I saw that. A friend of mine, when he heard about me doing this, he asked if I'd seen your first one and I hadn't, so he got a copy and we watched it together. You were really good in it. And that look you had," Manny shook his head, blowing out a breath. Jonathan's evil underworld character had a sick head tattoo. "That was hot."

Jonathan grinned. "My agent's boyfriend was my stylist for the movie. He put that together for me. I had these new hair implants, right, things were looking good for the first time in years, and then he goes and shaves the shit off. I was like, God damn it."

Manny laughed. "Those must really work, though."

"Yeah, pretty good. So is this what you want to do?"

"I think it is, yeah. Had what felt like a really good audition a couple weeks ago. Still waiting to hear back."

"Who's your agent?"

"I don't have one yet."

"Oh, shit. We need to fix that." Jonathan dug his phone out, scrolled to a number, and started composing a text. "What's your number?" Manny was tripping, but he answered. Jonathan finished sending the message. "This guy represented me when I was still with WWE. When I got the movie offer I didn't want to get a second agent so I asked him to handle it. Robert Anderson, he's a good guy. Smart as fuck. What will he want to know about you?"

"Um." Manny couldn't believe he was going to say this. "I've done some porn." He almost whispered it.

"Jeez, who hasn't? What kind?"

Okay, somebody else who wasn't freaked out about it. "Crossover solos."

Jonathan made a *pssht* sound. "That ain't nothin.' What do you use the money for? If you don't mind my asking."

Manny gave him an 'are you serious' look that made him laugh. "Training. Yoga, dance, weapons, kung fu. I work part-time at this gym in Hollywood, spin training. For a long time I worked for a caterer too."

"But now you're in a movie with me," Jonathan said, looking smug. "And you had a good audition. Tell me about it."

Adrian said, "At the restaurant, Mr. Morris."

Jonathan looked out the window. "Oh yeah, here we go. Tell me once we get seated."

The next day, Manny was out in the Valley having breakfast with Lauro at the filming house, giving him the 411 on dinner with the movie star. "Can you even believe that shit? I was *tripping*. The whole time."

"That's pretty wild. And it wasn't a pass?"

Manny shook his head. He wouldn't bet Jonathan was a hundred percent straight, but it didn't matter. "Far as I can tell he's just a friendly guy who feels like he got lucky and tries to pay it forward. He told me he lives alone."

"Maybe he likes to wind down from a work day doing something social, before going home alone. So did the agent call you?"

"Yes!"

"Dude!"

"I know!" They were both cackling into their coffee. "He's all, send me your kit, and I'm all, is there a glass slipper in here somewhere." A moment to breathe. "He said he's going to contact the production about a contract upgrade. Because of the improv. I said, should we do that? They didn't exactly ask me to. He said, doesn't matter. You did more than five lines. Even if they cut it back in the edit, you did the work. More to the point, they let you do it. They didn't say stick to the script. I was about to say how do you know but I figure Jonathan must have told him."

"You've got a way," Lauro said.

"What kind of way?"

"A way that makes people want to help you. Have you talked to Irv yet?"

Manny started to say 'about what' but then thought *oh*. "Not yet. If I get the part on 'Alhambra' I think I will." He changed the subject to the next scene he was doing, asking what Lauro thought about the back-story he'd come up with.

They ended up talking about it until Lauro had to get ready for a shoot. "Would you," he began, then stopped.

"What?"

Lauro sighed. "You know I've seen all your stuff. I think I see where you're going with this. Could I write something? Would you be okay with that?"

Manny blinked. "Like another scene?"

"No. Like a screenplay. Putting all those scenes together."

"Oh! Well, sure. Knock yourself out. I'm sure as shit not gonna write it, and Irv would rather change a tire than write a script."

"God, I know. Okay. Thanks."

"Let me get out of here so you can work." They shook hands, as usual. Manny wanted to hug the guy. He was so much more than a handshake friend. "Can I hug you? Or is that a thing you absolutely hate?"

Lauro smiled. "I don't hate it, and yes." It'd been a long time since Manny hugged a friend. It felt good.

A week after Manny's next soldier scene wrapped, Irv was at the filming house, bullshitting with his partners by the pool, when a text notification pinged his phone. He dug it out of his cargo pocket, read it, and sighed. Monica said, "What?"

"Figueroa got the part on that Spanish show."

"Good for him. Was that him?"

"No, that was Cyrus Garrett. Says the kid got himself an agent between then and now. Referred by Jonathan Morris."

"Whoa." Payton drank some beer, staring out over the pool. Thumped his chest, belched, and said, "Guess he won't be doing too much more here, will he?"

"Not likely." Irv sent back a reply, put his phone away, and reached for the bottle on the pool deck. His first thought should have been 'can I get any more work out of him before he leaves.' Instead it was 'will I even see him before he leaves.'

Cyrus said the cast would be assembling in September. That left quite a bit of time to shoot something else. He knew Lauro was working on a private project, a screenplay based on the soldier scenario. Irv would have liked to be in on that conversation. He'd still like to be in on it, if Lauro finished writing the thing. If he and Manny decided to try to do something with it. Something that did not necessarily have to be porn. Would Irv be willing to let them repurpose the Stroked material? Probably.

Maybe he should say so right up front, since Lauro was up-front about the project. Stroked owned the footage, but it wouldn't be the first time some of their material got licensed for other use. *Will I even see him. Will I ever see him.* Knowing this day would come, knowing he'd helped make things happen and could legitimately blame himself, was no comfort.

At least he did get to see the kid again. Manny heard about the Arabian Nights nonsense they were putting together and came up with a suggestion for a pictorial. It was pure torture, because it was bondage again, with Manny in makeup and jewelry like something out of ancient Egypt. There were strips of white canvas, and silky-looking ropes, and a blindfold. Sand on oiled, tawny skin. Plus a live snake borrowed from a neighbor at the Brewery. Irv was proud of the fact that he managed not to say (or do) anything completely out of bounds.

Manny was mentally prepared for it this time. He still hung out for a while afterward, accepting the chair and the blanket, with a cookie and a hot drink. When he was getting ready to go, he said, "You're really great to work with."

Irv said, "You too. I'll call you when it's ready for review."

Manny never asked Irv why he set up their review meetings. He'd started hoping it was for the same reason Manny always accepted the chance to review. Hoped he wanted to spend more time together, even though he was dressing it up like business. "I appreciate that. Be in touch."

"Yeah. See you." Irv closed the door behind his model, flipped the deadbolt, and leaned his forehead on the wall. *You are so, so fucked.* Letting the kid go without saying anything was going to be next to impossible. The smartest thing to do was schedule the review right up against something else, so he had to get Manny in and out fast. "He's just so, ungh," he said on the phone with Monica later. "Why? What is it about him?"

"Irv." Her tone was very 'what the fuck do you think.'

"I know. Wait till you see these pictures. You remember that one Nastassja Kinski did, with the snake?"

"Oh, you are *shitting* me."

"Nope. This snake is not as big as that snake, but it's still a fucking huge snake. It's this albino python that a neighbor has." The neighbor who'd promised to stay on-call till they were done and to immediately collect his pet.

"And Manny let you put this fucking monster on him?!"

"His idea!" Irv was half-laughing. "It's fucked up! He says he likes the way it feels. I'm all, you're out of your mind, but hold position while I get this shot." Monica was giggling. Irv sighed. "We're going to sell a million of those at the con next year."

"I suppose you're going to make wallpaper out of it."

"Can neither confirm nor deny," he said. Monica made a skeptical noise. "Thanks for listening."

September 2016

It was funny how easy it was to move out of that apartment. Manny hadn't even been there for two whole years, didn't have much when he got there, and hadn't added much since. His parents said he could store some stuff at their house. The full-size futon mattress was too old to be worth saving; it went to an acquaintance from the gym, who wanted to put it in the yard for his dogs. The bed frame and a few other bits of furniture went to Goodwill. When the shoot was over in February, he'd find a new place to live, and start fresh.

He wouldn't need much in Mexico. Clothes for when he wasn't working; his phone and laptop, with a solar charger; his guitar. The picture of Lobo would go with him, because he didn't trust his parents not to snoop through his boxes. All his other good pictures were on his laptop, or his phone. The cast liaison said there would be activities after hours but nothing would go very late, because out on location everything that needed electricity would have to run off a generator, which had a limited load. Manny got the message: they'd be living like old times. If you couldn't run your shit off batteries, you better love the simple life.

With that in mind, he dug out a couple packs of playing cards from way back and threw them in the truck. Somebody was bound to be up for poker. When they rolled back to base camp (a motel in Mexicali), he would bet everybody was going to be watching TV. Or fucking.

Of course that thought led him straight to the conversation with Lauro. He wanted to see Irv before he left town. Had to see him. If there was ever a time to make this potentially-embarrassing move, it was right before he was going to be gone for months. Lauro confirmed Irv was home, so Manny sent a text to ask if he could stop by; Irv said he could.

He left the apartment for the last time, found a cheap motel close to the freeway downtown that didn't look too sketchy, checked himself in. He didn't leave anything there, though. His duffel bag and guitar case fit behind the seats in the cab of the truck.

When he got there, it was kind of awkward. Manny couldn't read Irv at all. They talked for a few minutes about the new gig. Manny asked how Irv felt the first time he got a big shoot.

"I was sure it was the first step to an Oscar," Irv said, a little sourly, then forced a smile. "Excited, in other words."

"I'm excited too. And I couldn't have done it without you." Manny regarded Irv for a few seconds, not surprised but regretful that the older man did the predictable thing, shrugging it off. He couldn't have imagined those signs of interest, but the guy always deflected. Refused to take credit for anything, even though the amount of help he'd given went way beyond 'let's make money together.' Refused to indicate with a word or a gesture that he might welcome something else. Anything else. But he had to ask. "Could I take you out for dinner tonight?"

Irv blinked. He didn't expect that. They'd been working together more than a year and he'd been able to stifle every evil, inappropriate impulse. That was probably why he clung to 'kid' even though Manny was only ten years younger than he was. He looked every one of those ten years younger without the beard. His mouth looked *stop thinking about his mouth*.

What in hell was he thinking, anyway, asking Irv out for dinner? Whatever, it didn't matter, he was going down to Mexico in a minute and when he got back to L.A. he might or might not get in touch. Nothing in the contract said he had to. No commitment, just the way Irv had promised. He meant to say 'No need.' Instead he said "Sure."

Manny couldn't believe it. From the micro-expressions on that face he'd been expecting a No. It was such a relief that he smiled. "Great. How about Pace? I don't think I'm going to get much good Italian food south of the border."

They'd been out to eat exactly twice since their first meeting. Both times to the same place, Jerry's Famous. It was always full of agent and manager-type people with their clients, as well as of average folks and tourists. It was not an intimate place to eat, even if you went at night, which they didn't. Pace, on the other hand: people took dates there, or so he was told.

Irv should have suggested some other place. He didn't. "Sure." It was like he couldn't say anything else. Maybe it was that smile, which he didn't see very often. Which he had better stop thinking about immediately, because this was only dinner. That was all it could possibly be.

Manny didn't give the guy time to change his mind. "Let's go."

Irv didn't argue. He stood up, lifted his phone off the desk and slid it into his front pocket, patted his back pocket to be sure his wallet was there, and followed Manny across the room. On their way out he grabbed his keys from the dish on the entry table. Made sure the door was locked. Didn't say a word. Not when he climbed up into the passenger seat of Manny's ridiculous pickup truck (it didn't look so ridiculous in that one video, shot up in the hills), or as they were driving from the Brewery to Hollywood, or while Manny was parking. Not when they were waiting for a table. Then they were seated and the server was asking what they'd like to drink. Irv had his mouth open to say something and Manny got in ahead of him with a request for a bottle of wine. *A bottle, really*, Irv thought, but he still didn't say anything. He wondered what the server thought of this. Young, very good-looking guy with older, not-at-all good-looking guy. Well, she probably thought Irv was an agent or a manager, which he sort of was, at least for a minute. If she thought about it at all. Probably she didn't care. Her only concern was getting a good tip out of it. He finally got a word out. "Why." Only one word, and then he stalled.

Manny sat back, wishing the wine was already on the table. He sipped some water instead. On the way down here, while Irv was saying nothing in the passenger seat, he'd rehearsed what he wanted to say. He did not want to go to Mexico for five months in the same state of frustrated curiosity he'd been in for the past fifteen. Aside from that hookup with the guy from Shall We Dance, there hadn't been anybody. Since he started working with Irv, every time he thought 'maybe' about somebody, he thought *but I should tell them about Stroked*, and he didn't want to. It wasn't that he was ashamed of it, not really. It was only that he knew a guy would look at him differently, and expect him to be up for things he might not be up for.

And the truth was, for a long time now, when he thought about who he wanted to have sex with the answer was Irving. So here they were, and it was time to open his mouth. If his pass was rejected, they'd both have time to get over the awkwardness before he was back in Los Angeles.

"Because I like you. I wanted to spend my last night in L.A. with someone I like." All true. He could have said a lot more. He left it there, because 'my last night' could mean a couple of hours for dinner, or it could mean the whole night. He would much prefer that was what it meant. He'd be paying for the night at the motel whether he was actually inside the room or not.

Irv thought he heard some subtext, but it was so bizarrely unlikely that he dismissed it. He decided to treat this as just another business dinner. It would have been a great strategy if Manny were cooperating at all. But he kept doing and saying things that implied this was a date. An actual date, the kind of thing that men did when they were interested in each other on a personal level, and Irv was so not prepared to think that way.

He'd been doing a really good job staying professional with Manny, admiring from afar. But now here he was, leaning forward with his elbows on the table, smiling at Irv and *what the actual fuck, is that his leg?* Irv lost his train of thought because Manny's leg was undeniably against his. Calf to calf contact under the table. Had to be intentional.

The expression on Irv's face would have been funny if Manny wasn't in earnest. It went blank for a second after Manny moved his foot. Then his eyes closed on something like a frown, he shook his head, and when he opened his eyes again his mouth was a little bit open as if to say something. Probably 'what the fuck.' But he didn't say it. Now the expression changed and Manny had to say something. They'd been talking all along but in that bullshit business way. "Irving," he said, really soft. "Don't look like that. I'm not making fun of you. I don't have some hidden camera in here to make some nasty practical-joke clip about you. You are a nice guy, much as you try to cover it up. You're smart and interesting and funny. I like the way you look, and I want to see if I like the way you feel." His voice was super low then, and a bit uncertain. All of that might be more about him than about Irv. But Irv knew everything about him. Maybe all of that would fit into the rest of it somehow.

Irv's voice was low, too, and a bit rough. "You're out of your fucking mind." He looked to each side, leaned forward, and nearly whispered, "I don't want some pity fuck. I don't want a thank-you fuck."

"That's not what I'm talking about. Look, let's enjoy the rest of this dinner. Then I'll take you home, and maybe," he hesitated, because Irv's expression was not exactly saying 'sure, we'll go to bed, no problem.' Manny forged ahead. "Could I just hug you? Maybe kiss you? It's been so long since I did that, and it would mean something with you."

That got to Irv. He knew perfectly well Manny wasn't dating. Hadn't been dating. Had apparently given up on the whole idea of dating, which made no sense for someone as young and gorgeous as he was. *That fucker Angel*, he thought. It was amazing how one person could ruin a guy. He didn't think Manny wanted Angel anymore, not unless there had been some major soul improvement. But an unrequited crush could be hard to shake, especially after a guy lost the love of his life. "Did you see Angel when you went to give notice?"

"Yeah, I did." Manny sat back. He left his leg where it was, though. "He was a dick, as usual. And that is not what this is about, either."

Irv gave him a long look. "Huh." He drank some wine, topped up his glass (he wasn't driving, after all), and thought about it. On the one hand it would be truly insane to say no to someone like Manuel Figueroa. Even if it were once-and-done, that would probably be a good memory. On the other hand, if it were once-and-done, he'd probably never get the guy in front of the camera again. Well, he kind of didn't expect that anyway, not with Manny's acting career getting some traction. The part on 'Alhambra' wasn't huge, but it was regular. He'd be in every episode, which meant if the series backers picked up another order he'd probably get called back. It was a niche project, for sure. That wasn't necessarily a bad thing. Who ever

141

remembered cop number four from cop show number ten? Whereas these costume dramas on the streaming channels, even if they kind of sucked they were memorable, because they were different.

"Quit thinking about work," Manny said. He wasn't exactly smiling now, but his expression was warm.

"What else is there? Did you get any material from the producers yet?"

"Yeah." Manny accepted the change of subject. They might be talking about work, but Irv had not said No. He kept not saying No all the way back to the Brewery. When Manny parked the truck he didn't let it idle. He turned off the engine, turned his head, and looked at Irv. Mentor, friend, manager, guy who'd taken a confused gym rat and turned him into something close to an actor. If along the way that involved some pictures and videos Manny had to hope his family never found, well, he could live with it. They didn't respect him anyway. "You never tried to talk me into doing something I didn't want to do. I appreciate that."

Irv heard subtext again. Manny wasn't going to try and talk him into anything tonight. "Get out of the truck." He knew he sounded just like his dad, just like a fucking cop. It was no wonder he'd never had a love life worthy of the name. He opened the passenger door and hopped down, resenting the overly-tall vehicle all over again. It wasn't like Manny was all that tall. Five nine was a very useful height in film. Irv on the other hand was five seven, which was not a useful height unless you were perfectly proportioned and good-looking, neither of which applied to him. *What the fuck am I doing.* He slammed the door and stood there. A second later the other door slammed, and a few seconds

142

after that Manny was around the truck. Irv simply stood there not knowing what to do. The guy wasn't an idiot. He'd've figured out that this was tacit permission for the hug, maybe the kiss. *Holy fucking shit, is he going to kiss me.*

He didn't, not immediately. Manny lifted a hand, saw from the tiniest hint of a flinch that Irv was borderline freaked out, and continued the movement. Stepping in as if Irv's arms were up, as if the hug were offered. As if the guy meant to do more than submit to it. One arm over Irv's shoulder, the other sliding between his arm and his ribs until it wrapped around his back and Manny's body rested against his. That lasted almost five seconds, which felt like forever. Then, hesitantly, Irv's hands did come up. His arms closed around Manny. He made a muffled sound, something confused and all-too-clearly emotional. Manny let his cheek rest against Irv's hair. Felt him incrementally relax, the barrel chest expanding with a deep breath and then settling closer. He felt so cuddly. Manny closed his eyes, enjoying the moment. The men he'd been with, even Lobo, didn't cuddle. Didn't hug. Only the bro hug, that casual frat-boy thing designed to keep two men from getting too close. Irv smelled good, too, some weird mixture of tobacco and leather and cloves. It shouldn't have been enticing but it was. Manny turned his head a few degrees, getting his nose into that wiry, prematurely-graying hair. It was no wonder Irv had a complex. All he did was take pictures and video of men who looked better than average. Men who were every bit as artificial as Manny was. All the working out, the grooming, the classes on how to move, how to talk, how to seduce. That was what it came down to. Making the person on the other side of the screen feel like they had a relationship with you. It was

143

all in the body language, really. How you changed weight, how you breathed, how you touched yourself. Manny realized he was stroking his hand up and down Irv's back, and Irv wasn't pulling away. He dipped his head and put his mouth on Irv's neck.

"Fucking hell."

The words sounded startled. Also a bit breathless. He was still not pulling away. Manny was getting turned on. He brushed his lips over the rough skin of Irv's poorly-shaved jaw. *You just don't care, do you, or do you think nobody else does so why bother.* He heard a quick intake of breath. Manny hadn't kissed anyone for a long time. He was willing to bet it had been even longer for Irv. The one hand was still on Irv's back, the other was on his neck. Thumb under his ear, fingers wrapped around behind. Not gripping, not holding him still. If he wanted to get away he could. He wasn't moving.

Irv was barely breathing. Manny kept moving his mouth across Irv's skin. Up the side of his face. Across his eyebrows, down the bridge of his oversized nose. Not quite kisses, more like he was making a map using those lips instead of a pencil. Across his cheekbones. Irv's mouth was open. It felt like the only way he could possibly get enough air. He had a raging hard-on. So did Manny. This was so utterly fucking impossible. If the kid didn't kiss him soon he was going to have to *oh Jesus Christ thank God.*

It was meant to be another brush of his lips across skin, tracing the shape of Irv's mouth with his own. But he got caught there, with Irv's bottom lip between his, and he couldn't get away from that lip. For what felt like hours Manny alternated between bottom and top lip, tasting, licking, nibbling. Manny had coffee after dinner. Irv polished off that bottle of Ruffino. He still

144

tasted a bit like Chianti. "Mmm." It was the first sound Manny had made since he got out of the truck. And now Irv kissed him back. Head tilting, mouth open wider, inviting Manny's tongue and meeting it. One of his hands was on Manny's neck, the other arm tight around his waist, hand on his ass, pressing them together. Manny rocked his hips. They both gasped. "Irving."

"Manuel." They were in contact from foreheads to knees. Irv knew the next move was his to make. He couldn't argue with this. "Let's go up."

Yes, thank you Lord. Manny organized his hands. One into his pocket with his keys, clicking the lock button. The other reaching for Irv's hand. They walked across the parking lot, into the building, up the stairs and ramps and more stairs. The filming house in the Valley was all one level. It was like Irv deliberately chose a place to live that was the exact opposite. No huge walled garden here, with sheltering trees. No pool, and privacy only behind his locked door. Pavement and people. "Why the Brewery," he said. It wasn't really a question. They were at Irv's door, he was unlocking it, they were going in. Manny no longer cared why the Brewery.

Irv answered anyway. "It reminded me of this place in Queens near where I grew up. An early conversion. I'm going to the bathroom."

Manny nodded as he kicked off his shoes. He looked around as if seeing the place for the first time. A big open work space, with kitchen, bath, and laundry areas tucked under a sleeping loft. The only photo on the wall in the whole place was in the kitchen. It wasn't one of Irv's. It was taken by the previous tenant, also a photographer, who happened to be Victor Garcia's boyfriend. Manny wondered if Irv was ever tempted to hang any of his own photos. If he ever looked at the pictures of Manny. He flashed back to that first bondage series. Remembered how the ropes and chains felt against his skin. How the leather smelled. How Irv so carefully avoided his eyes when he had his hands on Manny. *You wanted me then, too.*

When Irv came out of the bathroom Manny had a foot up on the edge of the loft stairs, stretching. He had his eyes on Irv. Faintly smiling, handsome, unbelievable. Irv jerked his head toward the bathroom. He knew it was borderline rude. He was always that way, never had any social graces, and God knew this kid had seen him at his worst. If he still wanted to be here, it was in spite of Irv's worst. The idea was kind of breathtaking.

Manny passed Irv without leaving much space. Close enough to let his hand brush against the other man's. He didn't waste time in the bathroom, but he was as thorough as he could be. It seemed that Irv had decided they were going to do this, and 'this' might include quite a few things if Manny was lucky. He already felt like he'd been pretty lucky. That kiss would be a great memory for the next few months. *Finally I know what his mouth feels like.* When he left the bathroom Irv was nowhere to be seen. Manny walked softly to the kitchen; not there. He must be up in the loft.

Irv was in an absolute panic. He'd never brought a lover here. He'd only *had* one lover, here in L.A. Since then it was the occasional sex partner, usually a one-time thing, at long intervals when he couldn't stand it anymore and was willing to take the kind of guy who would take a guy like him. None of those guys were regrettable, but none of them were anything like Manny, either. He stood there in that modest loft by his modest bed, a bed that any fool could see usually had one man in it, and listened to the almost-soundless footfalls coming up the stairs.

Manny thought for a second that Irv was actually afraid. He still had his clothes on. Hadn't pulled down the sheet. Manny chose not to believe that meant he didn't want to do this after all. If he didn't want to do it, he'd be downstairs, standing by the door, saying 'have a safe trip.' He stepped over to the bed and pulled down the sheet. Then he pulled his shirt over his head. Heard a sound from Irv. Maybe that was the sound Irv always wanted to make when Manny took off his clothes. He unbuttoned, unzipped, pushed his jeans down. Kicked them out of the way. Went over to Irv and said, "I want to see you."

Irv almost said 'why' but managed to swallow it. He started on his shirt buttons. Evidently Manny thought he was taking too long; he pushed Irv's hands out of the way and had the shirt off a few seconds later. Then his hands were all over Irv's chest, fingertips brushing through body hair, mouth against his neck again, making soft sounds as if he actually liked what he was feeling, seeing, tasting. Irv turned his head and Manny kissed him again. It was different now. Hotter, hungrier, more possessive. His hands were at work on Irv's jeans. Irv had no idea where his own hands were. The only two things his brain could focus on were the kiss and the hand on his cock, stroking him through the boxers. When the kiss stopped he needed a second to catch up and realize Manny was on his knees. "If I knew this was going to happen I would've worn my fancy underpants."

Manny turned his head to the side, laughing. "You're so loco." His hands were up under the boxers. He tugged them down. "Ay sí, así papi." Irv had half a second to appreciate the sight of Manny on his knees

147

with Irv's erection in his hand. Then it was in his mouth.

"Holy Jesus." Thank God they had that conversation. This would be an awful moment to say wait a minute stop let me get a condom. Why did they even have that conversation? Oh yeah it was because of that fucker Angel and, oh Lord. *And I said I had a close call too and now I got tested every year even though I basically never had sex and Jesus fucking hell his mouth.* He was trying to think, trying to be mindful, trying to pay attention. It felt too good.

Manny was loving the feel of Irv in his mouth. He smelled like honey. Must be from that Burt's Bees lotion that was in the bathroom. Not completely free of vanity. His skin was firm and resilient. He acted like he was sixty years old sometimes, but he wasn't even forty. *You need more loving, that's all.* Irv was shoving himself into Manny's mouth, hands on his head, panting. A little bit vocal, the way a lot of men got when they were starting to peak. *Come on papi, come in my mouth, give it to me.* He had one hand clamped on Irv's ass and the other between his legs, stroking up behind his balls, feeling them tighten. "Mmm." He wanted to feel it. Wanted to taste it. That cock swelled even more. *Yes now yes there it is yes God YES.* He made another sound as Irv climaxed.

Irv barely heard Manny because he was so loud himself. He'd fully intended to get out, or to warn the kid, or something, but it took him too fast. And now he couldn't move at all because Manny was literally holding him still, one of those strong hands spread across his ass and the other one flat against his groin, keeping Irv's cock in his mouth. Swallowing with a stifled moan, lips tight around the base, a soft laugh when Irv's body jerked again. He slowly, slowly, God so slowly moved his head back. Lips still snug all the way to the end, and then licking across the tip. Irv watched the whole thing. "My God." They would make a fortune with a video of that.

Manny finally let go. Sat back on his heels, eyes closed, breathing through his mouth, so turned on he couldn't even think of what to do next. He felt Irv's hand stroking across his head and down his neck. "What do you want now."

"What do *I* want?!"

Manny laughed again, opened his eyes, and looked up. "Sí papi. What do *you* want. I'm already way ahead on what I wanted tonight."

"I didn't even know wanting something was an option." Irv patted his shoulder. "Get up. Get on that bed." He gave Manny a hand. They went to the bed. Irv stripped Manny's boxer briefs off, felt the wet spot as he dropped them on the floor. Pushed Manny onto his back, rummaged in the nightstand drawer for the lube, and straddled his thighs. "I seriously can't even believe this is happening right now."

"Are you gonna stroke me?" It was soft, a request framed as a question.

"You bet I am." Irv wrapped his slippery hand around Manny's impressive erection. "I've seen you do this so many times." Not nearly enough times.

"You think you know what I like, huh. Closer."

Irv glanced at Manny's face, his smiling mouth. He did seem awfully far away. He set his other hand down. Still too far. Onto his elbow, then letting his legs go. Stretching out, half on top of Manny, with their legs tangled and his hand at work. Manny pulled him in for a kiss. Not a super serious kiss this time; they were both too distracted. Irv was loving the feel of Manny in his

149

hand. He'd fantasized about this a lot. Watching Manny get himself off was food for a million fantasies. He did it beautifully. And now Irv was doing it for him. He was panting against Irv's mouth, hips moving. One arm wrapped over Irv's back and the other flung out, gripping the bed, all muscular curves and smooth tawny skin. Knee up, heel dug into the bed, moaning. "What do you want, baby."

"Tus dedos. Tu mano."

Well, Irv knew enough Spanish to get that all right. He shifted back, located the lube with his free hand, somehow managed to get some where he wanted it without letting go of that cock. Manny had both knees up, holding one leg open. Irv caressed, teased, rimming with his fingertips until Manny was whimpering. Then slow penetration with a finger, feeling the reaction at the same moment he saw it. Another, hearing the stifled cry. "Let me hear you."

Manny did. He let it rip with filthier Spanish than he'd ever used. Shoving his cock into Irv's hand, squirming into the pressure of those fingers. Feeling the climax build and build and then break. "Jesucristo!" He went limp, breathing hard.

Irv held still for a minute, lightheaded himself because he'd forgotten to breathe. Strongly wishing he'd had a camera ready, because he could get off to that for the rest of his life. He retrieved his hands, so gently it was nearly a caress. All he wanted to do was caress this man. Instead he reached over for a couple of tissues. Leaned down to lick Manny's softening cock, then nuzzle into the trimmed hair alongside it. Heard a soft laugh, felt a hand pulling him down. After a minute he sighed. "Why in the fuck did we not do this a year ago?"

"I don't know. We'll do it again when I come home." That was a little hard to believe, but so was the fact that he was lying here with his head on Manny's shoulder, arm draped across him. Manny's hand was stroking lightly up and down that arm. Irv was strongly tempted to kiss that perfect chest. After another minute he decided he might as well. "Mmm. Irving."

"Sí Manuel."

"Can I sleep here?"

"Yeah. Go to sleep." What an unbelievable night. And he wanted to stay over. Irv was still pondering miracles when he fell asleep.

CHAPTER 8

Irv woke to the scent of coffee, the sound of Latin music, and an epic case of morning wood. "Stop that," he said out loud. "He has to drive to fucking Mexico today." He deeply regretted not putting Manny face-down on the bed. He'd been incapable of taking that much initiative. That was the best blow job of his life, though, after the best kiss of his life, and beggars could not be fucking choosers. He could jerk off later, imagining all the filthy things he wanted to do with Manny. Oh lord, the guy was cooking bacon too. *I think I'm in love*, he thought, then literally smacked himself in the face. That was impossible. It was a figure of speech, that was all. Well, at least the erection was gone. He found a clean shirt and boxers, pulled his jeans on, and went downstairs. Into the bathroom first, then to the kitchen.

Manny was leaning against the counter, half his attention on the bacon and the other half on something on his phone. He looked up and smiled. "Hey Irving." Took a step or two, leaned in for a kiss. "Thanks for last night."

"Uh, you're welcome?" Irv had no idea why that came out sounding like a question. Maybe because if anybody should be saying thank you, it was him. "Smells good in here."

"I figured you wouldn't have bacon if you didn't eat it."

"You figured correctly. Expecting a black man not to eat bacon just because he's Jewish would be ridiculous." He got himself a cup of coffee, noticing the six eggs out on the counter. This should have been so awkward. One or the other of them should have been

152

trying to flee the scene. Instead, apparently, they were going to have breakfast together. "So, what route are you taking?" He didn't ask why Manny was driving instead of flying. The kid gave up his apartment; he'd've had to store his truck somewhere. More trouble than it was worth, probably.

"Taking I-10 over to Indio, then drop down past the Salton Sea to Mexicali."

"How long will that take?"

"I'm not trying to get there today. Not due till late tomorrow." Manny couldn't remember if he'd told Irv that before. They'd talked about the scripts, the cast list he received, the basics about the semi-remote locations between Mexicali and the Gulf of California. He'd done quite a few acting jobs now – legit acting – but they'd all been in or near the city. This was so new, so much, so huge. "I used to go to Mexico to ride."

"Rosarito Ensenada?"

"Mm-hmm. It's fun."

Irv snorted. The idea of a fifty-mile bike ride being fun was alien to him. He only did spinning classes because he hated running even more. Manny turned the bacon, inspected it, and started lifting the strips onto a plate lined with paper towels. He left the fat in the skillet. *If he cooks the eggs in that I'm going to propose, I just know it, oh fuck me there he goes.*

Manny knew he should have asked before he started cooking. But Irv had the stuff, and he was hungry. Plus, it might be a good idea to act like he thought this was normal and natural. Like this was something he wanted to do again. There was something he wanted to ask, but he would wait until after they ate.

Irv got there before him. "What are you planning to do on the holiday break? Going to stay with your folks?"

153

"Oh no. I don't stay at their house anymore."

Irv grunted comprehension. One of those situations. People could try to explain it all they wanted – try to excuse it, more like – but it all boiled down to 'ick.' For parents to feel that way about their own child was a thing he couldn't understand. Of course, he didn't have any kids. Didn't know what it would be like to invest hopes and dreams in some little person, build some kind of reality, and then find out that person had his own hopes and dreams. His own reality. "My parents were almost relieved that I'm gay. Dad was like, finding a girl might have been tricky."

"He did not say that!" Manny was horrified.

It made Irv laugh. He watched Manny scoop the eggs out of all that beautiful bacon fat, piling three on the slice of challah that was on each plate. "Not in so many words. But let's face it. I'm black, Puerto Rican, Jewish, and queer. When the Nazis come for me they're not going to know what the fuck kind of label to put on my sleeve. And on top of that I had to be ginger, short, and tubby."

Manny made a disapproving sound. He carried the plates past Irv and put them down on the room-spanning work surface. It was way too much to be called a desk. "You're not tubby."

Irv followed with their coffee. "I was twenty years ago."

"Whatever. Cómelo."

Irv couldn't remember being so hungry in the morning, especially after a dinner like they'd had. He felt lively. Literally full of life. He shouldn't feel this great when the person who made him feel great was about to take off for five months. Before he could think twice he said, "You could stay here over the break."

154

Manny set down his fork. Swallowed. Gazed at Irv, mouth open, waiting for words. "Really?"

Irv couldn't tell if that was relief, surprise, or horror. "If you want to."

"I wanted to ask. I'd love to."

"You're going to be careful out on location, right?" Another thing he should have thought twice about saying.

They were close enough to touch. Manny reached over and laid his hand on Irv's arm. "I'll be careful."

"It's just that it's out in the middle of nowhere and there's horses and swords and all that bullshit. Scorpions. Rattlesnakes. Whatever."

He cares about me, Manny thought with delight. Didn't call it out. Squeezed Irv's arm, retrieved his hand, and finished his breakfast. "Is it okay if I email you sometime?"

"Yeah, sure." Irv was delighted. If he got an email he'd have an excuse to write. It would be rude not to write. "You could send a picture if you wanted to." *Oh my God*, he thought, mentally rolling his eyes. *I'm a fucking teenage girl all of a sudden.*

Manny planned to do exactly that. A picture of him in costume. A picture with a horse. A picture in his tent, or wherever they put him, naked. He'd caption that one 'thinking of you.' Maybe he'd send a video. "I might."

Irv had no idea how those two words could sound so suggestive. He might send a picture. He might send a naked picture. He might send a picture knowing that Irv would be looking at it before he jerked off, or maybe while he jerked off. He might send a video of *himself* jerking off, not that Irv didn't have a bunch of those already, but those were different. Those weren't

155

for them. *Oh fuck. Are we 'them'? Are we 'us'?* Impossible. No way. Maybe he'd come back at the holiday break, maybe he wouldn't. Maybe he'd send an email or a picture, maybe he wouldn't. This was a case of 'take what you get and be grateful,' not 'imagine all the best-case scenarios that only happen to other people.' He kept right on telling himself that through washing the dishes, waiting for Manny to brush his teeth, and walking him out to the truck.

Then Manny put a hand on his face and leaned in for a kiss. "I'm going to miss you, Irving."

"I'll miss you too, Manuel." He went for a hug. Started it himself this time, knowing he was going to hold on too long. Feeling things he hadn't felt in twenty years, things he'd thought he would never feel again. Faced with the appalling possibility that he might be about to cry, he eased back and said briskly, "Do good work. And drive safe. Now get out of here before they charge you for another day at that shitty motel."

Manny kissed him again. "I'm going. Take care of you."

"Yeah." He watched the kid – his lover? – open the door, climb up, slam it shut. The engine started; the seatbelt went on; the window went down. "Get on the road, you've got a long way to go."

"I know it. Just wanted to do this." Manny held up his phone and took a picture. Irv's outraged squawk made him laugh. He waved and drove away. It wasn't until that night, when he was mentally revisiting the past twenty-four hours, that Irv realized Manny wasn't wearing his ring anymore.

That day and night on the road, Manny felt like he was driving off the edge of planet Earth. Once he left

156

the freeway he saw hardly any cars. Taking his time, exploring some back roads. He stopped for the night at a little motel in the middle of nowhere, the first one he'd seen after finding a barbecue joint at a crossroads. Only a few other units were occupied. The place had satellite, and there was nothing else to do, so he turned on the TV. Sent a text to Irv: *Miss you already*. Got back a reply before he turned off the light: *Miss you too*

In the morning he did his yoga. It was hard to focus because he was excited now. In not too many more hours, he'd be checked in at base camp, reviewing the package the cast liaison said would be waiting, about to start his career as a real actor. He wondered if Marco would be at base camp too. Then he wondered, with another rush of excitement, if Patrice would be there. They hadn't exchanged numbers, and the production had released only the top four cast members' names; he had no idea if she'd been cast as his wife.

Both questions were answered after he parked at the motel in Mexicali and walked into the lobby. A dozen people were milling around talking, mostly sounding as worked up as Manny felt. He was heading for the desk when he heard "Manuel!!" and turned around. Patrice crashed into him, laughing, throwing her arms around his neck. "Ay Dios mío, I'm so glad to see you!"

"Yo también, chica." He hugged her. "So glad it's you. When did you get in?"

"A minute ago. I flew down, there was a bunch of us on the flight. The tall guy drove himself like you. He was like, on that tiny-ass plane? No." She stood away a little, so he could see, and hooked a thumb over her shoulder.

Manny saw Marco over in the corner, talking to somebody. They made eye contact and smiled. Then he

157

turned his attention back to Patrice. "So what kind of prep have you been doing?"

She glanced away for a second. "Actually I had a medical thing I needed to do. So I haven't done a ton. They told me I don't have to ride, they're going to teach me how to do the mule cart thing. Haven't even looked at the packet yet," she said, forestalling his next question. "No clue about the schedule."

"I need to know where my truck goes. And something about food."

"You hungry? Yes Lord. I'm starving. The truck, though, there's a hangar about a block away. They rented this Quonset hut thing for the vehicles. There's signs. But here. Let's get you checked in, settle into our rooms, and then we can solve the food problem when we get back from the hangar."

"Okay," he said, amused. If Patrice wanted to come along he was totally okay with that. Though maybe she was sticking close for more than one reason. Another glance around the room confirmed the first impression: she was the only woman. Surely they would have more women in the cast? That village scene he'd read had women, and children too. Maybe those were all going to be extras or U5s, brought out to whichever location by the day. He turned toward the desk to start taking care of business.

By the time they got back from the hangar, everyone was checked in. All of them were directed to a restaurant not far away, for orientation. Manny half-expected Patrice to want to change clothes. When he left his room, she was waiting, having added only a jacket and some makeup to her traveling jeans and knit top. They walked down the street, hearing music everywhere. One song from somebody's car, another from a storefront, a live band somewhere close. It was all way too modern to start feeling like his character.

The whole restaurant was reserved for the cast and crew meeting. Name badges were issued as they went in. Someone said something about beer. On the way to find it, Manny spotted three other women wearing the yellow 'cast' badges. "You're not the only one after all."

"Thank Jesus." She still sounded nervous, though, and continued to stick close. He would have wondered about it if he weren't so busy meeting and greeting.

For the next four hours it was welcome speeches, jokes, food, beer, a presentation on the schedule, and getting the rundown on the locations. What would be provided, what wouldn't be, safety and hygiene, and the animals. "Oh Lord," Patrice murmured, halfway through that talk. "I know there'll be a chapter in my memoirs about the mule, but I forgot about the cat."

"This is a trip," he murmured back. "I've never even been on a farm." They both snickered. "I'm gonna be texting my man whenever we can get a signal, guess what kind of shit I stepped in today." She stifled a snort, hand over her mouth.

"Tell me about your man," she said later, when they were back at the motel. Both in Manny's room, drinking bottled water, mostly because neither of them had thought of finding a liquor store.

He scooted up the bed, leaning against the headboard. "It's a long story. Maybe I shouldn't even call him my man. I had my eye on him for a long time and we finally connected right before I left town."

"Hmm." She studied him for a moment. "Was it a make the move now and if it doesn't work we'll have some time to get past it thing?"

159

"Mm-hmm. Exactly that. We've been working together."

"What kind of work."

Do I tell her, or do I make some shit up. "Can you keep a secret?"

She huffed out a laugh. "You have no idea." After a second she nodded. "Won't leave this room."

"He's a partner in a porn business. Hired me to do some pictures, some scenes. Crossover solos," he added, because Jonathan knew what that meant so maybe she did too. "Nothing too far out."

Patrice didn't look horrified; she looked interested. "I thought about doing that, so many times. Even talked to some people about it once. They were kind of skeevy though, and their office was kind of gross, and I bailed out."

"He's not skeevy at all. His partners aren't either. It's all real professional. They never tried to get me to do anything I didn't want to do, and I've always felt respected. Safe. Then about six months ago, little more, I was talking to one of the guys on the crew and it was like, huh. I knew I liked this guy, right? But I started thinking of him a different way."

"Oh, I know how that goes. What's he look like? You got a picture?" Manny reached for his phone. Pulled up the picture of Irv and handed it to Patrice. Half-expecting her to laugh. She glanced up at him, half-smiling. "He wasn't posing for this picture, was he."

"God no."

"Pretty eyes. Older than you."

"About ten years older. I knew he was never gonna make a move. He doesn't think he looks good. Thinks

160

he's too old for me." She handed the phone back. Manny looked at Irv again, thought *he does have pretty eyes*, then set the phone aside. "I've waited a long time."

"Looking for the real thing?"

He half-shrugged. "Not so much looking. I had the real thing a long time ago. That guy." He pointed across the room to the picture of Lobo. "My first. He was killed in the military."

"Oh, honey. Shit."

"Mmm. Anyway I told Irv, having that changes your outlook. But I feel like I could have something with him. Something real."

"More power to you, baby. Well." She reached over and patted his leg. "I'd better get my beauty sleep. Enjoy having a bed while I can." He huffed out a laugh. "See you in the morning."

"In the morning," he echoed. It was a minute after the door closed before he got up to flip the locks. Everything started in the morning.

The experience on location was not difficult, exactly, but it was different. They were very isolated out there, with not a lot of services, and had to be self-sufficient. The catering truck, the shower trailer, the honeywagon, the medic's van. That one looked almost like a TV station's truck, with a satellite dish on the top. It was reassuring to see that. Most of them couldn't get a cell signal worth a damn, so knowing there was a way to call for help in an emergency made everyone feel more secure. All of the cast and crew were housed in tent cabins except Tiburon and the actress playing his wife; they had trailers. The only place the rest of them had real beds and indoor plumbing was at base camp.

Every one of them was glad to have the option of going back there when they had a day or two off the schedule.

Manny was never a camping kind of guy. His family did day trips into the local mountains like everybody, but never an overnight trip. Never anything where they'd have to buy special gear. This was 'close to nature' in a way he'd never been, and the fact that other people were right there every night didn't make the coyote song any less startling. They weren't exactly roughing it, though. The cabins were sturdy, the food was good, and people were always around to make sure the cast and crew had what they needed.

The first week was all costume fittings and rehearsal. There was a ton of physical training to do. How to move in the costumes, how to handle their weapons. Fights of various kinds, and religious behavior. There was technical stuff, including how to deal with the sound engineers; they were all going to be wired with mics. They worked on diction, pitch, and phrasing, learning how to pace dialogue and how to make sure everyone's speech had the same slightly-foreign, slightly-antique style to it. It might have been back to basics for a lot of the cast, but for Manny it was Acting 101. Plus there was all the business with the horses. Not every cast member was riding, but all of them had to be okay with the animals. It wasn't only the mounts, either. There were three dogs, a half-dozen chickens, a flock of trained pigeons, a couple of goats, and the cat.

The cat belonged to Patrice's character. Its handler would be bringing it out to the set only on the days it was needed. Patrice had to learn the cues for whatever cat action was required; most of the time the handler could give the cue, but sometimes a shot had to be framed wide. She got used to handling the mule pretty fast, took a picture for Manny when he was up on Saluki, and said, "Thank fuck I don't have to ride. You look really high off the ground."

Saluki wasn't super tall, but it did feel like a long way down. Manny was coached to ride differently, sitting up on the horse's withers with his knees bent like a racing jockey. After a day of that he had to spend an extra hour stretching. He wondered how Marco and Tiburon were doing; they were going to be on horseback for hours every day for the first few weeks.

Meanwhile, he and Patrice were going to have a lot of scenes together on the set that served as all the villages, occasionally with a woman who played a weaver, a guy who played a scribe, or a guy who played a barber. The barber guy was the real thing, too; getting shaved on-camera with a period-appropriate open blade was a new experience for almost everybody, and they all did it. In costume, in character, because this was a clean and well-groomed culture.

It turned out that Manny's prep for his character was spot on. He was the guy who went from village to village, finding out what people needed, working out a way to get it, and making deals for exchange. He was a schemer, a fixer, a man of his word but a man with changeable loyalties. Manny loved having the chance to create such a well-defined personality. A lot of it was on the page for him; the rest came from his interactions with the other actors, in character or out.

The scripts in general leaned toward intrigue, with dramatic and action sequences arising from political and cultural conflicts. The whole cast was getting an education. None of them had even heard of '13th-century Moorish Spain' until their agents sent the script. Some of their characters were Spanish, others were North African. The framing story for the series

163

was the fall of the Caliphate to the Kingdom of Castile. The writers had given it a twist toward fantasy, with clairvoyants, astrologers, and sorcerers to make the whole thing more exciting for a TV audience.

Religion was part of every character's daily life, whether Muslim, Jewish, or Catholic. That was new to most of the cast members, too. All of them would have identified with one or another modern religion, but none of them practiced daily observance except the three actual Muslims. When he mentioned that to Irv, he got back a text saying *I haven't been inside a synagogue since my bar mitzvah*. Manny hadn't taken church seriously since his confirmation. He couldn't relate to hearing a service every day, much less praying five times a day.

Once they started filming, things got complicated. This group of people went to this location, a different group to a second, while Tiburon and Marco were out on their horses with a mounted camera crew that included a guy flying a drone camera. The episodes weren't being shot in order, so the producers scheduled scenes based on efficiency.

Manny was constantly amazed by the complexity of it, and the intricacy of the details. The dialogue was filmed in English, but background chatter often happened in Spanish or Arabic or both. There were books everywhere. Beautiful manuscripts, bound or in scrolls, from tiny pocket books in linen or fine leather wrappers to giants that were stored in boxes with tilt-up tops. All the main characters had some kind of personal book as well as a personal weapon. Both were part of their costume, like the linen undergarments, the handmade shoes, and the richly-colored robes. Manny's robe was dyed with indigo that tinted the skin of his shoulders. He screen-capped Irv's comment on

164

the selfie he sent after a long hot day and saved it. If the series didn't get picked up for a second season, he thought he might ask about buying the costume. He had a feeling Irv could do something pretty sexy with it. Wondered if Irv would want to take any pictures over the break.

The cast got close fast. They might have bonded on any shoot, but this one was forcing people to bond. One of the guys said it was like a combination of boot camp and summer camp. The nights they spent out on location meant long evenings with nothing much to do but sit by a fire. Talking, playing cards, playing guitar; Manny wasn't the only one who'd brought an instrument. Marco mentioned he used to have one.

"What happened to it?"

"Girl I was kind of dating set my apartment on fire."

"Dude, *what?!*"

Marco laughed and told the story of the play he was in four years ago, and the cast-mate with bad ideas. "I was sure I was never going to get hired again, but the director on that project took me under her wing. Gave me some good advice."

"What did that boil down to." Manny was half-smiling.

"Manage your money, take all the classes you can afford, and try out for every fucking thing." Everyone around the fire laughed. Marco shrugged. "She was right, too. Anyway, I guess I need to get back in practice." He flicked a fingernail against Manny's guitar.

"You can borrow this one. I'll leave it for you when I get to go to base camp and you're still stuck out here." He shot a sideways glance at Marco, saw an eye-roll and a smile.

Patrice snorted. "Ooh child."

"Hey, he's second-billed, he can take it," somebody else said. "Okay, so Marco, what's your favorite thing about this so far."

"Being second-billed."

Everybody cracked up. Then Patrice said, "My favorite thing is working with Manny. No offense to the rest of y'all. And honey, you don't have to say your favorite thing is working with me." She patted his knee.

"I couldn't pick a favorite," he said. "I'm loving all of it. This is the job I've been wishing I had for the last ten years. If my man was waiting for me at base camp, it would be perfect." He got a little bit of bullshit about that, but he wasn't the only gay man in the production. It was the same kind of bullshit everybody got when they said something about missing somebody. "What about you," he said to Patrice later, when they were both in his tent with a battery-powered LED lamp, waiting till it was late enough to call it a night.

"What about me?"

"Is there someone you're missing?"

She stared at him across the tent as if she wasn't sure about his motivation. "No," she said after a long silence. "It's been a while. I've kind of been going through some shit."

"I'm sorry. It's just, you're so pretty. Hard to imagine you being single." He could have sworn she blushed, but the light wasn't good enough to be sure.

"Ten years ago I would do anything not to be single. But I'm over that now. I'm almost forty."

"No!"

She grinned at that. "Sí querido. I'm taking care of myself. Someday maybe I'll look around and say, you know what, it's time to get someone in my life. Right now having friends is enough."

"I'd like to be your friend," he said softly.

"Oh baby, you are. I'm so blessed." She reached across to pat his knee again. "But now I guess I'd better go chase the scorpions out my tent. Lord have mercy, people back in the city won't *believe* what we're putting up with." They said goodnight, and he watched her go. They both knew there wouldn't be any scorpions. It seemed there was a lot she wasn't saying, but she didn't owe him anything. He hoped one day she'd trust him more.

He did not expect to get the answer to almost every question all at once, by accident. They wrapped their part of a scene and were given the nod to go back to camp. After the shuttle dropped them off Patrice said, "I'm getting in the shower before everybody else in the world rolls in."

"All right. I'm gonna take a run, listen to some music." It was more of a jog than a run, what with the uneven terrain and the chance of rattlesnakes, but once in a while Manny liked the illusion of solitude that came with putting in earbuds. He was still listening when he walked up to the shower trailer and opened the door. Then he said, "Shit," and almost dropped his clean clothes.

"Fuck!" Patrice grabbed for a towel, covering herself. They stared at each other for a few seconds.

Manny blinked, realized she was looking at him like she expected him to hit her, and shook his head. Took the earbuds out. "Lo siento, I didn't realize you were still in here. Had my music on. You need a minute?"

She swallowed. Cleared her throat. "You've seen it now."

"Nobody else is back yet, I can step out." He started to do that.

"No, it's okay." She took a visibly deep breath. "You should know. I've been trying to think how to tell you."

"Patrice, it's none of my damn business."

"But we have to do that scene where we kiss."

He set his clothes on the nearest bench, wrapped the earbud cord around his phone and set that down too, sat beside the little pile and started taking off his shoes. Made eye contact. She was standing there waiting, clutching the towel so it covered her whole front. Before the silence could get too long he said, "Look. I'm a gay man playing straight. Haven't kissed a woman since I was sixteen. Never kissed anyone on camera. Gonna be awkward as fuck about it anyhow."

"Oh, right." It sounded a bit shaky. "No difference now that you know I have a dick."

"You've always been a woman in my mind, and that," he gestured toward the towel, "doesn't change anything." She started to cry. "Patrice, cariña, no llores." He wanted to go to her, wanted to hug her. But hugging in public with their clothes on was one thing, and this was something else. He didn't want to step over any lines. "So okay, you're transitioning. I'm glad to know. Now if there's anything you need from me, if I should be some different kind of way with you, you have to tell me."

"No," she said, sniffling. "You keep being your way. I have to get my clothes on." She turned away, dropped the towel, reached for her clothes. Manny stayed where he was until she was fully dressed and on her way out.

Then he reached out, not grabbing, only making the overture. "Hey." She half-turned, touched his hand in the way they were used to, her fingertips curling into his. He was reassured. "Meet at the food truck in fifteen?"

"Okay." Her smile was uncertain, but it was a smile.

The kiss scene wasn't on the schedule till the following week. Manny hadn't brought it up because he wasn't lying about feeling awkward. Now that he had this new information, he thought they needed to work something out. But what, and how, were beyond him. He would have asked Irv, or Lauro, if he could have gotten hold of either of them.

Fortunately, one of the producers opened the subject the next day. Manny and Patrice were done for the week and had three whole nights up at base camp ahead of them. They had their gear packed and were hanging around the catering truck, waiting for the shuttle bus, when the producer walked up and said, "Speak to you privately for a minute? Both of you." They looked at each other; Manny was pretty sure his face said 'oh shit.' Didn't speak, only nodded and followed the producer to his car.

That was how private conversations usually happened out here: somebody got in somebody's car. They closed the doors. Patrice said, "What's up?"

"You two have a scene next week involving physical contact and I wanted to check in. Make sure you're both comfortable with the scene as written."

169

Manny and Patrice exchanged another glance. Her face said 'I don't know, are we?' He said, "I was going to suggest we rehearse while we're at base camp. Work on some back story, stuff like that."

"He knows, Rodrigo," Patrice said. "He says he's fine with it."

"I am fine with it." Manny put a little emphasis on 'am.'

"Well, good." Rodrigo was twisted around in the driver's seat, looking from one of them to the other. "We cast it this way because two reasons. We liked you both in the parts separately, and we liked your chemistry in the audition. But we needed to get clear on the boundaries because, eh." He stalled.

Manny almost laughed. What was the guy going to say? We cast a trans woman to play your wife, her transition's not complete, but we were hoping you'd be cool with it because you're gay anyway? No way could he say that. He wasn't even supposed to acknowledge that Manny was gay. Gender was supposed to be a non-issue. Everybody knew it wasn't. "I am seriously fine with it," he said. "Patrice is who she is. I like her, I respect her, and if I screw up this scene it's not because of her. I'm gonna do my best for you." After a second when the others didn't say anything, he added, "But I do have a question."

Rodrigo looked cautious. "What's that?"

"When it comes to back story. As long as what we come up with doesn't affect the storyline that's on the page, can we kind of run with it? Or is there something we should know about where the characters are going?"

"All we got is what you know. Marco's going to ask you to move some information, and you're going to ask him for something in return. We're not looking to place your character on the political or military side of things."

"So I might ask him for something personal. Okay, good. You got anything, Patrice?"

"I, um." She paused with a strange look on her face, as if this was kind of cool but very unexpected. "Last time I was online I was reading up on women in this time period and I thought, why don't they have any kids. So I was thinking maybe the back story has to do with that."

"That's good." Rodrigo sounded surprised. "That's great. Work with that." Something caught his attention. "The bus is rolling in. Go on, get back to town."

"Thanks, Rodrigo." Manny reached between the seats to shake the guy's hand, then got out of the SUV. He waited for Patrice. Half an hour later, they were on the road to Mexicali with a busload of others who didn't have to be on location for the next two or three days.

They ended up taking the night completely off. Manny got on the phone with Lauro, and then with Irv. "Got called into a meeting today," he said, knowing Irv would blow a gasket. Half laughing when the questions started. "No, it was a good thing actually. Me and Patrice have a scene next week, it's our kissing scene. Yeah, only one. Marco's got a different woman in every village. Oh no, for real. He's like this combination lieutenant and consigliere and ambassador, and he's just fucking his way through Spain." Pause for laugh. "Tiburon, his character is married, they've got this whole political arranged marriage thing going but really hot with it. I mean, based on the script. We've seen some footage for

171

continuity, and a little from our own rehearsals. Like, see what you did here, don't do that." He waited, smiling, for Irv's laugh to wind down. "Anyway we've got a couple days off so we're going to work on back story for our characters. Patrice had this really good point, why don't we have any kids. We're traveling around, maybe there's a home base somewhere, but it seems like there would be kids. So I'm thinking maybe we're trying, or maybe we lost one. Make the scene about that instead of going for heat. They've got enough of that. Well, if we only have the one intimate scene, it's kind of, what's the word. Yeah, gratuitous. So what have you been up to?" He listened for a while, asked a few questions, trying to keep Irv on the phone longer. "It's good talking to you. I miss you. Yeah, two weeks to go. It's still okay if I – okay. No, I can't wait to see you. Did you get those pictures? The new ones?" A stifled laugh, and his voice a bit softer when he said the next thing. "Yeah, I was thinking about you. I'm gonna be thinking about you in a few minutes, here all alone in my room. See you soon, Irving. Bye." He disconnected with a sigh.

Back in Los Angeles, Irv looked at the latest pictures again, then put his phone down and spent some quality time with his hand.

CHAPTER 9

December 2016

Irv was incapable of settling down to anything useful. The text from Manny saying 'I'm on my way' came at noon on December first. Irv knew he couldn't expect to see the guy before the third. Told himself to be productive. The problem was, he couldn't concentrate. What with cramming in all possible filming so they could spruce up the house, he'd worked his ass off for weeks after Manny left. The minor renovations at the porn house were finished right before Thanksgiving. Nothing of his was scheduled to shoot till after Christmas, so he flew back to New York to see his folks for a couple of days. He didn't have anything to do. The only reason he even came home on the thirtieth was he knew when the 'Alhambra' shoot shut down.

He didn't know when Manny had to report back. It wouldn't be sooner than the fifteenth. The idea of spending two weeks together produced feelings he couldn't diagnose. On the one hand, it was great to imagine going to bed with Manny again, possibly more than once, potentially a lot more than once. He was fairly sure that was going to happen; the texts and emails that rolled in every time the guy landed at base camp were not of the 'make you guess' variety. On the other hand, what in hell would they talk about, or what would they do, when they weren't in bed? Because you couldn't stay in bed all the time.

Irv hadn't lived with someone since right after he came to Los Angeles. He couldn't remember how it was when he and that guy were new. Their beginning was overwritten by their last few months, when all they did (when they weren't in bed) was fight.

With all that running through his head, it was not too surprising that by the morning of the third, when the text came with Manny's ETA, the loft was cleaner than it had been since before Irv moved in. He had enough groceries to see them into 2017, he was better-groomed than he'd been in years, and he was so keyed up that another cup of coffee seemed like a really bad idea. As the time approached, he was so nervous that after brushing his teeth he opened the entry door and left it that way. It was better than the non-zero chance of smacking himself in the face with it when Manny got there. Then he sat on the stairs to the sleeping loft and tried counting backward from a hundred. It was better than pacing.

He was on his third hundred when Manny came to the door. Stepping through it with a smile, gaze going to Irv on the stairs. "Irving," he said. He dropped his duffle bag, closed and locked the door. "I'm going to the bathroom, and then I want you to kiss me."

Irv nodded, speechless. He watched Manny pass, thought *you move differently* with a sort of abstract interest, and hauled himself to his feet using the railing. Reminded himself to breathe. Wondered why in hell he was such a mess. Hoped it didn't show. He went to the kitchen, hoping his idea of a 'welcome home' wasn't the worst idea in the world. This wasn't Manny's home, they weren't living together, it was definitely the worst idea. He did it anyway.

Manny came out of the bathroom halfway expecting Irv to still be sitting on the stairs, looking as though he wasn't sure about this. Instead he was standing over by the couch, which was new. Big-ass couch, big enough for two men to lie down on, placed with one end close to the work surface. On that surface was a bottle of champagne, with a couple of stemmed glasses. *He wants to celebrate.* But his expression – something like cautious cynicism – didn't go with the bottle. It had to mean Irv was feeling insecure. If Manny didn't do something fast, if he didn't do the right thing, this could go sideways. He walked straight over to Irv, put his hands on the man's face, and kissed him. "Mmm." Just the way he remembered. "God I've missed you," he said against Irv's mouth. "It's so good to see you," against his neck. Hands on his body, had he lost weight? Undoing buttons, because Irv's mouth was on his throat now and Irv's hands were on his back. "Jesus you feel good." Thoroughly turned on, and Irv was too. Pushing the shirt off his shoulders. "Oh, papi, look at you." Did he look this good before? He must have. They were getting in each other's way now, each of them trying to get into the other's pants. Half-laughing, making frustrated noises. In a disorganized scuffle Manny got his shirt off, Irv got his pants off, and then he had Manny on the couch, pulling his jeans down, then his briefs.

"You shouldn't have sent me all those pictures," Irv said, from the inside of Manny's knee. "All I've been doing since we shut down the house is staring at those thinking about all the terrible things I want to do to you."

Manny wasn't thinking too clearly, but he managed, "Shut down the house?"

"Repainting, shit like that." From the smooth skin below Manny's hipbone. "I didn't get my mouth on you before. I've been regretting that."

"Me too. Irving."

"Manuel." They hadn't even properly kissed, not the way he wanted to kiss this man, but he was not

175

getting past this. He closed his mouth over Manny's cock with a ravenous sound.

"Oh *Jesus*. Irving. Yes, God, santa sangre tu boca, vas a matarme, fucking hell papi, yes, fuck, ahora." Manny ran out of words in either language. He kept making sounds, because Irv's mouth on him was heaven.

Irv was making sounds too, because Manny in his mouth was heaven. This beautiful perfect cock, the taste of imminent climax, Manny's foot on the back of the couch and his head flung back as he cried out. Irv took him all the way, feeling the pulse in his mouth and the gush in his throat. He breathed in roughly through his nose, held it for a few seconds. Then he swallowed. Manny's body jerked again, with another helpless sound. *I did that*, Irv thought hazily. This beautiful man could have come home to anyone, but he came home to Irv and was sprawled out naked underneath him. It was unbelievable.

He let go and crawled the rest of the way up. Manny's arms closed over his back, pulling him in tight. Irv kissed him. They each made a sound somewhere between a sigh and a moan. Irv was so hard it hurt, but he didn't want to stop kissing. *Did I ever want to kiss someone this much?* Another thought he shouldn't be having. Manny's leg was locked over his, they were both moving, the friction starting to tip over into too much. "Mmm."

Manny loosened his grip, stroked his hands down Irv's sides. Broke the kiss enough to say, "You need lube."

"You want me to come on you?" He could definitely do that. In about a minute.

"Do what you want. Come on me. Fuck my mouth. Get in me. I washed this morning." Washed inside, so he'd be clean, ready for anything.

"Were you thinking about that?" Irv couldn't help smiling. "Where were you?"

"Some motel. There was a drugstore." He didn't even know if Irv liked that. It's not as though they discussed it. But then, Irv probably didn't believe Manny was coming back until he actually walked through the door.

"What do *you* want."

"Everything." *Keep holding me, kiss me forever, love me.* He blinked. Those were not thoughts he'd had before, not consciously at least. Irv didn't notice; he was reaching over Manny for something on the work surface. To get there he had to push up a little, stretch a little. Manny got his hand around Irv's hot erection. "I want this in me."

"Jesus. Okay. I mean sure, if that's what you want." He felt Manny laughing. He was grinning too when he leaned down for another kiss, then sat back on his heels. "You look in-fucking-credible." Getting some lube on his fingers, expression intent.

"You too." Manny put his foot up on the back of the couch again. His other knee was bent, leg open, giving Irv access. A caress, the way he did before. Manny was already relaxed from that orgasm. It didn't take long to get him open. He was watching the whole process, watching Irv's face and the way he had to grip himself a couple of times. "Así papi. Ahora." Watching as Irv engaged. "Oh fucking Jesus."

"Mmm." If Irv opened his mouth to try to make a word something really godawful was going to come out. He wanted to close his eyes so he could fully

177

experience this sensation. He wanted to watch Manny's face so he could be sure the man was enjoying this. He wanted to take his time and make the most of it. He wanted to go wild and lose his mind, get to his climax as fast as possible so they could rest up and do it all over again as soon as possible. Manny had one foot on Irv's back, he was gripping Irv's arm, eyes closed, lips parted. Irv changed direction. Slowly, adding a little lube as he pulled partway out, then sinking further in. Manny's ripple of reaction, his breathless moan, told Irv he'd hit the spot. He put his other hand down. Short strokes, concentrating, it had to be too soon for the kid to come again but by God Irv was going to do his best. He pressed all the way in, got his mouth on Manny's. Rocking his hips. It was almost too much, but he could feel Manny's cock, hard against his own belly. His breath, getting short. *You did miss me. You did save it for me. You do want me.* They weren't really kissing. Mouth to mouth, vocalizing, gasping. Irv wasn't in full control now. He was on one elbow, Manny's feet locked over his back as he ground in. "Okay," he managed. It was a question.

"Don't stop." Manny wanted to come again, but he didn't need to. He needed to feel Irv, feel him everywhere. "Come for me, papi."

"I want you." Incomplete sentence. All he could produce. Couldn't find the rest of it, 'to come for me again.' He couldn't believe he'd held it this long. He pushed up, locking one arm so he could get the other hand on Manny's cock. Christ, yes, a little wetness on the head. He spread it with his thumb, felt those hips jerk under him. He didn't stroke, only held that cock and said, "You move." And Manny did, pressing and squirming the way he did when it was Irv's fingers inside him. Using Irv, who didn't have to move at all

178

from here on out because the sight of that, and the feel of it, was enough to make him stop breathing altogether. He saw Manny's balls draw up, felt his cock swell, heard something like a sob. Then it happened, Manny convulsed around Irv, and with one great heave he was coming. He shouted something. Manny made another wordless sound. Irv nearly collapsed. He caught himself on his hands. Waited a few seconds, head hanging, while his heart rate settled down a bit. Slowly pushed off, disengaging, sitting back in a floppy, trembling heap. "Jesus. All right?"

"Mmm."

That wasn't enough of an answer. "Manuel. Seriously. That went hard. Are you all right."

Manny slowly straightened his legs, wriggled his back, propped himself up on his elbows so he could see Irv more comfortably. "I'm going to still be feeling it tomorrow, but I'm fine. That was some *fucking*, pendejo." Irv huffed out a laugh. "Besame, Irving."

"For a minute. Then I need a drink."

"God, me too." It was quite a few minutes of mostly holding each other, with some kisses of the soft, glad-to-see-you variety. The kind Manny imagined about a million times while he was in Mexico. He thought Irv must like this kind of kissing too, or he wouldn't be doing it. Irv didn't seem like a guy who did favors when it came to sex stuff. Manny felt his thoughts veering off – maybe this wasn't entirely, or only, sex stuff? – but he dragged them back on track when Irv got off him. Patted his chest and headed for the bathroom to tidy up. Manny took his turn a few minutes later. When he finished Irv was dressed again. He had the champagne open and the glasses full. Handed one to Manny. They tipped the rims together,

179

sipped, eyes on each other. "Mmm, that's good." Manny set the glass down and got dressed. They sat close together on the couch, not talking.

Or not right away. About halfway down the glass Irv sighed and said, "Was that reckless? What we did just now?"

It was hard not to flinch at the implied question, even though Irv's tone was neutral. Not an implied accusation. Manny said, equally neutral, "No one else has touched me." This was clearly not the time to say 'I don't want anyone else to touch me.'

"Good. That's good. Look, I'm sorry, but you know I'm not exactly a party animal and you were down there all that time, you've been alone a long time, you're young –"

"Irv, for God's sake. You act like you're a million years old sometimes."

"Well, that's how it feels sometimes." He didn't mean to say that. "Cards on the table. Condoms outside this room." He didn't want to say that. He wanted to say 'don't let anyone else touch you.' It was clearly not the time to say anything like that. He didn't even know he wanted to say it, until that moment.

Manny kept his expression neutral, wondering if this was 'I won't be jealous if you fuck other people,' or if it was 'I don't care if you fuck other people.' Because he could have sworn those were two different things, but this was not like any other situation he'd been in. He couldn't remember if he'd always been so off-balance when it came to figuring this shit out. Then he realized he hadn't tried before. He and Lobo figured everything out together, and nothing since then had been a relationship. And he wasn't sure what kind of relationship this was, but it was some kind. Best to take it one question at a time. "Sí, claro."

"So tell me about this Patrice character." There were more pictures of Manny with that person than with anyone else. Irv hadn't let it get to him too much, even though Patrice was really good-looking, because the body language said 'friends,' not 'lovers.' Also he was pretty sure she was a girl. "She's a girl, right?"

Manny smiled. He settled back, relaxing. "Patrice is a girl. She plays my wife on the show. She's transitioning. I saw her one time at the shower trailer and I could tell she expected me to say something mean. I never knew anyone transitioning before." They talked about that to the end of the first glass of champagne. Talked about other people on the shoot to the end of lunch, and the end of the bottle. Then Irv made some coffee, and they talked about the work the partners did on the filming house. He showed Manny bits and pieces of the things he'd filmed or photographed during the fall, talked about what was in the queue for January, asked a couple of random questions that led to deciding on a movie to watch after dinner.

That turn to the conversation was entirely reassuring. Irv didn't have to worry about finding something to talk about if they had movies to watch. And boy, did they ever. The first one – at Manny's request – was 'Come Again,' the Rick/Zane nostalgia feature that was such a big hit for Stroked last year.

"Haven't seen this since right after the awards," Irv said before he started the DVD.

"You're always busy. I was too, that was right when things were starting to happen." Manny shifted over so his body was up against Irv's. As soon as Irv

181

started the disc, he put his arm around Manny's shoulders. *That's what I wanted*, he thought, smiling to himself. All those weeks in the desert with nothing to do after his scenes wrapped, he'd had plenty of time to think about what he wanted.

Irv tried to be objective, but he was too happy with the film. His idea, Monica's suggestion about the backstory, Lauro's script, committed performances from Rick and Zane: it all added up to one of the best things they'd ever released. Fifteen months after launch, it was still selling.

He was also happy about the immediate situation. First that Manny showed up, second that the guy was all over Irv, third that they had weeks to relax into this. One great night (and their first night was really great) had set the bar awfully high. A disappointing follow-up was so likely that Irv tried not to expect anything else. *Not disappointed*, he thought, glancing sideways at Manny's face. Once the disc ended, he'd start a conversation about why he thought the movie was good. See what Manny thought about it. See if there was any residual interest in making more scenes for Stroked.

They didn't get around to that conversation right away, because after the movie there was some mild but satisfying fooling around. Then, after breakfast the next day, Manny started the conversation. "So I was thinking about what might be next. I mean, if you still wanted to do any scenes with me."

After an astonished second, Irv said, "If I *want* to?" Manny laughed. Irv shook his head, making a 'can you believe this guy' face. "Of course I want to. Where you want to take it? Still with the El Vaquero thing?"

"People liked those," Manny said. "The country, the horses, there's not a lot of that in your catalog."

"It's not that easy to get secure outdoor film sites that don't cost a truckload of money. If Red was charging us to use the stable we wouldn't be going out there. So, what else do you think you might want to do? What would be different?" They brainstormed about it for nearly an hour, Irv taking notes along the way because they went on some interesting tangents, before he set that aside and suggested watching a classic Western.

There were so many great films Manny had never seen. The whole three-week break became a film festival, punctuated with food (including dinners out several times a week) and lovemaking (almost every day, in a variety of ways). Once Manny suggested Irv tape them. Another time it was Irv's suggestion. He'd never done that before, because he thought he was the opposite of photogenic, but after seeing the first one he got over it. Saying so made Manny laugh for so long Irv finally had to kiss him again to make him stop.

They broke it up with a day out in the Valley. Manny went out on a trail ride with Red and his wife Mary. Irv stayed behind at the stable, lying in the hammock, napping off and on. It was a much-needed few hours of solitude and silence. He'd been living alone for a long time, and even though it was great having Manny at the loft, he'd missed having time to be the grouchy old troll he'd gotten used to being. That thought was clear in his mind when he woke up from one of those mini-naps. Since he didn't have anything else to do, he went to take a leak, refilled his water bottle, and returned to the hammock to think about things.

He had not set out to be a grouchy old troll. He wasn't even forty. Had he somehow settled into a persona, a role he thought made sense for a pornographer who was (unlike Monica and Payton) never going to be mistaken for one of his models? It fit, for the guy who never made a pass at a model. The guy who never had a boyfriend. The guy with film-school cred and a body of legit work that nobody cared about because it didn't make money. That guy was *supposed* to be a cynic, wasn't he? Disillusioned, mercenary, unsentimental?

The trouble was, he didn't actually feel like that anymore, if he ever did. He still had ideas about work that might be considered art. Still had dreams. Or maybe it was more accurate to say he had dreams again. It was a scary place to be, because he couldn't lie to himself. He had dreams because of Manny, and dreams that depended on another human being were the most dangerous kind of all.

At the end of this break, Manny would go back to Mexico. At the end of the shoot, he'd return to L.A., and they'd have to see if this was truly a relationship or if it was convenience, mixed with loneliness, mixed with lust. The fact was, Irv would take option 2. He could tolerate being someone's convenience. It was better than being alone, at least when the someone in question behaved as though he genuinely liked Irv.

That was sure how it looked when they rode in again. Manny smiled the second he saw Irv, calling out, "Papi, you got to go easy on my ass tonight, Freyja wore me out." Mary and Red were cracking up. Once the horses were squared away they all went down into Van Nuys for dinner at the Warners' house. Manny had been there before, for this or that session of weapons training. This time he got the welcome-friend tour, with the history of how Red came to live there. He was trying to buy the place now, and there was a whole story about that too. Then Red and Mary asked him a ton of questions about the 'Alhambra' shoot, because co-star Marco Hidalgo was a friend of theirs, and there were more stories.

It was very late when he and Irv finally got home to the Brewery. They were both quiet on the way, while they were washing up, and as they got into bed. "You look tired," Irv said.

"Mm-hmm." Manny was half-asleep already. "You want something?"

Irv thought *do you think you need to pay for this with sex?* He kept his tone level, put a little smile into it. "Go to sleep." It was one of those moments that could have gone either way. Turning aside from each other, and waking up knowing this wasn't really much of anything; or turning into each other's arms and waking up knowing it might be everything.

Manny rolled onto his side, slung an arm across Irv, kissed him briefly but warmly, then laid his head on Irv's shoulder. "Had a great time with you tonight," he said drowsily. "Buena noche cariño."

Irv blinked. *Did he just call me sweetheart?* "You too," he said very softly. He wasn't at all sure that Manny was still awake enough to hear it. Wasn't even sure which part he was echoing. *Oh bullshit of course you are.*

The next day was typical, if anything about this situation could be called 'typical.' Coffee, some fooling around, breakfast. A trip to the gym, where Irv got on a bike, Manny ran on a treadmill, and they both spent some time in the weight room. Then a shower, back home, and a movie. Manny fell asleep halfway through. Irv turned down the volume, watched to the end because he was incapable of not doing that, and considered calling his parents.

185

Instead he went over to the desk and pulled up the script Lauro had been working on for months. The one that ran with the yellow-ribbon scenario. They'd been talking about it here and there; Irv was doing his best not to push it too far in one direction or another. Plus they both felt it was, in a way, Manny's project, and he might have ideas about where to go with it. That conversation hadn't happened because Lauro was taking a cross-country road trip. It was his first-ever vacation since he signed on with Stroked. Irv knew there had been some texts going back and forth, but Manny wasn't acting like this was top of mind right now.

Irv was glaring at the empty brackets where a heart-rending reunion scene should be when his phone buzzed; it was his mother. Irv glanced over at Manny, confirmed he was still asleep, and picked up. "Hey Ma. I was thinking of calling you. Wanted to say Merry Christmas before you and Pop head down to the islands. How's the weather." He listened for a minute, enjoying the rant about New York in December. "Yeah, I won't tell you what it's like here. No, I'm fine. Keeping my voice down because I have company and he's asleep." He knew what was going to happen next. His mother always got excited when Irv had company.

Manny was less than half awake. He heard Irv's voice, softer than usual. Lay there with his eyes closed, feeling more relaxed than he had basically ever in his life, hearing rather than listening.

"Yeah, he's a friend." Irv waited for the barrage of questions to end. "Yes, that kind of friend. You remember that model from the clip? The soldier thing, yeah. Mm-hmm. It's never a good idea to get involved with a model but he started it and I, well. Because me and relationships is historically a shitshow, you know

186

that, Ma. I'm hoping we'll stay friends. I don't know. He's got a pretty major job right now. Shoots down in Mexico. The star is a big name down there. Co-star got an Emmy nomination last year. Manny's learning a lot. Mmm. He's a good physical actor. Still figuring out how to use his voice."

How to use my voice, Manny thought, more fully awake. He didn't have big speeches in 'Alhambra.' Hadn't been given a lot of direction as to line delivery. Now he thought he should have been paying more attention to the others. He could work on that in the back half. And then there was that comment about relationships. Irv wasn't saying he didn't want one.

Irv was still talking. "I invited him to stay here during the break. His family lives out in the Valley, but," a shrug in the voice. "I don't know if they actually threw him out of the house when he came out, but it doesn't seem like he goes through the door now. No, he wasn't lucky like me." A soft huff of a laugh. "Oh, you'd love him. He's a sweetheart."

I'm a sweetheart? Manny almost opened his eyes then, almost made it clear he was awake. But Irv thought he was crap at relationships, and Manny wasn't sure where they could go with this, and he was positive Irv wouldn't have said some of those things if he knew Manny was listening, so he stayed quiet.

"If he asks, yeah. I'm not going to ask. No. I'm not making suggestions, really. There's a power thing. Well, no, I'm not his boss. Oh yeah, the stuff with the horses is legit. We were just out there yesterday. Uh-huh, Red Warner. He's still a monster. He's making the big bucks now."

Manny thought this was a good place to act like he was waking up. He rolled over, stretched, made a soft

187

sound. Moved his head to make eye contact, smiling a little.

Irv noticed. He let his volume come up a little. "Yeah, good to talk to you too, Ma. Give my best to Pop. Have fun in Puerto Rico. I thought I'd go up to San Francisco for a few days after my friend goes back to work. Yeah, get some stock footage, see some friends. Then it's back to smog and porn." He laughed out loud. "It's a living, Ma. Love you too. Bye now." He disconnected, turned his head, made eye contact with Manny. *Would you come back.*

Manny couldn't decipher Irv's expression at the moment, so he said, "I missed the end of the movie. Was it good?"

Irv raised his eyebrows and said, "Have I played you anything that sucked?"

"No." Manny was smiling. "You watched it to the end, didn't you. I can catch it some other time."

"I'll start it over. You can fast-forward to where you crashed. I've got some shit to do for the site anyway." He re-started the movie on the second monitor, tossed the remote to Manny, and turned to business.

A couple days after that, Irv was watching the end of his time with Manny approach and trying to distract himself. They were sitting on the couch with a sports movie on – one of Irv's favorites of the genre, 'Love and Basketball' – and he started a conversation about fitness for some reason. Manny said something about how good Irv looked. He waved it off, of course, which got a rude word in Spanish and an eyeroll. Then he remembered that impression he'd had when Manny first walked in, which had been refreshed several times but generally when they were doing things other than talking, and said, "You move differently now. What's up with that?"

"Oh. That's because I haven't been biking. I had these coaches for a while, a yoga guy and a ballet guy. You remember." Irv nodded; Manny smiled. "Wanted to fix my posture, but the real reason I went to see the yoga guy was to ask him about you. About whether I was crazy to be thinking about calling you. Anyway, they tried to fix my posture, gave me all these great exercises to do. But I spent so much time like this." He hunched over, mimicking the position of being on a bike.

"And you haven't spent much time doing that since this summer, huh. You're still doing the exercises?"

"Oh yeah. And everything on the show is walking, or riding, and I'm in scenes all the time with people who are taller than me so I'm always reminding myself to be taller." Irv made a disgruntled sound; Manny grinned. "I like being the tall one."

"Go fuck yourself."

Manny laughed. "I didn't tell you, I met the guy who used to have this loft."

"Where'd you meet him?"

"On the set for 'Countdown.' He was there one day hanging out, taking pictures. He lives with the co-star, Victor Garcia."

Irv sighed on the inside. This was definitely a not-great part of having a lover who was an actor: he was going to be around amazing-looking people all the time. "And what did you think of him."

"You ever see him?" He meant in person.

189

"I've seen both of them. I went to Andy's last show, the one he did here last fall. That's where the picture in the kitchen came from." He was not, absolutely not, going to verbalize his general impression, which was 'Jesus Christ those guys are hot.'

"He's too tall," Manny said, watching Irv. He was pretty sure the guy had no idea how much his face gave away. Manny was not going to say 'he's super sexy' because it would make Irv feel bad. Besides, it was irrelevant. "Those guys should be married. They're so in love." He changed the subject, because all of a sudden those words – married, love – seemed like they were written in neon. "The day Mr. Martin was on set Victor and Jonathan got up to some nonsense. They were hanging around with a bunch of us and started doing this thing like they were in character, almost their real lines, but so filthy. I mean, *filthy*. We were all busting up."

"Well, if somebody could impress *you* with his filthy mouth, it must have been pretty filthy."

"You make me filthy," Manny said, moving in close and getting his hands on Irv. The monitor went to sleep long before they thought about looking at it again.

They'd both made it through the whole three weeks without really talking about what they were doing or how they were doing it. It was such a short period of time. Not enough to spell 'boyfriends,' even though it seemed to go beyond 'friends with benefits.' Manny couldn't decide what to do, or what to say. He made the first move asking Irv out to dinner. Irv made the second one, inviting Manny to stay. It was his turn again, and he needed to do it before he was packing his bag for the drive. He didn't want to actually be in the loft when he did it, so he suggested going out for lunch after their last trip to the gym.

Irv was at the point of actively suppressing possibly-unwelcome invitations, so he was glad Manny made that suggestion. He made some remark about the guys at the gym on their way out. Then, "No sign of Angel this time." *Why did I say that.*

"I wasn't even looking," Manny said honestly. "He's, like, irrelevant. Are we dressed good enough for me to take you to Pacific Dining Car? I always wanted to eat there."

It was pretty hard to dress badly enough to get tossed out of a restaurant in Los Angeles, even an upscale one. As long as a person was fully-clothed and clean, that is. "They won't throw us out." And if Manny wanted to buy Irv a twenty-dollar Cobb salad, that was fine with him.

They had a short wait to be seated, but before long their order was in and it was time for Manny to do the thing. "I've had a great time with you, Irving. Thanks for letting me stay."

"My pleasure." It probably sounded a little gruff.

"Would it be all right if I crashed with you for a few days again at the end of the shoot? Just till I can find my own place," he added, thinking that might make Irv more likely to go for it.

Thank you Lord. "Sure, that's fine." Irv drank some water. That was perfect, actually. Take a minute to get re-acquainted and figure out if they wanted to keep seeing each other. Or rather, if Manny wanted to keep seeing Irv. He wondered what the guy was planning to do. Go back to work at the gym? Keep hitting the auditions? He had some good credits now, and some connections. Would he actually want to shoot

191

anything else for Stroked? Should Irv even encourage that?

Manny watched Irv think. Those micro-expressions again, little clues to what might be on his mind, but nothing that really invited a question. "With all those movies we've been watching, I realized I never noticed a lot of stuff. Like, I'd notice what an actor did with a line or what they were doing in an action scene. Especially those, I guess. Then you pointed out what Alan Rickman does in 'Die Hard.' I'm going to think about ways to communicate like that, in between lines."

"Good. That's good. Do you guys rehearse, down in Mexico?"

"Some. There's a lot of moving parts sometimes, so it's like here's your business. Moving from point A to point B, and whether you're carrying something. Sort out the traffic pattern, stuff like that. But not really the fine points of how we react to each other. I mean the supporting cast. Marco and Tiburon, they do a lot more rehearsal. I'm going to try and watch when they're doing that."

"I'll bet that guy was pissed when Hyundai came out with those cars."

Manny made an I-don't-know face. "I think he did ads for them."

"Wonder what GMC would think of that thing you did in the back of the truck." Manny was cracking up. Irv watched that, trying not to let on how much he was going to miss this.

And the very next day, it was over, at least for a while. He walked Manny out again. Gave him a hug again. Stood still for a long, sweet kiss. This time there was no maybe I'll write, maybe I'll send a picture. Irv chose to believe. The kid hadn't let him down yet. And he really needed to stop thinking 'the kid.'

"He's turning into a real actor," he told Monica on the phone the next day. "The way he talks about his character. What he and his show wife do to prepare."

"Did you talk about him doing some more stuff with us?"

"Yeah, we talked about it. But when he comes back I'm probably going to tell him he shouldn't. That show, it's going to drop in April. If he comes to the con, somebody there is going to recognize him, and that might not be good for him."

"His decision," she reminded him. "Maybe the thing won't get picked up, anyway. If it's just the one season, so what."

"Well, it's not like the people in charge don't know he was doing stuff with us. But still."

"You're overthinking this. The stuff he's done, some people would say it's only erotica."

They were so desensitized. He wanted to laugh, but this was actually serious. "Sure, if we took out the explicit parts, everything we do is erotica. Besides, even if I took the explicit stuff down now, somebody somewhere has a copy."

She sighed. "Yeah, okay. I feel like you think you've screwed him up somehow, and you should know better. Look at what's happening for him. That's because of you. So if he wants to do another scene or whatever, let him."

"Mmm. We'll see. Maybe I should stay out of the decision, but I can't not weigh in. He probably would never have thought of doing porn if I hadn't walked up to him. I'll at least tell him what I think, because I'm a fucking decade older and that gives me some perspective." He sighed. "It's blowing my mind that this is even a thing. Him and me."

"I keep telling you, you have a lot to offer. Everything I've seen from him tells me he's smart. He doesn't waste time on people who aren't good for him. So he thinks you're good for him. But if he didn't *like* you, he would not be fucking you. He went a long time without fucking anybody. And you know you weren't his only option."

Irv couldn't exactly argue with that, even though it was the part that blew his mind the most. "I'm starting to believe in it."

"Good. So let's talk about how to freshen up our catalog without El Vaquero. Let me get Payton on the line." They started talking about the half-dozen new people who'd joined the roster in the past year. Irv gratefully fell into business.

CHAPTER 10

Manny took his time driving to Mexico. It was an easy trip even without an overnight stop, but taking it slow let him enjoy this remote part of SoCal. And it helped him get in the right head space. Away from the city and everything that meant, into the wide-open empty landscape. Now that he knew his way around the world of 'Alhambra,' the drive felt like going back in time, if not hundreds of years. He stopped for the night at a small, isolated motel. Nothing was near it except a shabby taco stand and a gas station. Manny got himself some dinner, went to bed, and thought about the show instead of watching TV.

At base camp in Mexicali he collected another fat envelope from the producers, hauled his gear into his room, then drove the truck over to the hangar. A few of the cast members made noise about that before, wanting to take their private cars on location, but the producers said No. Manny didn't care. It wasn't like you could drive back and forth to Mexicali every day. They were starting really early a lot of the time, or going into the night. And there sure wasn't any other reason to go for a drive out in the desert.

The first ten weeks of the shoot, half the challenge for most of the cast was getting used to being out there. This next eight weeks ought to be easy. They were familiar with the sites, with their costumes, with the props and animals, with each other. Manny was actively looking forward to seeing Patrice and Marco again. He liked to think that at the end of things, they might keep in touch. He'd sent Marco a text from L.A., only because he was online one day and saw the guy had gotten married in Las Vegas. Patrice was texting him all along.

She arrived with a bunch of others again, all on the same plane from Los Angeles. Manny was in his room with the door propped open to signal he was there. This time there was no big meeting; everyone was on their own for dinner. They were all expected to skim through their packets right away, so if there were any major questions or problems about the schedule, Rodrigo or another of the production staff could try to deal with it before they got on the bus.

With that in mind, Manny asked Patrice if she wanted to have a working dinner. They spent a couple hours at the restaurant down the street, going through their stuff, comparing notes on the scenes they'd already done and how those would relate to the new ones. "Fuck my life," Patrice said, flopping back on the banquette. "I thought shooting out of order was no big deal, but now I'm seeing how we've, like, *evolved*. And we have to match that in the shit that's back in time. Jesus, Mary, and Joseph."

"God, I know. It's a good thing you kept all those notes early on. I didn't start doing that till halfway through. I'd be fucked for real."

"Speaking of fucked, how was your break? How's tu hombre de ojos verdes?"

Manny drank the rest of his beer, smiling into the bottle. "He worked me over." Patrice laughed. "It was good. I think we have something good."

"Going back to him at the end of this?"

He nodded. "I asked if I could crash with him till I get my own place. Thought he might want to offer, but it was my turn. Didn't want to leave it up in the air."

"You want your own place?" He shook his head. She gave him a 'thought so' kind of look. "Think he might ask you to stay for good?"

"I don't know. I kept catching him looking at my hand. I used to wear a ring Lobo gave me. They weren't going to let me wear that for this, so I put it away before I came down the first time."

"Planning to start wearing it again?"

He glanced over at her, then away. "No. And if he asks, I'll tell him why."

Those last eight weeks flew by. They all had a groove now, solid in their characters and used to the routine. Everybody got just enough time back at base camp to avoid cabin fever. Manny worked with Patrice on tuning their scenes to the right levels, watched and listened when the more experienced actors were doing dialogue, and soaked up the craft like a sponge.

People were starting to speculate about whether they'd get picked up. The platform that ordered the show was being cagey about it in the entertainment press. But a couple weeks before the end of filming, they got the word: second season was a go. Everyone was excited. Most of them wouldn't know for sure that they were going to return until contracts landed in their in-boxes. They were excited anyway. Manny sent an email to Irv that amounted to 'holy shit.' The answer was nothing but a 'glad to hear it.' He chose to believe they would celebrate properly when he was back in Los Angeles.

Irv was actually thrilled about the series getting picked up. Even though it meant Manny was definitely not going to turn into a down and dirty regular for *Stroked*. Unless his part didn't get carried forward, but from the sound of things Irv thought that was unlikely. It was the kind of character that could be used a lot of ways, and he must be turning in the right performance.

They wouldn't spend eighteen weeks developing the character if it wasn't working. It would have been easy to kill off the trader and replace him.

All the episodes would drop at once, or so his industry contacts told him. They were going to do a red-carpet launch event in April. Plenty of promotion in early summer, trying to snag an Emmy nomination or five. If it hit, it could be a multi-year gig. Years of Manny spending the winters in Mexico, then coming back to Los Angeles. If he stayed with the series, he could take his pick of other projects that filmed over the summers. And maybe, just maybe, he'd want to spend some of that time with Irv.

It was too early to fantasize about shit like that, or so he told himself. The emails back and forth weren't going into detail about what they might do. Manny hadn't opened any kind of discussion about where he might want to live.

The ideal (for Irv) would be to keep him right there at the Brewery. Manny might well be open to it, but he'd be working, and while this place was fairly central it was pretty tight when it was set up for a shoot, which most of the time it was. If Lauro hadn't moved to the apartment at the filming house, that place would be good. But he had, and that seemed to be working out great for everybody in the company. *Talk about it when he gets back*, Irv told himself. The one thing he needed to be clear on was that he wanted Manny at the loft. Anything else would be a lie.

Besides, it was the practical thing. He said that to Monica and she laughed in his face.

Manny didn't really need to be hanging around on the final day of filming. His last scene wrapped two days before, and he could have taken the shuttle bus back up to Mexicali then. But he decided to stay, because Rodrigo said he could, and he wanted to get the most out of this experience. So he sat on the bench by the parking area, watching Tiburon and Marco play their last scene and then ride off into the literal sunset. It was the second take, because Tiburon's horse was a jerk the first time. They'd had a long day; both horses were tired and irritated. In addition to wrapping several scenes that were almost entirely mounted, the production was doing some scenery prep for the next season. They'd built some fast-and-cheap masonry structures, and now they were breaking those up to be instant ruins. The breaking-up was done with explosives. The noise had everyone on edge.

The scene played out. Tiburon rode off. Marco went a different direction, along a wooden fence. It was a zig-zaggy thing built of what amounted to little more than rough-edged boards with their ends stacked, and two more in an X to brace every joint. The set people called it a worm fence. Not a nail in sight, but no-one could say for sure that it was period-appropriate. The main reason they used it was they could transport all the wood from one site to another, assemble the fence without any hardware or post-holes, and take it down again without too much fuss. It created the illusion that this wasn't a barren, unpopulated desert, and provided some interesting structure for certain shots. They had a whole village at one site; that was partly built of stone and adobe. The rest was made of easily-rearranged polystyrene blocks that looked like stone. The one site served as all the different villages, with a bit of re-dressing.

Manny was thinking absently about how smart the modular approach was when the director said "Cut!

That's a wrap on season one. Great job everyone," a rock-breaker went off, and all hell broke loose.

With that explosion, Marco's horse Carmen had had enough. She reared up, twisting. Marco lost his seat and went off, right onto one of the joints of the fence. He hung for a moment, turning grotesquely, then thumped to the ground on the far side. Everybody started yelling. A secondary camera operator said "Shit!" and started running over there.

Manny was on his feet, bolting for the medic's van. He banged on the door. "Carlos! Get your shit! Marco hit the fence."

"Fuck!" The door opened a few seconds later. Carlos had a bag of gear in one hand; he passed it to Manny and reached back for another. "Where?" He had a sat phone in one hand. Manny pointed. Carlos could see people converging. He spoke in Spanish into the phone, finishing with "Prisa."

They both ran. It wasn't far, maybe an eighth of a mile. When they got to Marco, they were winded mostly because of fright. A gang of people was standing around, half of them taking phone pictures. Marco was lying still and was covered with blood. Manny sucked in a breath. "Jesus, Carlos, what the fuck."

"Marco? Marco, are you in there?" Carlos pulled on exam gloves and did a rapid assessment for airway and circulation. "He's breathing, pulse is okay, where's this blood coming from." Manny was opening the medical kit, laying out the most-likely-needed items on a clean plastic tray. He heard, "Madre de Dios."

Manny looked over as he tugged on a pair of gloves. Carlos had the costume cut away from a jagged tear. He was peeling the fabric back from a terrible wound. "Did the wood do that?"

"Must have. Saline." Manny handed it over. Carlos cut the bag open and let it spill all over the wound. "Best we can do for cleanup here. The chopper shouldn't be more than fifteen minutes. Have you ever done an IV?"

"No, the Red Cross training was like advanced first aid but not that advanced." Manny was giving thanks he'd at least done emergency-response training before heading down here the first time. He knew what all the gear was, and how to handle it. At the time he'd only been thinking it was an easy way to get a little boost in his rate.

"Okay. We're going to try to wrap him up to minimize the blood loss. Then I'm going to get a line in. Can you help me with the wrap?"

"Sure."

"Good. Then I'll put you on monitoring his vitals, okay?"

"You got it." They went to work. It took both of them, and most of the gauze and tape in both bags, to pull the edges of the wound closed and strap it tightly. By then others had brought up a stretcher. They transferred Marco, who was not quite unconscious, onto the cleaner surface. Manny focused on the blood-pressure cuff, the pulse oximeter, and Marco's breathing while Carlos set up a saline drip. Four guys carried the stretcher back to the landing zone with Manny and Carlos walking alongside.

"It had to be the big guy," one of the volunteers said.

Marco muttered something that sounded like "Fuck you." Manny and Carlos exchanged a glance; that comment was a good sign. The helicopter was already in sight when they slogged past the production vehicles.

Carlos arranged to follow the medevac crew in his van. He said, "We'll be going up to the Hispano Americano in Mexicali. Get in touch when you get back to base camp, all right?"

"Sure."

"Thanks for your help, Manny."

"Any time. Get him out of here." He backed away from the copter as Carlos jogged over to his van. He was shaking now that it was over. Somebody patted him on the back; he turned his head to see the horse boss. "Hey Gabe."

"That was kind of intense. You doing okay?"

"Yeah. How's Carmen?" Manny told himself it was silly to be concerned about Marco's horse, but she was a nice horse. It wasn't her fault some idiot blew something up right at that moment.

"She's fine. My assistant will have her boxed up as soon as the vans get here."

"Better see what's going on." They walked around the line of vehicles again. The shuttle bus was pulling in. So were the trucks and trailers that would move the animals to their respective homes. The catering truck was already gone. Manny hadn't even noticed it leaving. "Damn, I was hoping for a snack."

"You're all packed up, huh. Come over here." Gabriel took Manny over to his own truck. First he retrieved a packet of wet wipes and an empty plastic bag. Manny peeled off the exam gloves and scrubbed away the blood on his forearms; he hadn't even noticed it. All the waste went in the bag while Gabriel rummaged in a cooler behind the seat and pulled out two bottles of Coke. Next came a couple of cold cheeseburgers with grilled tomato and onions.

He handed one to Manny, who devoured it. "God, that's good. Thanks. I owe you."

"You going to be in town tomorrow?"

"Yeah, I think I'll start the drive back day after."

"Cool. I'll check in with you. Go get on that bus."

"Gracias."

"De nada." Gabriel waved him away. Manny started for the bus.

The ride back felt longer than usual. Considering he'd barely done anything that day, Manny was exhausted. He sent two texts once he was back in his room at base camp, showered, and more or less relaxed. The first message was to Carlos, to check on Marco. That wasn't entirely reassuring, because the answer was that the big guy had been moved to Sharp Memorial in San Diego for surgery. But he was alive, and stable enough to be moved, so those were good things.

The second text was to Irv. Short and to the point: *Hey Irving I'm back in Mexicali. Can you talk?*

Irv got the message and thought *Uh-oh*. That 'can you talk' could mean a bunch of things that weren't great for Irv. Except Manny used his whole name, which was generally reserved for intimate moments. He didn't bother texting back, simply called. As soon as Manny answered, Irv said, "Are you all right?"

"I'm fine. A little shook up. We wrapped today and there was an accident. Marco Hidalgo got hurt."

"Shit, how bad?"

"Not sure but there was a hell of a lot of blood. He was riding along this crazy fence, one of the rock-breakers went

203

off, and his horse dumped him right on a fucking post. Tore his back open like a chainsaw."

"Fuck!"

"Yeah, that's what we all said. I helped Carlos get him situated. By the time the medevac people got there he was ready to transport. They brought him here first, but I hear they took him to San Diego for surgery."

"Jeez, that's not going to be great for the production."

"Not for the guy who set off that firecracker, that's for sure."

Irv snorted out a laugh. "Sorry, shouldn't laugh."

"No, God, please do. It was a fucked-up day all along because they were doing that shit between takes. All of us were like, fuck those guys, they couldn't do that after we're done?"

"Yeah, I guess whoever scheduled that, his ass is in a sling." Irv thought of something else inappropriate to say and managed not to say it.

Manny might have read his mind. "Our guys who were carrying the stretcher said, it had to be the big guy."

"That's what I was thinking."

It was good for a laugh, which Manny really needed. "He is fucking huge. He's even taller than Red. Lost weight since he was on 'Flagship' though. He was so built on that."

"Hey."

Another laugh. "Come on, you know you'd put him in front of the camera."

"Of course I fucking would. He's like the Mexican Dwayne Johnson. So he's not so built?"

"No power gym out on these locations, and it's impossible to gain weight on gazpacho and guacamole. He looks amazing on a horse. Or when they get busy with those swords. Tiburon's great, too, but Marco's really been showing up."

Irv knew about the fight choreography. "Ever spar with him?"

"With someone seven inches taller than me? Half again my weight? Claro que no." Manny listened to Irv laugh, thought *God I wish I was there already*, and said, "I'm sure his sword is epic but I'm looking forward to yours."

"You don't say. When will that be?"

"I'm starting back day after tomorrow. Can I come straight there?"

"Yeah, do that. You going to be able to sleep?"

That gave him a warm feeling. It always did when Irv let slip something soft. "I'm winding down now. By the time I see you I'll be all loose." He let his tone go a little bit wicked.

"Oh really. And you're going to take your slow-ass time getting here like before, so I have to think about that for three days, huh?"

"Three nights. I want you thinking about me all three nights. I've been thinking about you."

"If I think about you for all three nights you're not going to be able to walk for three days after you get here."

"Well, you've got that nice couch." It made Irv laugh again. Manny felt so much better. He wanted to say something else, didn't want to push it. Maybe after they had time to settle back into being together, he'd know if he could say it. "Okay papi. I've been up since five so I'm going to sleep. Want me to call you on the way?"

Irv knew he should wave that off. He couldn't. "Yeah, do that. Get some rest."

"You too."

"Oh, right, after that conversation." Irv heard Manny laugh and disconnected, because if he didn't he was going to start saying all kinds of things he shouldn't say.

Manny was pretty much ready to sleep, but he sent a text to Patrice anyway: *You still here? Big mess on set today. If you're around let's get some breakfast*

A reply pinged in almost immediately: *WTF happened? Yeah I'm here*

Accident, Marco's hurt. Probably on the news online already

Shit fuck and damn! How bad?

Pretty bad

You shouldn't be thinking about it before bed. Stop. Turn on the TV and watch something stupid till you fall asleep. Watch some wrestling

Yeah okay

See you in the morning OXO

Thanks querida OXO

A day in Mexicali to decompress felt like the best idea ever when Manny woke up and realized he didn't have to go anywhere. He got in touch with Gabe and Patrice first thing, determined that both of them were in the same mood he was, and organized a meetup at a breakfast place. He walked over to the hangar for his truck, collected Patrice, and went to eat approximately everything.

Two hours later he leaned back in his chair, feeling lazy and overfed, smiling at his friends. "God, that was good."

Patrice swallowed the last spoonful of flan, stifled a belch, and said, "I feel like I should have taken pictures of everything we had on the table." They surveyed the wreckage. Gabe still had a mouthful of sweet-corn pudding; all he could do was nod.

Manny rolled his neck, stifling a yawn. "Feels like I could go right back to bed. Regret it if I do, though. Where do the horses go now?"

Gabe said, "Tiburon."

Patrice blinked at him. "Does he have a ranch?"

"Pretty much. Big place north of Mexico City. Has a whole staff down there. All I got to do is catch up to the convoy, make sure everybody gets settled in, then keep tabs on them till it's time to move again. It's not too far from me."

"I'm going to miss Saluki."

"I'm *not* going to miss that fucking mule," Patrice said.

"Aw, she likes you."

"Likes me?! Was there a day that pinche puta didn't either drool on me, chew on my hair, pee on my foot, or push me out the goddamned shot?" Manny and Gabe were both cracking up. "If they bring me back I'm asking for hazard pay. Hmph."

Manny reached over to tug her hair. "You could ask to ride."

"Do I want to ride? How we get all our shit from place to place if I ride?"

"Depends on the scripts, I guess." Manny drank some coffee. "If they go with the idea that Marco gives us a house, maybe it's only me riding around all the time. Maybe I've got an apprentice, and you stay home with the baby."

"Lord have mercy." Patrice played with her spoon for a few seconds, thinking. "Huh. That could work. I wouldn't get as many scenes with you, though, would I?"

"Probably not."

Gabe lifted his chin to signal their server. "You're supposed to be taking a day off, not thinking about the job."

Patrice gave him a look. "How long you been in show business, Gabriel?"

"Long enough to enjoy a day off." He and Manny fake-argued about the bill for a minute, but Manny got hold of it in the end.

They all shook hands outside, promising to stay in touch. When they were heading for the truck Manny asked, "Does that really happen?"

Patrice shrugged. "Sometimes. It's like any job. You make friends while you're working, then after you leave and you're not seeing each other it kind of fades. How long did you work at that gym?"

"Four years."

"Still in touch with anybody?"

"Not really," he admitted. "And that was only last summer."

"Hmm." It was half a laugh. "I worked at Jiffy Lube for twelve years and nope. Not a single person. Part of it's how big L.A. is. Work was in Hawthorne, I lived in Westchester. That's not so far apart, but the people I worked with lived anywhere from Inglewood to Gardena. When you're trying to get to your second job, or your kid's school, or whatever, there's no meeting up for dinner or drinks. It is what it is."

"You still live in Westchester?" They were in the truck now, cruising back to the motel.

"No, I moved out of there. I'll be staying with a friend in Silverlake this summer. Got another thing to do." She made a complicated gesture that Manny interpreted as having to do with her transition.

"That's not far from the Brewery. If I end up staying there, maybe I could come over." He'd almost said 'maybe we could meet up,' but whatever kind of thing she was having done, she probably wouldn't be feeling like running around town. He glanced over; she was smiling.

"Yeah, that would be nice. So you're driving back tomorrow."

"Uh-huh. You flying?"

"I haven't booked it yet. Wasn't sure how long I'd want to hang out here."

"You could come back with me," he suggested. "I'd like some company on the road. Usually break it overnight, but we don't have to."

"Overnight, huh? It's not even two hundred and fifty miles!"

"Yeah, but you know that travel time estimator is bullshit. Google Maps was all, it's four hours the whole way. Bullshit," he said again. Patrice was snickering. "Took me two hours just to get to Ontario the first time. I didn't want to leave at the crack of dawn or worry about getting here on time. Wanted to, you know, ease into it."

"Good strategy, I guess. Sure, I'd be cool going back with you. Could give you a break with the driving."

"My big ol' truck?"

"Child, please. I drove every damn kind of car while I worked at Jiffy Lube."

"I can't picture you doing that."

"You can't, huh? I was good at it, though. Grease monkey by day, diva by night." She did a Z snap.

They laughed about that, and about Manny's races, and about the differences between growing up in San Fernando and Miami all the way to Los Angeles. Manny sent Irv a picture before they got on the road: *Driving up with Patrice. Be there tonight if that's okay*

The reply he got was very encouraging: *If by okay you mean best news I've had all week*

Irv considered and discarded about a hundred words to describe the way he was feeling as the clock ticked down to Manny's ETA. The word he finally settled on was 'elated,' and then he spent a few minutes wondering if he'd ever felt that way before.

The past five months might have been as educational for Irv as they'd been for Manny. Thinking about what could possibly happen between them, or for them, sent him on an archeological dig through the past twenty years. On most of those long winter evenings alone, instead of editing or otherwise preparing something for Stroked, he was going through all his own work. Going back forever, creating an organized archive, and journaling the process. He still hated writing, but not as much as he did a year ago. Forcing himself to verbalize about various projects and experiences went a long way to clarify what he wanted to do in the future.

He'd talked to Lauro half a dozen times about content. They hashed out some fresh approaches to stock scenarios. And they talked about the soldier story. Lauro had been in touch with Manny, too. All that was really left to decide was if this was going to be a collection of loosely-related scenes, or a real movie. For option two, they needed to film some through-story involving the soldier. If they went with another man, there'd be a much smaller potential audience. Neither of them wanted to make that call; the project wouldn't exist without Manny, so they wanted him to decide.

Everything else hinged on that. If Manny was down with making a fully-explicit feature, he was probably also down with more pictorials or scenes for Stroked. If he looked at Lauro's script and said 'this is a mainstream movie' then he'd probably need to get out of the porn business. The industry was forgiving, but only up to a point. Porn was a thing people might do before, after, or instead of having a mainstream career. Not a thing people did alongside legit film and TV work.

So along with organizing his archive, Irv spent some time assembling non-X-rated versions of Manny's pictorials. Looking at those images through the lens of erotica, or even fine-art photography, meant choosing different material. He got Lauro involved with that, too, because a pictorial that didn't exist for the sole purpose of getting someone off needed a different reason to exist, or in other words story.

He'd been surprised to the point of astonishment when Lauro requested a print of one of the images. "For you?"

Lauro gave him an embarrassed look accompanied by half a shrug. "The thing is, they're really beautiful images, and he's my friend."

"But *that* one?" They were both looking at the image on-screen. It was one of Irv's personal favorites, one that he was willing to bet would be a massive seller in Manny's future fan-club store. The white shooting box had been draped with fabric that said 'Middle East' without being too specific. The only prop in it was a brown leather camel saddle Payton came up with for the Magic Carpet Rides series (no one asked him exactly where he found it).

Manny was nude, lying lengthwise on his back on the saddle. Upper arms bound to it with strips of white canvas. Feet on the floor, toenails painted gold, a dusting of sparkling white sand up the side of his leg. Irv had an extra cushion on the saddle, a little longer than the actual thing, because those brackets that went on the camel humps had finials. Torture to lie on, and this wasn't about pain. This was about the sensual drape of Manny's upper body. Lovingly lit, golden-brown skin covering those sleek curves of muscle.

The albino python was on top of Manny. Part of its lower body wound around his downstage thigh. Its head hovered alongside his neck, gorgeously set off by the beaded choker he wore. Red and blue and gold, nearly two inches wide, fringed with tiny gold coins, from Monica's collection. Manny's lips were parted as if he were breathing through his mouth, which he might have been; his eyes were half-open. The snake's body hid Manny's privates from the camera.

Irv's other personal favorite from that session was a head shot. He'd taken it against the sky-blue drop sheet behind the fabric drapery, lit as if by the sun. Framed from the upper chest, showing the choker and the fancifully Egyptian eye makeup. Manny was looking right at him when he took that shot. Very faintly smiling, eyes slightly narrowed, so much intention in his gaze that Irv couldn't quite believe they weren't lovers at the time. Couldn't believe he hadn't seen it.

There had been no reason at all to take even one head shot, never mind the half-dozen others from that session. Lauro didn't mention it, probably because he knew perfectly well how far gone Irv was. Now he was waiting, probably expecting Irv to make some kind of joke. Instead Irv said, "You're right, it is a beautiful image. What size print you want?"

And then of course he ordered two, which meant he had to decide where the hell to put his copy. In the loft, Manny would think he was just wank bait. In the bathroom, everybody who came into the damn place would think 'wank bait.' So Irv hung the print in the kitchen, and moved Andy Martin's photograph from somewhere up on the north Pacific coast to the bathroom.

He opened the main door a few minutes after getting the text saying *Just dropped Patrice in Silverlake, on my way*. This time he didn't have champagne waiting. He had a bottle of something expensively Italian, to go with the colossal amount of takeout from Pace keeping warm in the oven. Maybe that was sentimental and goofy, but it was also practical; Manny was getting in around dinner time, and they weren't going to want to go out. Irv was pretty sure he wasn't going to want to go anywhere for at least twenty-four hours.

When Manny stepped through the door he looked toward the stairs as if he expected Irv to be sitting there again. Then he turned his head and smiled. "Glad you got that chair?" He set down his guitar case and duffle bag, closed and locked the door.

"For so many reasons." Irv set down the book he hadn't really been reading, pried himself out of the recliner, and met Manny halfway across the room. "Mmph." The only sound he could make with Manny's mouth on his. Walking backward slowly until his shins hit the chair again. Collapsing into it, pulling Manny with him, still kissing. The chair wasn't really big enough for two, but they made it work.

After a while Irv loosened his grip enough that Manny could squirm into a comfortable position and gaze at him from a few inches' distance. "What smells so good?"

"Dinner. Ordered from Pace." God, that smile. Those deep dark eyes, that expression, this *man*. "I'm really glad you're here."

"Me too."

"You want to stay?"

Manny blinked. "You mean … what do you mean."

"I mean," Irv began, then stalled. Swallowed. *Just say it, the worst that can happen is No*. He took a steadying breath. "I mean you don't have to look for your own place unless you want to. I'd love it if you stayed here. With me."

Manny laid a hand on Irv's face, breathed his name, leaned in for another kiss. Soft, slow, tender, trying to communicate everything he wasn't sure he should say yet. At least he could say, "I want to. Yes." It was another few minutes before he started disentangling himself. "You ready to eat?"

"God, yes." He'd been too keyed up for lunch. Every time he looked around the loft, he got hung up on whether this was the kind of place where two men could live together. It was stupid, because he knew plenty of people here at the Brewery who cohabited. Most of those couples – he shied away from the thought; were he and Manny a *couple*? It seemed so unlikely – involved one person who worked at home while the other had an outside gig or two. Well, they could talk about that. Later. He accepted a hand up out of the chair, patted Manny's ass, and followed him to the kitchen. "So Patrice is staying in Silverlake." Not really a question, just an attempt to change the subject.

Manny was staring at the picture on the wall. "Irving?"

"Mmm, yeah."

Manny glanced over; Irv was blushing; the temptation to give him some serious shit about putting this pin-up on the wall was strong. Instead he said, "I forgot how big that snake was." Then he turned around and started getting things out of the oven. "Yeah, Patrice has this friend who's a stylist. Dolores. They've known each other a long time. Anyway, there's another medical thing this summer and Dolores said she should stay with her. Shouldn't be living somewhere alone, you know. It's not a big place but Patrice travels about as light as I do. She's got some shit in storage, like me."

"With her family?"

"No. Her family's back East. They're not close. I didn't ask a lot of questions."

Irv took some plates down off the shelf, flatware out of the drawer. "You think she doesn't like talking about it?"

"Mmm." Manny gave a half-shrug, dishing out chicken parmigiana with a side of spinach lasagna and a pile of grilled Caesar salad. "You got enough for like three days here, papi."

"Once I get your clothes off, not planning to let you put them on again for a while." Manny laughed. Irv was grinning, opening the wine. "Did Lauro send you his script?"

"No, is it done?"

"He wants to talk to you about it. Talk to us. Thought I'd see if he wants to come over sometime soon."

Manny covered the takeout containers again and picked up his plate and a glass. He'd somehow missed Irv pouring the wine. They took the meal over to the desk, kicking task chairs into position. "That would be good. I thought about it some while I was down south." They ate in contented silence. The food was excellent, the wine was perfect, and Manny couldn't remember ever being happier.

After washing up, they negotiated where Manny's gear would fit in. Irv told him to take a good look at how the place was set up. "We didn't really do that last time," he said. "I mean, I know you noticed."

"Yeah, I noticed." The biggest difference from the apartment at the porn house was the way most of the DVDs were hidden. The wall-spanning work surface had a wall-spanning shelf above it, loaded with Irv's books. Aside from that, the walls in the main space were bare and white. "Did you get rid of a lot of the movies?"

"Mmm. About half. There's so many clips online now, and a lot of those movies, I was only keeping them for one scene." Irv heard Manny snicker and rolled his eyes. "Not usually the sex scene." Another snicker. "Anyway, that stack is stuff I thought you might want to see before I give it away. The rest of the collection is in the closet under the stairs. Made a deal with myself, if I'm going to buy a new hard copy I have to get rid of something."

Manny finished putting away his clothes, thinking about that. "You used to watch a couple movies most days."

"Well, I was hoping." Irv stalled again. Manny was staring at him, one eyebrow up. "Okay, I was hoping you'd want to live here with me, so I'd have something to do besides watch all those movies, all right? I mean, it seems like you don't mind going out with me."

"Irving, for God's sake." Manny closed the distance, going for a hug this time. Easing back, enough to cup Irv's face in his hands, giving him a light kiss. "There's so many things I'd like to do with you. It's been a long time since I had someone I wanted to do things with."

Irv had to clear his throat before he spoke. "Me too."

CHAPTER 11

He probably shouldn't have been surprised that Manny took the whole 'doing things together' thing very seriously. A week into cohabitation, there was a new giant calendar on the wall in the laundry area with all Irv's shoots written in. If Manny had a meeting or an audition, he said he'd write that in a different color. They agreed on regular days to go to the gym together, chose days to go out to dinner or a movie or whatever, and had a conference call with Lauro. That led to setting up a dinner meeting at the loft for the three of them plus Patrice.

"You remember what I sent you before we did the last El Vaquero scene," Manny said after they got the dinner plans finalized.

"Yeah, I remember."

"Can I tell you about an idea I had?" Irv made a 'go ahead' face. Manny leaned back on the couch, turned halfway toward Irv. "When Patrice and I were getting ready to do that kiss scene, we had to come up with our back story. That reminded me of the idea I had, that maybe El Vaquero and his soldier signed up together. Even then I was thinking, the way you edited those scenes, it really wasn't laid out that my soldier was a guy or a girl. It could go either way."

Irv abruptly understood where Manny was going with this. "You were thinking, because you like working with Patrice, maybe she plays your soldier?"

"Right." Manny let that sit for a moment. "If I get called back for the second season, she will too. We'll know before the first season drops. Neither of us would have to take another job between now and then."

Especially since he was living with Irv. He didn't need to say that.

"You said she's got a procedure this summer."

"Right. But that got me thinking, what if the reason my soldier comes home is she got hurt?"

"Whoa." Irv thought about it. "You think she'd be okay with that?"

"I don't know. I wanted to run it by you. It's," he hesitated for a second. "There's so much reality in this already."

"Mmm. I know there is." They both thought about it some more, staring at each other. Irv was mostly thinking how brutally real that would be. If they could shoot in the hospital for sure, but even if it was only during Patrice's recovery. What it would actually be like for a young officer who'd expected that to be her career. Recovering at home on not much money, wondering what happened next.

Shooting over the first week after she was discharged, they'd get all the pain, all the emotional turmoil, all the needing-help-and-not-wanting-it. She'd barely have to act at all, and Manny wouldn't either. It was plain as day how much he cared about her. Irv told himself not to dwell on that. This new thing of theirs was going to be a series of negotiations, and he was determined to start each one from Together. "You should talk to her before this dinner thing. If she's up for it, all we'd really need to do is tell Lauro where the script is going and mark up the calendar." Then start on permits, work a deal with Patrice's friend to use her house – did she have a house? – and sort out any other locations. Once Lauro had the through-story and last act written, they could figure out where and how to

219

shoot the necessary scenes from earlier in the relationship. Irv was getting excited.

Manny watched Irv's face. If the guy was this wound up about it already, he was going to go off like a rocket when he met Patrice. "I'll go see her and talk it over."

Her first question, of course, was "So are we talking porn?"

Manny glanced over. They were sitting next to each other on Dolores' front porch, feet on the steps. In the sun, with Mexican coffees in hand and Dolores' big mutt of a dog sprawled out behind them with its back against their butts. "It doesn't have to be. We'd be using some footage I've done for Stroked but it can be edited so it's not explicit."

"Huh." She sipped her coffee and thought about it. "You must have remembered what I said. Thinking about doing that, back in the day."

"Well, yeah. But still. Irv's down with making this an R feature. He'll set up a separate LLC if you want to do it that way." He swallowed some coffee. "I just had the idea because we do good work. We get along. And I can see you as a soldier. You're tough as fuck. You do what it takes." She made a pleased sound. "There'd be at least one love scene. But what we film together, we can fake it. I don't know if I'm your type, anyway."

She snort-laughed. "About that."

"I can make it work with a girl." He was blushing.

She leaned in to nudge his shoulder with hers. "I really appreciate that you think of me as a girl."

"You *are* a girl. You're so much like this girl I went out with in high school, it's not even funny."

"She wasn't Puerto Rican, I bet."

"No. Her family was from Guatemala." They were both quiet for a minute. "The thing is, if it's porn, we don't need much else. The scenes between us, whether they're in bed or not, those are the movie. We might need a few scenes with other people. Like here we are with our friends at a house party before we go to boot camp, here you are out on deployment with your squad. But we wouldn't need big action scenes." He glanced over again to make eye contact. "You know what a legit movie about a soldier is like."

"Yes Lord. Explosions and helicopters and Jesus wept."

"You want to see the script so far?"

"Yes." Her tone said that was the stupidest question ever.

He laughed. "Okay, I'll email it to you. Then you have to tell me before dinner if there's anything you don't want to talk about, so I can tell Irving. He'll want to know who you are."

"He wants to be sure I'll be good for you."

Manny blinked, turned his head, tapped her knee. "What do you mean?

Patrice made eye contact again. "Everything you've told me about him? He's gonna want to be sure I'm not here to fuck up his thing with you. He's in –"

"Don't say it!"

"What, like don't jinx it? Manuel Figueroa."

He laughed under his breath. "I know. Soy estúpido."

"You've got it bad, chico."

So, so bad, he thought. He was looking at the future again, and it was scary. Except it was also great.

221

Every day, from waking up with Irv to going to bed together, was great. They gave each other shit about their workouts, their bad taste in music, their cars. They argued about the best way to get from here to there, or whether pineapple belonged on pizza, or what the good parts were in movies. They didn't disagree about a single thing that was important. He told himself to keep a lid on it. Because even though they'd known each other for almost two years, what they were doing was new. Irv hadn't lived with a lover for a long time, and Manny never had before. This might just be the honeymoon. Once they got used to it, they might stop liking each other so much.

Or maybe they wouldn't. Maybe they were right for each other, and this was the right time.

Irv surprised Manny with an actual dining table on the day of their dinner meeting. He blinked at the room after closing the door, loaded down with grocery bags. "Chairs, too?"

"Borrowed from one of the neighbors." Irv chose to disregard the amused expression on his lover's face. "That's how we do it. I hear when Andy had a wrap party, he'd borrow chairs from all over."

"Makes more sense than everybody buying their own," Manny said agreeably. "Guess I'd better get in the kitchen." They could have ordered in, but he wanted to cook. The loft kitchen was utilitarian, uncluttered, better than the one he had before. It had one of those big stainless-steel commercial sinks with two basins and a built-in drainboard. The cabinets on either side were topped with stainless steel, too. So easy to keep clean, not like the shitty old 4x4 tile at his apartment. He flipped the switch for the track lighting and got to work.

After setting the table, Irv stayed out of the way. He had business for Stroked, plus an email from his mom to answer. That took a while because she wanted to know everything about the new living situation. Trying to express how he felt without going overboard was tough. He rewrote his last paragraph about a dozen times.

I know you've been hoping, for a long time, I'd find someone. Well, we're talking, and we're not saying everything yet but we are saying things like 'next year.' If this show of his does well enough, this could be the next few years. He's easy to live with. Easy to be with. I never had anybody easy before. God knows I'm not easy. Anyway, I'll keep you posted. Take care of you and Pop.

He read it over again, shook his head – it wasn't going to get any better, and their guests would be rolling in any minute – attached a copy of that pseudo-Egyptian head shot, and sent it off.

Two hours into dinner, they were on a second bottle of wine, picking from the copper braiser sitting in the middle of the table. Not much remained aside from scraps of onion, carrot, and mushroom, but they all kept going back in, chasing shreds of short ribs. Manny leaned back in his chair, glass in hand, smiling across the table at Irv. "I never had company for dinner like this before, can you believe it? If I had a friend over, we'd call out for pizza or something."

Patrice swabbed out the pan with a piece of bread. "How'd you learn to cook? Because honey, you can *cook*."

Manny ducked his head, pleased. "My mother taught us the basics. Or, you know, gave us jobs in the kitchen so we had to learn."

"This was really good." Lauro set down his glass, easing his waistband and looking somewhat regretful. "Set the bar pretty high."

"My contribution," Manny said. "Irv's the director, you're the writer. Patrice is the face."

"The what?!" She pressed her hands to her cheeks.

Irv bit back a laugh. "Nobody's going to wonder why Manny would wait for you."

"Jesus fuck, I guess we're talking about porn now." All the men laughed. Patrice was fanning herself.

"I know he told you it doesn't have to be porn." Irv gave it a second. "What are your thoughts?"

"Okay. Well, I liked the script. I'd like to see the scenes that Manny did with you. What you're building off of. You know I've never had a part like that. Where I'm one of the main characters."

Irv shook his head. "Doesn't matter. I've checked you out."

"But this last thing, it's the biggest thing I've done as a woman."

"Doesn't matter," he said again. "Manny thinks he could play this with you, and he would know." Manny gave him a warm look. "How about we have some coffee and talk about it for a while."

Lauro and Patrice said "Sure" and "Okay." Manny cleared the table and started the coffeemaker while the others took turns in the bathroom. After his turn, he joined them at the table again. Patrice was sitting across from him now. Lauro had a notebook and pen ready.

Irv glanced over at Manny and said, "Did you tell her about Lobo?"

"Yeah, I did."

"Okay, so she knows where you're coming from."

"Well, sort of." Manny addressed Patrice. "The first scene we did, this whole thing wasn't really a thing. It wasn't until we did the second one that we both started thinking, hmm. It was me alone in the house, and for whatever reason we both thought, this is the guy waiting for his soldier to come home. So we scored it with 'Tie a Yellow Ribbon,' and then the other four scenes were all starting from that same idea."

"Damn, y'all. Well, I really want to see them now. Six?" Manny nodded. Patrice looked at Irv. "I'll bet you were dying to get him in a couple scene."

Manny and Lauro laughed. Irv half-shrugged. "To be honest, I had mixed feelings about it then and I still do. Yes, I thought he might really hit that way. But he's trying to make it as a legit actor, and a couple scene is less forgivable to a lot of people. We've talked about the pros and cons, me and Manny. If we make this thing X-rated it could be a notable piece of work. High profile, not much competition. If we make it R-rated, we're up against projects with much bigger budgets. Not likely to place it anywhere except streaming, and it could get buried."

Lauro stirred. "There's always the possibility of doing both. Make it X-rated, do an R edit. A lot of people could relate to this story who wouldn't be comfortable buying an X-rated movie."

"The existence of an X version would mean instant notoriety, though," Irv said. "And if an R version gets picked up by a streaming platform, that's going to be more money than we'd make selling an X version. Plus it's going to be something you can put on your legit resumés." They were all silent for a moment. Irv had the distinct impression that Manny and Patrice, for

225

whatever reason, had both been thinking of going explicit. He hoped like hell it was only curiosity. "I'm thinking maybe we shoot a scene with the two of you, and you can decide after. Maybe by then we have a completed script, and we can talk about it again." He glanced at Lauro.

"It won't take me long if act three is Patrice coming home wounded. Is that where we're going?" There was some discussion about that. Lauro took notes. When they seemed to have exhausted their current ideas, he looked at his watch. "I have a shoot with Payton in the morning, so I'd better go. This was great, though. I'll get to work."

Manny walked him out, gave him a hug, and promised to come visit soon. When he closed the door and turned around, Irv had relocated to the couch. Patrice was in the kitchen. "More coffee?"

She came back out with a glass of water. "Not for me, sugar. That's a hell of a print in there."

"Irving knows how to take a picture," Manny said, smiling. He got a drink of water himself, then joined Irv on the couch.

Patrice sat at the other end, legs curled underneath her. "I wondered if I could give you some background," she said, looking a little uncomfortable. "I mean, Irv, I'm assuming everything Manny knows about me, you know. That's okay," she added, when Manny winced. "If I ever have a boyfriend he's gonna hear everything I hear."

"Whatever you want to say." Irv had his arm over Manny's shoulders. Manny was slouched down, half-leaning on his chest, cuddling. No other word for it, even though he was looking at Patrice. Irv got the idea there was some kind of message here.

226

"It's not so much," she was saying. "What you need to know for us to work together. This thing I'm doing this year, it's the last thing. There was another thing last year, and these," she touched her breasts, "the year before that. I basically haven't been with anybody since I started the work. So Manny's kind of my only man since then and I might get a little clingy but it's only 'cause I'm scared and not because I'm trying to take him away from you."

"You didn't have to tell us that," Irv said after a minute. He didn't dare look at Manny right then.

"I know. The thing is, you're trusting Manny to me, and I'm trusting myself to him. This thing we're talking about, it's a thing I haven't done. The closest is that little kissing scene down south. I may have triggers that I don't know about, that's all."

Manny squeezed her fingers. "One thing I can promise, if anything doesn't feel right, we stop. No matter where we are or what we're doing."

"Thanks, honey." She sniffled a little. "I'd better get out of here. Dee said, keep the car as long as you want, but she's probably thinking I'm on my way to Vegas."

They could tell she was trying to lighten it up, so they went along with it. Manny gave her a long hug at the door, murmured something to her. She kissed his cheek, waved to Irv, and left.

The next few weeks were busy. Irv had a ton of stuff to get ready for AdultCon. Manny was talking to his agent Robert and the casting folks, getting a line on a few gigs. He told everybody he was still up for work as an extra as long as it was skilled. Until there was a schedule for the soldier story, he was at liberty. A few meetings (including with the financial advisor he never

227

needed before) didn't take much time. To keep busy, he downloaded a collection of public-domain patriotic songs and started working up his own versions for the soldier story. He'd learned a ton of music in Mexico, but who knew if any of it was out of copyright.

He also went back to Kevin for a tune-up on his yoga routine, then to Dmitri. Talking Irv into going along to the Sunday morning class at Shall We Dance took some doing. Manny rewarded him with brunch at a WeHo diner. As they walked back to Irv's car, he said, "You ever miss living over this way?"

Manny glanced over, amused. "No. I wasn't on the Westside long enough to feel like this was my place. You ever miss the house?"

"God, no," Irv said with feeling. "The pool, okay. All that commotion all the time, no. It made sense for a lot of years but there was no privacy. I remember one time I took a guy back there and he was like really?" The second he said it, he wished he hadn't.

Manny patted his back. "He wasn't a dick about it, was he?"

"Eh. Not really. But I didn't tell him about the house, so he thought I was renting that apartment."

"He didn't know you co-owned everything, huh."

"Right. Well, that didn't mean much at the time. We're all in better shape now." The partners were in great shape, actually, which was something Irv hadn't brought up. The question of whether Manny should pay rent had been dismissed. He was in charge of feeding them, which from Irv's point of view was working out great, and which he seemed to enjoy. Was this the time to mention that the house would be paid off by the end of this year? That the partners were discussing hiring a new P.A. and offering Lauro a different position? That one of the other things on the table was a new erotica division, for hard-R material that could be sold through mainstream channels? That the whole reason they started talking about it was this soldier story? Maybe not. Soon, but not yet.

Manny could tell Irv had things to say. So did he. And pretty soon he'd say those things, but not yet.

A few days later, Manny was out in the Valley to get properly caught up with Lauro. They had dinner at an Indian restaurant, then headed back to the filming house so they could talk in private. With a heat lamp on, it was nice out by the pool.

"You move differently," Lauro observed after they were settled on loungers with coffee in hand.

"Irv said the same thing. It's because I'm not biking. I feel like I breathe better, all the time."

"Are you actually taller, or is that an optical illusion?"

Manny laughed. "When I really lift up through my back I can be five nine and a half now. But it's an illusion. It's just me making space in my spine. Couldn't do that before because my chest and shoulders were so tight."

"Tell me what you liked best about the shoot."

"Oh, man, there's so much. I love Patrice. Working with Marco and the rest of them. Learning every day. Riding almost every day. That horse, he's such a dick, but we get along."

"What makes him a dick?" Lauro was smiling.

"Well, for one thing, he's a stud. Like, for real. His whole life was about fucking from age four to age eighteen. He's twenty-two now and he still looks at the other stallion in the pool like, I could take you."

"Could he?"

"Oh, no. Not a chance. Saluki, he's a bony old man now. Brittle. That's why they gave him to me, because I'm the lightest person in a mounted role."

Sure it is. Lauro shook his head slightly, but didn't comment. "Is the other stallion Tiburon's horse too?"

"Uh-huh. He's a Friesian. Tops Saluki by about four hundred pounds. Almost half again his weight."

"Holy shit!"

"Yeah. Marco's horse Carmen, she's even heavier. Taller. Every time I see them ride out I think, teenage girls are gonna love this show." Lauro laughed. Manny was grinning. "I saw a Gypsy Vanner like Carmen in a parade once when I was a kid and I was like Will Smith in 'Independence Day.' Got to get me one of these. But she's so fucking big."

"How's he doing, have you heard?

Manny knew he meant Marco. "He's all right. Gonna be in physical therapy till the minute we go back to Mexico. I mean, if I go." He kept slipping up like that, assuming that he and Patrice would be back for season two. His agent hadn't heard anything yet.

"You don't think they would have given you a hint if they weren't bringing you back?"

"How would I know? I never did a character with a name before."

"Yeah, okay." Lauro sipped his coffee. "So I met someone." Super casual, like this wasn't a big thing.

Manny sat up fast, turning to put his feet on the ground, staring at his friend. "We've been talking about fucking *horses* when you had this to say?"

230

Lauro set his cup aside, grinning, but made a 'hold on there' gesture. "It's just, it's new. I don't know what might happen. Maybe nothing."

"Tell me."

So Lauro told him. "You remember when you went to Chrome for that cowboys and tango dance thing. And then we went last summer for the martial arts thing." Manny made a 'get on with it' face. "I went by myself for the holiday show from the Underground Cabaret. It was called 'Angels' and some people in the audience wore costumes. I guess that happens a lot. Anyway, there were two people in these really subtle outfits. Not wings or whatever, it was all about makeup and hairstyle and, I don't know. One of them was definitely a girl. The other one, I couldn't tell. It didn't seem to me like they were a couple. Had a chance to talk to the girl for a minute. Told her I liked her costume. She said, you should come to the January show. I said I might."

"And you did."

Lauro nodded. "I got a ticket for Sunday night and went in thinking nothing would happen, because usually nothing does, right? But she was there, by herself, and we sat together for the show. Then we hung out in the lounge upstairs until closing time. I was so wrecked the next day. Totally zoned out during a shoot."

"What's her name." Manny's voice was soft, because he could see how much Lauro liked this girl.

"Tani Chen. She's a receptionist for an accounting firm in West Hollywood. The person she was with in December is a co-worker. They share an apartment. He's gay."

"Did you tell her about you?"

231

"I had to, didn't I?" After a few seconds of staring at the pool, Lauro turned his head. "I said, look, Tani, you need to know something. I'm heteroromantic but I'm asexual."

No sign of trauma. Manny blinked at the current of hope and happiness, flowing from Lauro through him like a wave of adrenaline. "And she said?"

"She said, holy shit, you're kidding, me too. So we've been on a couple of dates."

"That is *amazing*. God, that's so great." He wanted to ask if Lauro had told Tani about his work. But maybe it didn't matter.

Lauro answered the unspoken question. "I told her about Stroked the third time we met up. She said, give me a minute. I was dying inside. She was staring at me while she drank her margarita and I could *see* her thinking. Then she finally says something, and it's 'how boring is that.'"

Manny laughed. "I guess you said, it's pretty boring."

"Uh-huh." They settled back on the loungers and started talking about the soldier story.

March 2017

Irv wasn't actually surprised that Manny and Patrice said he could videotape their conversation. If he were going through a transition like that he would want some kind of record of how he was feeling about it. And she'd been going through it for a long time. His mercenary commercial side wanted to tape it, partly because she was so accessible. She probably looked like a girl when she was a growing up. Definitely looked like a girl now. Still, Irv didn't know how anyone had the guts to go through the change. If hearing it from her was helping him get it, maybe someday they could release a clip that would help other people get it.

Because he was open to the conversation going in whatever direction it went, and because they'd already discussed so many things, he had Patrice review his standard agreement. She gave him a sharp look after reading it through. Then she went to talk to Manny in the corner for a few minutes, real quiet so Irv couldn't hear. Their body language told him everything. When she came back over, she asked him for a pen and signed the papers. "Manny says you won't fuck me over," she said. "He likes you. He trusts you."

"This ain't the Seventies," he said. "We're in this together or not at all." He tucked the document into his messenger bag, thinking. "Where you want to set up?"

Manny could almost read Irv's mind. He thought that Manny and Patrice were going to get up to something. And weirdly, even though they weren't here to work on the soldier story, it didn't seem to bother him. Manny couldn't decide if he *wanted* Irv to be bothered. They hadn't had that conversation. That 'are you planning to fuck anybody else' conversation. Or maybe it was, 'do you *want* to fuck anybody else.' Manny had about a thousand chances while he was in Mexico, but that kiss-and-cuddle with Patrice was as close as he got. Was Irv interested in seeing that? Was he looking at Manny as just another model right now? *Do I want him to stop me.* "Could I talk to you for a sec?"

"Sure."

"Take a look around, Patrice. See where you'd be comfortable." She smiled back at him and waved him

233

away. Manny crossed the room, took Irv by the hand, and led him into the kitchen. "I want to say something to you."

"Okay?"

"Me and Patrice, we got close. We're friends."

"You and I are friends, too," Irv said cautiously.

"Is that all, though?" Irv's eyes went wide. Manny gave it a second. "I care about you, Irving. I haven't been with anyone else since we started working together. And I'd be exclusive with you if you wanted."

Irv heard a whole lot underneath those words. "Manuel." He wrapped an arm around his lover, heart painfully full. It might be the worst time in the world to say this; it might be the best. Only one way to find out. "I am that absolute cliché of a guy. You ever hear of a thing called 'Pygmalion?'" He could tell from the blank look that the answer was No. "Ever seen 'My Fair Lady?'" A confused shake of the head. "Okay, gotta find my own way to say this. I wanted to help you make something of yourself. Find yourself, then become the best version of yourself. Be successful on your own terms, and be respected. I wanted all that for you. I still do, and I want you to be happy, because I love you."

Manny sucked in a breath. "Irving."

"You don't have to say anything. You don't have to say it back. It doesn't even matter if you love me back, I'm gonna love you anyway." His voice went wrong on that. He swallowed and looked away, blinking. If he could have he would have left the room, but Manny was holding him too tight. A long hug, both of them breathing unsteadily, and then Manny's hand on his face as he went for a kiss. It was soft and sweet, like their very first kiss.

234

After a minute Manny moved an inch or two back, rested his forehead against Irv's, and said, "I love you too. I do. I don't care if it's a cliché. You're the first man since Lobo who's treated me like a whole person, but that's not all of why."

"Who cares why?" They both laughed a little. "Okay, Manuel. Here's the truth, and here's the deal. I haven't been with anybody else since I met you, and I don't want to be. Back in December I had a moment where I thought, I don't want him touching anybody else, or anybody else touching him. I wanted you all to myself. But I got over that. Me loving you doesn't mean you're on a leash or in a box. It doesn't mean I own you. If you want to get busy with someone else, all I really care about is you play safe. If you want to get busy with Patrice that's fine. If you let me put it on video and sell it, hey." Manny was laughing under his breath. "All that time you were doing those solos I was thinking, goddamn, if he let someone else touch him he'd be a gold mine." Manny laughed out loud. "I know, I'm a disgusting old horndog and all I care about is money."

"Claro que no," Manny pointed out. "You've been telling me I shouldn't do any more scenes."

"Well, let's think about it. Just because we tape something doesn't mean we have to release it."

Manny nodded. "We best go find her before she thinks I'm having second thoughts."

CHAPTER 12

They started with how Patrice got the part on 'Alhambra.' That terrifying reveal, and the back-and-forth (involving her agent and, briefly, her lawyer) about whether they would even let her audition for the trader's wife. An hour later, the conversation had gone from basic history through twenty years of ways and means. Manny and Patrice were on a double lounger under the pergola; they each had a drink in hand. "I couldn't afford the surgery until recently," Patrice said. She swirled the ice cubes in her Cape Cod. "Until I got in the union and got some health insurance. Lord, was I happy to get my titties!" Manny cracked up. She swatted him on the arm. "Cállate! I looooove my titties. They're nice, aren't they Irv?"

"You are not supposed to be talking to me," he said, trying not to absolutely guffaw.

"Oh who gives a fuck about that. Everybody knows somebody's behind the camera. I should get my phone out. Get all meta on your ass. I'm taking a video of you taking a video of me."

"What was that like, though? I've never had surgery." Manny bumped his shoulder against hers. "Did it hurt a lot?"

"It hurt like fire, baby. They had to stretch the skin. It was so many trips back. This little implant, then a little bit bigger. I didn't want big ol' giant titties. All I wanted was enough. But I was sore, it was a mess. If I didn't have someone helping me around the house then, I would have been one sorry bitch."

"You look great, though. The scars hardly even show."

"Was I lucky? I've seen some awful scars. But I'm so close now. Only the bottom things left to do." She shivered a little, because those things were major.

Manny wrapped his arm around her shoulders. "How do they even do that? I mean it's none of my business. You don't have to tell me."

"Child, please. If I didn't want to talk about this shit I would have slapped you back six months ago. You are sweet as sugar. Isn't he, Irv?"

"Yes, he is."

"This is the part everybody freaks out about. It's like, okay, titties. Everybody and their sister gets fake titties. But when you're talking about cutting your dick off, they go OH HELL NO. And that's what it is." She shrugged. "That thing's got to *go*. I can never feel like a real woman while I've still got a dick. You want to hear how they do it?"

Manny wasn't sure he did, but he said "Yes" anyway. Then Patrice asked Irv if she should show the camera what she meant, and he nodded.

"Okay." She stood up, kicked off her high-heeled sandals, unzipped her jeans, and peeled them down. "Commando! Woo hoo!" Manny and Irv both laughed. "I like it breezy, y'all. Here we go." She sat down again on the edge of the lounger, legs apart, one foot up. Irv moved around to frame the shot better. "Now you see, I've had the orchidectomy. Balls go bye-bye, don't need them. Since then the hair situation really changed. And speaking of hair, I've already done the electrolysis, and that hurt like a bitch too. That's because some of this is going to get turned outside in, and don't nobody want a pussy that's hairy on the inside. They go in right here. Make an incision. They keep as much of the skin here as they can, the scrotum.

237

They take the penis out of its skin. Trim down the urethra." She glanced up at the camera. "That's what you pee through, children. They make a clitoris. Did you know a woman's clitoris is like a tiny little penis? Yes Lord. So if everything goes right, I can still orgasm that way. I keep my prostate, my G spot. And they use the tissue from the penis and scrotum to make me a vulva." She put her foot on the ground, knees still apart. Cupped her hands between her legs. "It's going to hurt."

Manny shifted in behind her, wrapping one arm around, cheek against hers. Her tone had been matter-of-fact, but she was trembling. Possibly from the stress of talking about this. "No way to make it not hurt, is there. How long will you be in the hospital?"

"A few days. It's a fuck of a lot of money. I've been saving twenty years to do this."

"Damn, girl."

"I had to decide between what they call a vaginoplasty, where they build me on the inside, and vulvoplasty. The second one is less invasive, less risky, less expensive. It doesn't let a lover get up in you that way."

"Which did you choose?"

"Vulvoplasty. I've lived my truth with a dick for forty years. What is essential for me now is to see and feel the body I always thought I should have. Being fucked like a woman, for some people it's essential." She turned her head, smiling at Manny. "I decided it wasn't for me. I'm real curious to find out how the vulva works, though. One of my girls told me she gets off better by having her man rub his dick on her vulva than by having him inside her." She glanced at the camera again and said, in her best teacher voice,

238

"That's *frottage*, kids at home." Manny snickered. "I had my doubts about the other way, because a real vagina gets juicy and a built one wouldn't. And when I thought about it, I was like, okay. Oral works. Anal works. Frottage works. A hand job works. That's as many ways to play as I ever had. And it's not like I wouldn't tell somebody. Pull the old bait and switch. That's a good way to get beat up."

"I got beat up once. Have you ever been?"

She nuzzled Manny's face. "I've been beat up. I've been raped. I've been having the bad part of being a woman all my life." They were both quiet for a moment. "A couple of friends are like, call me when you're ready. They want to try out my new pussy." Manny pressed a kiss to her neck. "Mmm. How about you, vaquero? You ever done a girl?"

"Sure." He mumbled it against her shoulder. On the other side of the camera, Irv thought *oh, here we go*.

"You call yourself gay, though." Patrice twisted around a little to see him better. Not enough to pull away from Manny's arm, only enough that her legs folded together.

"I haven't thought about it for a long time." Manny was looking at his hand, resting on Patrice's ribs, or possibly at her bare thighs. "I guess yeah. I always knew it was boys, and then men. But girls don't gross me out. I dated girls in high school. I had sex with girls. Only went all the way once, and I was scared to death she would get pregnant. It was my first time using a condom, it was before I had sex with a boy. I was like, this is ridiculous. But you have to. It's," he shook his head. "So, what. Is that bi? I don't know anybody who

239

says they're bi. I thought that meant you want men and women equally."

"I guess it does. Because a lot of us can *function* with either, right?"

"Right." They gazed at each other at close range. "You're so pretty." Patrice blushed, trying to wave it off. Manny was grinning. He was aware of Irv in that moment, glad they'd had that conversation. Glad the man knew if he kissed Patrice right now it didn't mean he wanted Irv less.

Patrice took the lead. "Irv, honey. You mind if I kiss your sugar baby?"

"Not at all. But how about we cut here, and take a break." He almost regretted saying that. They were probably both a little worked up from that heavy conversation. If they wanted to come back to it in half an hour, fine. In the meantime, they could all get hydrated, refreshed, whatever. Patrice did kiss Manny, on the cheek, before they got off the lounger. She wriggled back into her jeans. Irv carried the tripod and camera in, then went to the powder room, leaving the other two bathrooms for his subjects. From there he went to the kitchen to see what they had to eat. You couldn't always guess how long a shoot was going to go, and people worked better when they weren't starving. Or thirsty. Or jonesing for coffee. The place was always stocked.

Manny met up with him there a few minutes later. "Hey."

"Hey yourself." Irv stood aside, making way for Manny to help himself to whatever. He assembled a plate of cheese and crackers, carved up an apple, regarded Irv thoughtfully while he started to eat. "What?"

"Is this where we start?" He meant for their movie.

Irv watched Manny for a few seconds, thought about erotica, decided he thought that was the way to go. "Tell you what I'd really love to shoot."

"What's that."

"Glamour stuff. Soft lighting, lots of undressing and kissing and hands. Romantic. Like, ninety percent foreplay. Then if you two wanted to take it further, figure some angles. I want to be able to sell this mainstream." He could tell from the way Manny's shoulders relaxed that they were on the same page now. "Want me to get Lauro over here to help out?" Irv knew he was around.

"Yeah, that'd be good."

A few minutes later, Lauro joined them and they started brainstorming the story. "Maybe this is right before you go to boot camp. After the house party. You've been together a while. You're sure about each other even though you personally aren't sure about the military for a career."

Manny nodded. "We're excited, a little bit scared. Looking at a big life change and wondering what it'll mean for us, like that dialogue scene you sent."

"You could do that as voiceover."

Manny thought about it while he ate some more. It was good they could do this with Lauro; the timing was right. "What kind of costume do you have here for girls?"

"That's what I was about to ask!" Patrice came into the kitchen. "When I put these jeans on today I wasn't thinking of getting on camera." She'd carried her shoes in from the pool deck and chucked them in a corner of the living room with her tote bag. She was still as tall as Irv.

241

"Irv was just saying he'd like to do some glamour with you. Or with us. Love scene more than sex scene. Were you thinking that way?" She was freshly made-up and definitely looked camera-ready.

"Mmm, I had to get my face on, that's all. What do *you* think?"

Manny glanced at Lauro, who told her the idea for the scenario. She clapped her hands, held them clasped at her chest. *Good, that's what she wanted too.* "I never did even a pictorial with another person, but we trust each other, right?"

"Of course," she said, looking amused.

"Here's how we could work it." Irv made a few logistical suggestions. The four of them could handle the set dressing and the gear just fine.

After they had the room set up, Patrice looked around, sighed, and admitted, "I don't even know what will happen. If I'd get hard. I don't want it to look like I have a dick."

Irv said, "No one will know, I promise."

"How about we only shoot you head to toe from the back," Manny suggested. "Full nudity, but not full frontal."

She looked relieved. "Yeah, okay. That's good."

Irv agreed. "Let's get you in costume and get started. We've got plenty of time."

"Nothing but time," Manny said. "And maybe a shot of something." The bar cabinet was fully stocked, too.

"Ooh child, yes. Let me see what's in this closet." Patrice waited for Irv to lead the way. Manny got into the Army Rangers tee shirt they'd acquired for his last solo scene. Added eye makeup so it would look like

242

this was late at night, post-party, a little bit drunk maybe. Jeans, bare feet, ready to go. Patrice came back in wearing a cotton sun dress that showed off her shoulders and legs, with kitten-heeled sandals instead of her own towering shoes. "This way I won't be taller than you," she said. "I know you like to be the tall one."

Lauro was snickering as he set the tequila bottle and shot glasses on the dresser. Manny rolled his eyes and said, "Let's get to work."

Irv thought, when he looked at the video again the next day, that it was kind of a breakthrough. It was filmmaking, not only videotaping. They took it slow, with multiple setups, which meant by the time Manny and Patrice finally got down to business they were both really ready for it. Her orgasm was definitely real. She did that as beautifully as Manny did, those big eyes closed, lips parted, neck arching while Manny made a happy sound from between her legs. When Irv asked Manny about that later he said, "She didn't get hard, so I couldn't tell at first if what I was doing was gonna work. Had to learn how to read that situation. Wild."

"The camera loves her. When it's released, though," he shook his head, whistling. Manny was half-laughing. "There's going to be a whole Reddit about was that real."

"Yeah." Manny leaned back against the headboard, gazing at Irv thoughtfully. "What about the rest of it?" They'd tried a few different things before deciding on how Manny should finish. And that was real too, with his cock between her thighs, carefully framed.

"It looked like you had a fantastic time."

Manny was slightly embarrassed. "It's been a really long time since I did that."

"You can do it to me anytime." Manny laughed. Irv was grinning. "The look on your face was epic. You were like, oh *yeah*." They both giggled. "You're really great together."

"And you seriously didn't mind? I mean, it was kind of a special occasion, but still. If it's bad for us, you and me, I won't do that again once we're done with this."

Irv set the laptop aside, got a hand around Manny's arm, and tugged him over. Both of them wriggled until they were lying down, Manny with his head on Irv's shoulder. "I'm really glad we had that talk before everything started. Glad you gave me such a perfect opening to tell you I love you. It may be part of how weird I am, but I seriously didn't mind. Especially after we said those things. I enjoyed watching the two of you, I think it's going to be a great piece of film when I get it cut together, and I'm okay with more things like that happening if you decide you want them to."

"Part of that is we both know she's super clean, isn't it." Manny's voice was soft.

"Well, yeah. Not everybody's going to come through the door with a medical file. Plus, you told me about her in advance. I knew you were friends, knew you were attracted to her. I had time to get used to that idea, up here on my own. And to top it all off, I like her. She's righteous. She has a good reason for wanting to celebrate her body, and I'm not the man who's gonna say find someone else to celebrate with. She trusts you. She decided to trust me. It's an honor."

Manny kissed his chest. "You're right. That's how I felt. I didn't put that word with it, but that's it. You know what else I like about her?"

"What's that." Irv was brushing his fingers up and down Manny's arm. He really loved this, the cuddling, lying in bed together talking.

"I like that she's so real. She's like you. Her hair is her hair, her nails are her nails, her face is her face. You can tell she's older than me but, I don't know. I think she's beautiful."

"Not like me, then."

Manny swatted him. "I love you for you. Nobody else looks like you."

"Thank God."

"Cállate! Estás loco!" He hitched himself up. "I love your mouth." He kissed it. "I love your freckles." He kissed those. "I love your foxy eyebrows." More kisses. Irv was laughing. "Those foxy green eyes. I love your big ol' nose." They were both laughing. "I got a big ol' nose too."

"Yours works a little better with the rest of your face." The last word was muffled because Manny was kissing him again.

The soldier story was only one of the projects they were all working on, but it was the one they thought about most. Lauro finished the script and made a scene chart; Irv formed a company, got a few friends involved to help finance the thing, and started booking locations. Manny and Patrice rehearsed a lot, in between auditions or other business. They wanted to work out a complete story so they knew everything that wasn't going to be onscreen. The misunderstandings or fights, the start of their relationship, the things happening with each of them while they were apart. That led Manny back to the conversation with Irv the day they filmed the main love scene. He brought it up to Patrice one day when he was over at Dolores' house. "Do you think we're exclusive?" He meant their film characters.

She looked down at him from her position on the couch. "You're getting pretty good at that yoga shit," she observed. "I don't know. I kind of doubt it. Would you have been, really?"

Manny shook his head slowly. "Me and Lobo weren't, not after he went to boot camp. We said all kinds of things to each other about the future. We said I love you. It was like, things might happen but you're the one I'll always come back to. The one I want to live with someday when we get our shit together. I didn't go with other guys while we were together in high school. But he left when we were eighteen. He only came home a couple times after that." He didn't need to add 'before he died.'

She nodded sympathetically. "I hear you. Did you tell each other about people you hooked up with?" He shook his head again. "Kept it to yourselves? So when you were talking, it was all about you."

"Uh-huh."

"What made you think of that right now?"

He shifted to another position, shrugged. "I talked about it with Irv. Told him I'd be exclusive if he wanted."

"What'd he say?"

"Said he didn't want anyone else but if I did it was okay with him. As long as I'm safe." Patrice clicked her tongue. Manny grinned. "I don't really want anyone else either, but that was right when you and me were about to get naked." She laughed. "What about you?"

"What about me? Oh, you mean was I ever exclusive with someone? Mm-hmm. Never did me no

246

good, but." She shrugged. "I was always looking for my one and only. My Mr. Right. Finally figured out I was better off with Mr. Right Now."

He didn't quite buy it, but he steered them back to their fictional relationship. They could use that tension – being in love but knowing that there were other people while they were apart – to shade their scenes. Now he was curious about Irv, though. When he found the right moment, he'd ask.

Even with some confidence that there wouldn't be a better moment, Manny was glad he didn't actually have to ask. They were lying on the couch, halfway-watching a scene Irv just finished editing for the site. "You're getting as jaded as me," Irv said. "Not even turned on, are you."

Manny lifted his head off Irv's chest to make eye contact. "Twenty minutes ago you had my dick in your mouth." Irv laughed. "We were doing sixty-nine right here." He slid his hand down Irv's body. "Yeah, you're done for a while too." They were both ignoring the playback, grinning at each other. "I really like this."

Irv knew what he meant. "I like it too. It's so different from the other time I lived with someone."

"What all is different." Manny laid his head down again, thinking Irv might speak more freely without someone staring at him.

"Well, for starters, we were both in school. I was doing my master's in film studies and he was in law school." Irv hadn't really thought about Drake for a long time. Hadn't ever mentioned him, he realized. But Manny told him all about Lobo, so Irv owed him. "It wasn't as bad as I thought," he said after a minute to think. "I mean, for a while I thought, jeez, that sucked.

247

Over the winter when I was organizing my shit I started thinking about it another way."

"Like how?"

"Like, I remembered we weren't actually boyfriends." He felt Manny's belly jump with a stifled laugh. "No kidding. For a long time I was all, that was a terrible relationship."

"You ever talk to him?"

"No." He regretted that now. "The last six months or so we did a lot of yelling at each other. I honestly can't remember whose fault it was."

"Maybe nobody's," Manny suggested. "What do you think he'd say about it?"

"Fuck if I know." Irv realized he was curious. "Reach me my phone."

Manny thought *really?!* but sat up enough to stretch over to the desk surface and get hold of Irv's phone. "You still have his number?"

"No, but he'll be easy to find." Irv got busy Googling. Before long the phone was ringing. He put it on speaker, not at all sure he knew what he was doing but positive he'd tell Manny all about it anyway.

After two rings someone picked up. "Drake Gardner's office."

"Hi, my name is Irving Morton. Drake and I were at UCLA together. I had a question for him if he has a minute." He knew 'at UCLA' would be taken to mean they were in law school together.

"Just a moment." The line went silent.

It really was just a moment before the line went live again. It sounded like speakerphone. "Irv?"

"Drake, hi."

"Do you need a lawyer or is this something else? We haven't spoken for, Jesus, fourteen years?"

"Close enough. Honestly I have all the lawyers I need but if you have a minute I could use some help filling in a blank in my memory."

"Hang on." Manny and Irv heard a slight rustle and then the click of a door closing. After a second Drake was back on the line, now obviously holding the handset. "I've got ten minutes."

"How do you like San Francisco?"

"It's good. What are you up to?"

"Making porn." Irv waited for the laughter to die down. "It's a living. Anyway, I spent part of the winter organizing my past life because I was planning to ask someone to live with me."

"Is he living with you?"

"Yeah, he's right here. Say hello to Manuel Figueroa."

"Hello Mr. Figueroa."

"Hi Mr. Gardner, call me Manny."

"Sure thing. Call me Drake. Listen, this is super weird."

Irv stifled a laugh. "I know, I'm sorry. Quick rewind. You had the apartment and there was a roommate-wanted ad. That's how we met, right?"

"Right."

"Who made the first pass? I have this idea it was you."

"It was totally not me," Drake said, sounding amused. "Not that I didn't want to. You were hot as fuck back in the day. Still look like that?"

249

Manny propped himself up to see Irv's incredulous expression, tried not to laugh, and said, "I don't know what he looked like in grad school but I think he's hot as fuck now. He made the pass?"

"He came in from some film-student bullshit and he was all worked up. There was booze at the thing. I was on the couch watching something instead of reading cases and I'd had a couple beers too. I was like, how'd it go. He was all, we were screening our shorts, and then he kind of pounced on me."

"I did?!"

Manny and Drake both laughed. After a second, the lawyer said, "You were like, I've been meaning to do this. Next thing I knew we had our pants off. Good grief, I can't believe you didn't remember that."

"I did," Irv protested. "I just thought you started it. I remember us fighting a lot toward the end. Did I start that too?"

"No, I did. I was in third year and looking at moving up here. I wanted you to come with me."

"Oh, shit, that's right. Manny, don't get old, you forget stuff. I was the asshole. Were we both seeing other people or was that just me, too?"

"We both were." Drake's tone was still amused. "We weren't calling each other boyfriend. It was all, this is my roommate. Friends with benefits. But I would have gone for more."

Irv made an 'eek' face at Manny. "I'm sorry. Can I give you a general apology for all the bullshit I pulled? Because I'm sorry."

"No worries. It wouldn't have worked out. I wanted a security blanket. Guaranteed roommate, guaranteed person to sleep with. Someone I knew, because the next step was going to be so much new stuff and I didn't want to be alone for it."

Irv blinked. "Damn. You've really thought this through."

"Did some time in therapy."

"Seeing anybody now?"

"Uh." There was a pause, as if Drake were considering whether he should answer. "Actually, sort of. I met someone three years ago when I was down in L.A. for depositions. He was staying in the same hotel I was. Another lawyer. He's from India."

Irv instantly started his mental recorder, thinking this was a great setup for a new scene for Stroked. "What was he doing in L.A.?"

"He was here as a tourist mostly. Came over for a wedding. The widow of his longtime partner was getting married."

Irv picked up his head to frown at Manny, who made a WTF face. Irv had no idea. "What the fuck?"

"Rabi was in a long-term relationship with an architect who was married to a woman. Being gay is basically illegal in India."

"Still?!"

"Yeah, still. Anyway. The architect was killed in a worksite accident. The widow already lived here in L.A., and she was in a relationship with someone here. She and Rabi were friendly. So he came to the wedding."

"And you met. Can I put that in a scene?"

"Jesus, Irv!"

Manny stifled another laugh against Irv's chest. Irv ran his hand over Manny's head, smiling. "No identifying characteristics, I promise. The scenario is great though. So, he's still in India?"

"We're working on it. Anyway it's been unexpectedly great to talk to you but I have a conference call in just barely enough time to go take a leak."

"Can I call you again sometime? I get up to SF."

"Sure. Bring Manny. If I want to see what kind of porn you make, where do I go?"

Irv gave him the website address. "Nice talking to you, Drake. Thanks for giving me the time. And good luck with Rabi."

"Thanks. Good luck to you, too." He disconnected.

Irv and Manny reorganized themselves, sitting up, staring at each other. After a minute Manny said, "So you remembered about half of what happened there."

Irv sighed, leaning his head on the back of the couch. "I was such an egomaniac then. Everything was about me. It's no wonder I didn't want to remember being a dick. He's a nice guy."

"Yeah, sounds like it. Show me that website, where you found him." Irv navigated back to it, found Drake's bio, turned the phone so Manny could see it. "Hmm." Irv stifled a laugh. Manny studied him. "He had more hair in law school?" Irv laughed out loud.

April 2017

The chauffeured SUV was idling at the end of a line of similar vehicles, all waiting to decant their passengers at the 'Alhambra' red carpet. "I am about to pee my pants, I'm so excited," Patrice said. "And if it wouldn't mess up my makeup, my nose would literally be pressed up against this window."

Manny patted her thigh. "This is crazy, right?" His other hand was tight in Irv's. He was glad Patrice asked to ride with them instead of going in her own car. She glanced at her buzzing phone. Manny nudged her. "Dolores again?"

"She's mad as fire."

Irv laughed. The stylist would have been Patrice's plus-one, if not for a previous commitment. "Too bad about that wedding."

Patrice made a huffy sound. "I'm just glad y'all let me come with you."

"Wish we could tell people about our project." Manny was so charged up about the soldier story, it almost overtook this event on the list of Most Cool Things in Life. Almost, but not quite. The SUV edged forward again. There was a mob of press where the vehicles were stopping. He and Patrice had been given copies of the press kit, so they knew what people would be seeing today: the first two episodes, and then a trailer for the other eleven. They'd each be getting a swag bag, which (rumor had it) would include the whole season on DVD. Manny couldn't wait to watch it all. He was dying to know what Irv would think. Would it show, how Manny got better? Had they managed to blend in their performances well enough? Would Irv think he was good in it? Maybe it shouldn't matter, but it did. He was the whole reason Manny got the job.

The next event was going to be less nerve-wracking. Manny was invited to the premiere of 'Countdown.' And of course, Irv was his plus-one for that, too. They wouldn't be walking the red carpet for the press; they'd be in a separate lane, heading through to the guest entrance, to sit and wait for the name cast to come in and introduce the movie. They'd both been to premieres as guests before, but Manny was still really looking forward to it. By then Patrice would have had her surgery, and they'd have started filming the third-act scenes for their movie. He couldn't quite believe all this was happening.

"Wish I could go to your next one, too," she said, as if she'd read his mind.

"I'll take you to see it once you're on your feet," he promised. The SUV moved forward again. Any minute now. "I look okay?" He turned toward Irv as he spoke.

"You look sensational." The new tuxedo fit like a glove, and of course Manny had the perfect body to wear a tux. His hair was super-short, just long enough to look like hair and not stubble. He'd let his beard grow for the past week, which meant he looked almost exactly the way he did when they met. *But now he's mine*, Irv thought, mind blown all over again. His sexy lover, his favorite model, and better-every-day actor, starring in the first legit film Irv had made since 2005. "And here we go." The SUV stopped and security people reached for the passenger-door handles.

Patrice was first out, facing the press with her chin up and a wide smile. She was wearing a dress provided by Red's friend Lesley. It had exactly the right exotic, antique flavor to it without being a costume. Her hair was up, showing off a gold-plated diadem set with red-orange stones and a pair of matching earrings. Manny thought she looked gorgeous. He took a picture with his phone. Took another, of the whole red-carpet craziness. Turned to smile at Irv. "Can you believe this?"

Irv wanted to say 'I'm so glad you're getting to have this experience' but now was not the time. He just smiled, moved toward the offered hand, and looked down the line to see what was happening. Somehow he was not expecting horses. Marco Hidalgo (still recovering from the on-set injury) was there with his wife, both in costume. It looked as though they were talking to a huge horse. "Jesus, is that thing bigger than Red's?"

"She is big." Manny was even more excited now. He figured he would have been given a heads-up if Saluki were there, so he wasn't surprised not to see the old horse. But he could see Tiburon's black stallion down at the far end of things. When he looked around again, Irv was six feet away. "Wait, where are you going?"

"I was going to hang back, let you walk with Patrice."

Manny gave him a narrow-eyed look and reached for his hand. Gave the other one to Patrice. "All together." They started down the red carpet.

Irv wasn't expecting to get any sense out of his TV stars at the end of the event, and he didn't. There was an after-party, which wasn't much of anything aside from music and a buffet of finger food, except there was another screen back there showing rehearsal clips. He kept catching himself watching that, waiting for Manny to show up on screen, instead of watching the actual guy. But it looked as though Manny and Patrice were having fun catching up with their cast-mates. The contracts had gone out, and all of the name characters in the first-season cast would be returning. Irv was glad the show was going forward, glad Manny and Patrice would get a chance to build on the work they'd done in the first season. He heard about it all the way home.

Then he took a day off to binge-watch the whole season with Manny. Now he knew where some of

Patrice's ideas came from, for staging the scenes where she was deployed. And now he could really appreciate the work Manny put in on his voice. "You did a great job taking all that on board," he said at the end of the day, when they took a walk to shake out the kinks from all that couch time. "And good job modulating it from start to finish."

"Thanks." Manny was truly pleased. "When we started up for the second half, Patrice had all these notes about where we were in the first half. Shooting out of order like that, I would've been lost. Like, did I develop this piece of business here, or there. Did I talk to her that way then, or later."

"How much of your own stuff did you get to see?"

"They ran it for us at camp. Rodrigo, one of the producers, he was in charge of continuity. So he'd come in with his laptop and we'd have a meeting. Like, here's what we're shooting tomorrow, and here's what it goes with. Lifesaver."

"You did good."

"What did you like best?" It probably wasn't fair to ask. How could anyone remember, after watching all that.

Irv didn't even have to think about it. "That scene in the last episode where it's implied Patrice is finally pregnant, or pregnant again. She goes to get that basket of whatever out of the cart and you stop her."

"Oh yeah." Manny smiled. He liked that scene too. Where he said, go tend the fire, you are too slow. The brusque tone of voice combined with the expression of concern. Taking the basket out of her hands, heaving it to the table set ready for market day. Then walking past her at the fire, brushing the back of his finger lightly down her cheek as they made eye contact. Sharing the tiniest of smiles. "That might be our last market day together."

"Could be." Nothing was spelled out, but it was a good bet the trader's wife would have a house and servant in the next season, courtesy of the nobleman's second-in-command. A reward for the unofficial courier work the trader had done, or was doing. "You had a chance to talk to Marco last night."

"Yeah. He's doing good. He and Cameron are doing a bunch of shit this summer. I'll bet he wishes she could stay at base camp. I was wishing you were down there."

That shouldn't have pleased Irv as much as it did. Would Manny want him to visit? Should he suggest it? *Just say it.* "I could visit. Once you get the schedule. If you've got a couple days off in Mexicali, I could fly down."

Manny stopped walking, which since they were holding hands forced Irv to stop too. Turned, gazing at him for a long moment with a look softer than any he'd given Patrice on the show. "You would do that?"

"I'm going to miss you." No point not saying it. Apparently it was the right thing to say, because Manny tugged him closer and kissed him.

CHAPTER 13

May 2017

It was far from the first time Irv had gone to see a movie with no interest in the actual movie. Well, he had *some* interest in 'Countdown;' the advance buzz was good and, if nothing else, it had Victor Garcia to look at. More to the point, it had the traffic-jam scene with Manny, which was over much too fast to suit Irv. Even though the editors made it look as though he was riding about ten miles. The swag bag didn't contain a DVD, so he was going to have to buy one later. Maybe they'd put a behind-the-scenes feature in, about how that craziness was shot.

The premiere was kind of huge. There were hundreds of civilian guests as well as all the cast and crew. The movie's star Jonathan Morris introduced the film, cracking a few jokes about his slow ascent from pro wrestler to cable-movie villain to headliner. He brought his co-star up for a few minutes. They both showed up at the after-party, too, acting like they'd been friends all their lives. Irv glanced at Manny. "Are they for real?"

"Uh-huh." Manny was smiling. "They like each other."

"The big guy's waving at you. Go say Hi." He sent Manny in that direction, watching him make his way through the crowd, then watching the short conversation that followed. He got distracted for a second by Victor and his boyfriend, laughing at something on the far side of the room, before both of them headed for the exit. A minute later Jonathan was moving that way too, scooping up a nice-looking woman from another little knot of conversation. Irv looked for Manny again, spotted him, watched him approach. *Jesus he's gorgeous.* "What'd he say?"

"They're heading over to Miami in a minute to make the sequel. He was all, sorry you can't be in this one too."

Irv blinked. That was awfully nice. "Did you tell him about your show?"

"Uh-huh. He was like," Manny had to stop for a second to compose himself, putting on Jonathan's voice. "Oh yeah I've been watching that, heard about it from Garcia. Did you know he was in a play with that guy Hidalgo? How much shit is there on set?" Back in his own voice. "I was cracking up."

Irv was too; it was a good impression. "How much shit *was* there?"

"I'm trying not to remember," Manny admitted. "Glad I'm not on the livestock crew, that's all I can say." He caught hold of Irv's hand. "I don't think this will get any better. Ready to go home?"

"Why, have you got plans for me?"

Manny leaned in, speaking with his mouth against Irv's neck. "I always have plans for you. Venga." He couldn't resist taking a little bite. Loved doing that when they were out in public, getting them both stirred up. And he knew it always knocked Irv sideways, being treated like a sex object. He did some more of that on the escalator down to the parking garage, standing on the step below with his hands under Irv's tux jacket, teasing around his waistband, gazes locked. When they got to Irv's car Manny pinned him against the side. Full-body contact, kissing as if they were saying goodbye forever. He didn't stop until some driver honked at them and Irv started laughing. They both had to adjust themselves before getting in the car.

"I need to take some pictures of you in that tux," Irv said as he locked the loft door behind them.

"How about now?"

Irv turned around. Manny definitely had his 'we're about to fuck' face on; if he wanted to be on camera for it, Irv was not about to say No. "Gonna strip for me?"

"I'll strip." Manny took a few steps backward, toward the stairs. "Maybe you could strap me in." Raising his hands, gripping the railing suggestively.

Oh Jesus fuck. Irv swallowed. "Think that bow tie would make a decent blindfold?"

"Let's find out." Manny's voice sounded husky. They stared at each other for a few seconds. Then they both moved. Irv headed for his camera, yanking a tripod out from under the work surface. Manny went for one of the light rigs, setting it up with a diffuser. They each took a turn in the bathroom. When Manny returned to the main room, Irv was still in his tux, doing something with the camera. A pile of black leather straps was at his feet. The red recording light went on. That must mean he was in frame. "What's the story?"

"Fuck if I know. I ran off with the groom at a wedding?" Manny laughed. "You're James Bond and I'm the bad guy?"

"I saw that scene."

Irv came out from behind the camera, grinning. "We've made that scene a bunch of times. None of those guys were as hot as you."

"You make me hot."

They never used weapons, not even toy ones, so Irv forced Manny back by stepping into his space. "Stop trying to distract me, Mr. Bond." Backing him toward the stairs. "Now strip."

"If you think I can't escape in the nude, you're sadly mistaken." Manny had no idea if his accent was even close to right.

Irv almost died. Where the hell did Manny learn an English accent? Oh yeah, Red's wife Mary. *Focus*. He had to remind himself to breathe any time they played like this. "No stalling, Mr. Bond. Those shoes won't take themselves off." *And I'm not kneeling at your feet, not yet*.

Manny took his time, moving with slow deliberate grace. He'd learned that over the past two years, how to pace it so the camera had time to focus. Setting up the best frame-captures. Shoes off, staring arrogantly at Irv, waiting for the next command. Jacket, thrown at Irv, who caught it and instantly flung it at the recliner. Fortunately he'd dragged that closer. The trousers went next.

Irv was trying not to actively drool. He'd put a yellow gel on the light, going for that sodium streetlamp vibe since the rest of the room was dark. "Get that tie off." Catching it, tucking it in his pocket. "Now your shirt." Irv let that fall at his feet. Manny's skin looked so fucking edible he wanted to lick it. "As always, admirably fit, Mr. Bond."

"They don't give the double O to just anyone." Manny shifted his body, knowing how his muscles would catch the light. He should have felt ridiculous standing there in snug black boxer briefs, dress socks, and his new wristwatch. But he was in character as a man who could kill somebody with his bare hands, and thanks to Red and Kate he could play that now. "You won't mind if I check the time? I have somewhere to be." He started to raise his hand, the watch glinting suggestively in the light.

In a flash Irv was there, grabbing Manny's wrist and twisting. He went with it by reflex, but it was such a surprise that he was pressed face-first against the staircase before he knew what was happening. Irv's fingers at his wrist, the watch coming off, replaced by one of those leather cuffs. Hauling him around again, the cuff chained to the railing. "Not so cocky now, Mr. Bond."

I'll show you cocky, Manny thought, breathing through his mouth, trying to make his expression look vicious instead of insanely turned on. He faked a struggle as Irv fastened his other arm to the railing. They were both panting a little when Irv stepped back, rolling his neck. His back was to the camera and his eyes were asking if this was all right. Manny gave the tiniest nod, with the tiniest smile. Arching his spine and settling his hips, drawing Irv's attention to his massive hard-on. He didn't know how he managed not to laugh at Irv's expression, or at the silent 'fuck' the man shaped with his mouth, or at the way he had to adjust himself. Manny had a pretty good idea what was next. He did some more fake-struggling, swearing while Irv fastened on the collar, chaining it to the railing. Got his legs around Irv, grappling with him and pretending to kick. By the time that scuffle was over, Irv had Manny's briefs off. While he was catching his breath, Irv buckled on the ankle cuffs and chained them together. It was only slightly less uncomfortable than it looked; Manny was genuinely restrained now. And even more turned on.

Then came the blindfold. Not the tie; Irv had considered it, then discarded it as too thin. He wanted Manny's vision completely obscured for what came next. If this were a scene for Stroked, it would raise the stakes. Make the viewer wonder if this was going into

S&M. He stepped back, leaving Manny exposed to the camera.

After a few silent seconds Manny heard the faint sound of the camera's pause button, then Irv's voice. "You okay over there, baby?"

"I'm good. What're you doing?"

"Changing the camera angle."

That meant Irv was going to edit this later. Was he going to suck Manny off? Did he want that to really show up? What else was he going to do? Manny shivered a little. Even with absolute trust, being restrained like this – and blind – always shook him. Of course, that was part of the fun. He heard what sounded like Irv's shoes coming off, then next to nothing for a long moment. The faintest brushing sound, some kind of movement.

Irv watched Manny's body reacting to the tiny sounds Irv couldn't help making. Shoes, obviously. Taking off his jacket and tie. Undoing the top button of his shirt, rolling up his sleeves. Going to get a few things for the next part of the scene. God, he wished this could go on the site. Mostly because he knew it was going to be great. Irv might not be the sexiest man alive but with Manny in the picture nobody would complain. He was so tempted to say something when he stood at arm's length from Manny, watching him breathe. Instead he laid the tails of the flogger against his lover's thigh. Manny's whole body reacted: back arching, arms flexing against the restraints, chin going up. A sound, something between a grunt and a swear word. Irv brushed the tails up to his chest. He would never actually hit Manny; they'd talked about that. It was a hard limit for both of them. But after some experimentation they'd determined that Manny really got off on waiting for the touch. Waiting for Irv's touch, specifically. Being touched by other things while he was waiting made him frantic. And pushing him closer to the edge made Irv crazy.

He used the flogger for nearly ten minutes. Always light touches, dragging the deer-hide tails everywhere. Leaving Manny untouched for unpredictable lengths of time, then making contact again until Manny's chest was heaving with audible breaths. His erection was nearly vertical, flushed dark and dripping. Irv couldn't take it anymore. He tossed the flogger on the chair with all the discarded clothes, picked up a cushion and dropped it in front of Manny. Went to his knees and touched. The lightest touch, fingertips on the outside of Manny's knee, stroking up to his hip.

Manny felt Irv's hand – finally, skin against his own – and said "Oh *Jesus*." Almost a moan. Definitely a prayer. "Irving."

"Manuel." He said it with his face pressed into Manny's crotch, the 'L' sound turning into a lick up the side of that gorgeous package. Dragging his tongue across the slit, taking the head into his mouth, barely hearing his lover's cry. Both hands on Manny's hips now. He knew this wasn't going to take long. All he had to do was kneel here with his lips snug around this world-class cock, pressing with his tongue, opening his throat and breathing noisily while Manny fucked his mouth. God, the scent of him, the sound of him swearing, the change of shape and texture as climax neared. And the taste. If this were going on the site he'd pull off, let the camera see Manny come. But this was for them, so he stayed right where he was. Making a sound, a slightly-choked echo of Manny's, as the ejaculate hit the back of his throat. Another sound as he swallowed. Then he was on his feet, taking off the blindfold, kissing Manny hard. Unclipping the chains on his wrists and collar. Collapsing to the floor with Manny on top of him, still kissing.

Manny was only about half-sane at the moment but he could feel Irv's erection against his hip. He didn't want to stop kissing, so he got one hand down to Irv's fly and worked the trousers open. Slid his hand inside, wrapped it around that erection, and made a sound into Irv's mouth that meant 'go.'

A minute or so later, Irv had both arms wrapped around Manny. He was still on his back on the cold concrete floor. They were still lazily kissing. His shirt was a mess of sweat and come. Good thing it was machine-washable. A few more minutes passed before Manny changed position. "God *damn* this floor is cold." He shifted over, found that cushion, sat on it while he got the cuffs and collar off.

Irv made an affirmative sound and pushed himself up. "All right, baby? You need a minute?" In the chair, he meant, with the blanket. He always asked.

"I'm good." Manny sat there with his knees up, arms draped over them. He felt like cooked spaghetti, but he was fine. It was so different to do this, the restraints and the blindfold, when Irv touched him. "What am I going to see when we watch that? What were you doing when you weren't touching me?"

Irv laboriously got to his feet, shot a grin sideways as he tottered to the camera. "Putting a stranglehold on my dick so I wouldn't come." Manny laughed. Irv turned off the camera. Went to the light rig, switched that off. "Fuck, I'm exhausted."

"Me too. Let's go to bed." Manny stood up, checked in with himself, confirmed he was fine. He'd be even better once they were cuddled up in bed together. He slung an arm around Irv and steered them toward the stairs. "I love you."

"I love you too. Oh, fuck, I hate stairs." They were both still giggling when they reached the top.

June 2017

Irv didn't mind when Manny said he was taking Patrice out to see 'Countdown.' He wouldn't have minded even if Lauro and his girlfriend weren't going too. The past few months had been the best of his life, but an afternoon and evening alone were not unwelcome. After all those years living on his own, he still wasn't used to actually living with someone.

Manny knew, of course. He had a little bit of the same thing going. To counter all the things they did together now, they both scheduled time to do things separately. Plus they had work. Manny was keeping up with his various coaches, doing some riding out at Red's place, and picking up a job here and there. Irv was putting in about thirty hours a week of photography or filming for Stroked, another twenty or so on editing and site maintenance. It felt like he was cruising now that the soldier story was so far along.

They had nearly everything they needed in the can. The thought made Irv roll his eyes at himself, because of course this whole thing was shot on digital video. There was no 'can.' There wasn't even tape. Instead there was a binder full of page protectors, each one holding highlighted sheets of Lauro's scene chart and the SD card with the original shots. Everything was already loaded into the editing suite (and the backup drive), but Irv wasn't ready to start cutting it together.

Now that Patrice was up and around they only had one thing to shoot. It was going to be a bookend scene at the filming house, with the same gang of background actors they'd used for the going-away-to-boot-camp party scene. About half of those people were models for Stroked; the others were cast by Cyrus Garrett. His assistant Rita was going to be on hand to wrangle everything.

Once that was done … well, Irv wasn't entirely sure. There was always porn business. He was a little too busy to be developing anything new for the erotica division. The partners had sort-of-agreed that they should aim to release one hard-R title every year, which meant something should be in pre-production soon. A meeting was in order. Maybe Lauro had another screenplay in the works that they hadn't heard about. Or maybe Irv should get off his ass and reach out to a few of his legit contacts. He had more of those than Monica or Payton did.

One of them was, unbelievably, Jonathan Morris. He'd heard about the soldier story from Manny, which proved that Irv's lover knew how to work the system. The only time they'd been in the same room was at the 'Countdown' premiere. Somehow in that five minutes he managed to tell the movie star about the movie *he* was starring in. A couple weeks later, when Morris was already over in Miami starting work on the sequel, here came an email about a young streaming platform that was looking to acquire content. It had picked up a documentary Morris did voice-over for, and he knew some people. Even better, he was offering to put Irv in touch with those people. All he wanted was a synopsis and a rough trailer.

So Irv was working on the trailer while Manny and the gang were out on the town. Lauro already had a synopsis put together; he'd compiled the credits, too. Irv dithered for a few minutes about whether they needed that last scene before he did the trailer, but ultimately he decided to close it with the proposal. Manny on his knees in front of Patrice in her wheelchair. Tears on both faces. Patrice as lovely as a woman could be when she was in a hospital gown, hair in a ratty ponytail, no makeup. Thin and hollow-eyed, with a real bandage over the real wound from the IV in her hand.

Then he second-guessed himself and called a few people. Monica was not much help; Payton was no help at all. Finally Irv called Red, who picked up after so many rings Irv thought the phone must've been dropped out on the riding trail somewhere. "Hey Irv."

"Hey yourself. Am I interrupting?"

"If you were interrupting I wouldn't have answered the phone. I'm in the shop. Playing around with some prop design in between gigs."

"Glad I caught you. Listen, I have a stupid question." He heard a low laugh from Van Nuys. "Yeah, I know. I'm editing a pitch trailer for our soldier movie."

"Do you have a title yet?"

"We keep coming back to 'Honor.'"

"Yeah, that's good. So what's the question about the trailer."

"If I include a shot from the proposal scene, is that giving too much of the story away? Like, major spoiler? I've never cut a trailer before." They made so few feature-length things, and there was no point making a trailer for a short.

"Well, neither have I." There was a brief silence while Red thought about this. "Does the shot include Patrice saying yes?"

"No."

"Hmm. I think for a pitch that's probably good. I mean, you're signaling a happy ending, right? But you don't want to just hand it to them."

"Uh, okay. Yeah, I guess. I mean, we're marketing this as an erotic drama and Lauro made the synopsis read like a romance novel. But like the back cover copy, where there's that little bit of a question of whether they get their happy ending. You think that works?"

"Let me ask the expert." Another pause, not silent because Irv could hear Red calling to his wife. A brief off-mic discussion, of which Irv could hear little beyond an 'ooh' from Mary that sounded kind of enthusiastic. He was smiling when Red came back to the phone. "She likes it."

"Great. Thanks. So, uh." He stalled.

"What?"

Should I ask this other stupid question, or should I get the hell off the phone. Irv sighed. "When did you decide to ask Mary?"

"Ask her what? Oh! Ooh."

Red's sound of comprehension trailed off into a laugh; Irv almost disconnected. "Never mind, I –"

"No don't hang up. Um, I'm actually kind of, what. Touched? Yeah. That you asked me. Don't tell anybody I said that. I asked her the day after we said I love you, but Lesley kind of prompted it. So, not an expert here. Have you been saying that?"

"Yeah, a few months now. But it sounds like the one thing meant the other thing to you."

"It kind of did. Mary moved in with me a minute after 'Green Darkness' closed, and two months after that we were talking in the middle of the night and we said the L word, and then literally the next day Lesley said, so when are you getting married, and we hadn't even talked about it, because it was the next day. But after a minute to think, it just felt like if this, then that. You know?"

The funny thing was, that almost made sense. If they were in love, then marriage should at least be on the table. "Thanks, big guy. I'll let you get back to your power tools."

"Keep me posted." Red disconnected. Irv stared at the phone for half a minute, wondering when – and how – he should ask. Oddly enough, 'whether' was not in question.

Manny had the idea that Irv was talking himself into doing something. With everything they had going on, he doubted it had to do with the two of them, so he minded his own business. Lauro had come in with an idea for a new erotica screenplay (or, more accurately, with a half-written screenplay) inspired by his girlfriend's BFF and that guy's boyfriend. The Stroked partners talked it over and couldn't see a downside to having their second R feature be about two guys. If it didn't sell to a streaming platform or some other distributor, they could always market it through their own site. So that was in the works. Irv was busy editing 'Honor.' Manny had picked up a part in a raunchy rom-com shooting out in Ventura, so he was going back and forth for a few weeks. That led to trading in the truck, because its fuel economy was crap, and amazingly he now had the time and money to do better.

Patrice was taking it easy in L.A. They were planning to drive down to Mexicali together in

September. Manny's new Honda CRV would get its first road trip. It was so different, looking ahead now. Knowing that he'd be home with Irv at the holidays, and then at the end of the shoot.

But maybe before he planned on Los Angeles for the holidays, he should ask Irv the big question. Do it the same way he did the other thing, right before he left. That way if Irv said No, they'd have some time apart to get over it and get back to normal. He'd be okay if Irv said No. He'd still come back. Still love him. He just wanted that out on the table.

September 2017

Irv was losing his grip. Time had gotten away from him, and he never found the right moment. He didn't even have a ring, and he was pretty sure Manny would want one. If he said yes. He should have asked earlier. Like, as soon as he got the idea. Shouldn't have left it to the last minute, as if he expected Manny to say no and wanted to be able to slink back into his cave to get over it before they saw each other again. Could he wait till the holiday break? He probably should. The mental hamster wheel was driving him crazy.

The day before Manny was due to leave, they went to the gym together. They were spending the whole day together, because it was going to be weeks before they saw each other again, and Irv couldn't have concentrated on work anyway. He could barely concentrate on his workout. Then Manny suggested going to Pacific Dining Car, like they did the year before. Irv said "Sure," knowing it came across wrong.

Manny knew Irv well enough that the gruff tone didn't bother him. He knew the guy was not looking forward to Manny being gone. And there was this persistent feeling of unfinished business. Well, Manny's business should distract him from whatever was bothering him. Either it would be a big embarrassing fail, or it would be a really great day. The only middle ground he could imagine was a 'let's talk about that later.' He could live with that.

He waited until they were done with their meal, sitting around with coffee. Shoulder to shoulder in the booth, because with separation staring them in the face, they needed to be close. Manny took a breath, ran through the words he'd rehearsed about a thousand times, and dug the ring out of his pocket. Placed it on the table in front of them.

Irv saw it – so familiar, that silver ring stamped with SEMPER – and blinked. What the hell did this mean, after a year? There was so much subtext here he didn't know where to start parsing it. "Something you want to say to me?"

Manny made eye contact. "Irving. I love you. I'm always gonna love you. Maybe this is a bad idea, because someone else gave this to me." He nudged the ring with a fingertip. "But it meant love then, and it meant always. So I wanted to ask if you would wear this for me until I can get you a new one. Wear it for me until you marry me. Whenever that might be. Will you marry me?"

Irv swallowed hard, breathed through his mouth for a few seconds, and hoped his eyes didn't look as wet as they felt. "I was going to ask you, goddammit." He was staring at the ring, but he felt Manny's silent laugh. "When?"

"Is that a yes?"

"Yes, goddammit, it's a yes." He picked up the ring, wondering if it would fit. A little bit snug, but tolerable. And he could re-size it. "I don't want a new one. I want this one."

Manny lunged at him, kissing his fiancé in a way that was really inappropriate for a high-end restaurant in broad daylight. They were wrapped up tight in each other's arms for a minute after the kiss finally ended. He knew his face was wet, and was pretty sure that wasn't all him. "I love you."

"I love you too. They want us to get the hell out of here."

"We don't even have the bill yet."

"Yeah, they just dropped it off." They both snickered. Irv eased back. There was some face-wiping. Some fake-arguing over who would pay the bill. He let Manny win. "Holiday break?"

Manny knew what he meant. It would be so great to go back to L.A. in the spring knowing he was going home to his husband. There was no reason in the world to wait. "Las Vegas?"

"I'll look at some options, send you an email. We can finalize things when I come down to visit."

"Make sure your parents can come. They won't be mad we haven't met before, will they?" They'd talked on the phone, but that wasn't the same.

Irv snorted. "Not a chance. They'll be like, finally."

"Then maybe we visit them in New York next summer. I've never been there."

Irv kissed him. Nudged him out of the booth. They stood up to go, walking out into the afternoon hand in hand.

THE END